THE HOUSE OF LIGHT AND SHADOWS

LAUREN WESTWOOD

Boldwood

First published in Great Britain in 2025 by Boldwood Books Ltd.

Cover Design by Katie Tooke

Cover Images: Shutterstock and Alamy

A CIP catalogue record for this book is available from the British Library.

Paperback ISBN 978-1-83656-968-8

Large Print ISBN 978-1-83656-967-1

Hardback ISBN 978-1-83656-966-4

Ebook ISBN 978-1-83656-969-5

Kindle ISBN 978-1-83656-970-1

Audio CD ISBN 978-1-83656-961-9

MP3 CD ISBN 978-1-83656-962-6

Digital audio download ISBN 978-1-83656-963-3

This book is printed on certified sustainable paper. Boldwood Books is dedicated to putting sustainability at the heart of our business. For more information please visit https://www.boldwoodbooks.com/about-us/sustainability/

Boldwood Books Ltd, 23 Bowerdean Street, London, SW6 3TN

www.boldwoodbooks.com

To Eve, Rose and Grace. Sisters forever.

I have seized the light, I have arrested its flight.

— LOUIS DAGUERRE

Look at this life – all mystery and magic.

— HARRY HOUDINI

I

Don't look too closely. Things are not as they seem.

I lift the glass plate from the fixing bath, potassium cyanide dripping like tears. The windows glow red through the black bombazine. Outside it is daytime, spring, nearly summer. But this is a room of perpetual night. Darkness and shadows: the place where the magic happens.

The smell of bitter almonds floods my nose; already, the change is happening. From the blackness, light appears. First abstract, then sharpening into an image. A moment in time captured forever. A tiny sliver of immortality.

Through the years, tastes have changed. From the weird to the wonderful, the sordid to the sensational. I have tried to accommodate them all. I have captured moods, images, light and shadow. But is any of it real?

The image continues to evolve, the dark lightening, the light darkening. Two women, my sister and I posing together. We are seated on the velvet chaise longue, a potted palm and paisley drapery in the background. I am on the right; my sister is to my left. Our hands are clasped together: mine bare and hers gloved.

My sister's expression is gentle and serene, her beauty captured forever the instant the flash went off. In the photo I too am smiling, happy...

But don't look too closely at my eyes.

Only they reveal the truth hidden underneath.

1

SIXTY LONDON WALL, LONDON

The timing could not be worse.

I'm literally halfway to the conference room when Carrie, my assistant, calls out. 'Kate, you've got a call on line one. It sounds important.'

'Take a message,' I bark. I'm early, as usual, but time, tide, and the partnership review board wait for no man – and certainly not a woman. I'm up against Kevin and Dave, and although the party line is that all three of us can make equity partner in this round, the smart money says it's more likely to be one of us, max.

I really need it to be me.

'It's about your sister.'

'My—'

The heel of my shoe catches on the carpet; I grip the wall to steady myself. *Your sister.* I haven't heard those words for almost ten years or allowed myself to think their corollary: *my sister.*

Emma.

'She's in hospital, apparently. I think you should take the call.'

The room spins like a carousel. I stumble back to my office, sinking down in the swivel chair as Carrie puts the call through.

My mind is racing, but my hand moves in slow motion as I pick up the receiver. I think I say something – 'Hello', probably. A man's voice sounds in my ear: good diction; posh accent.

'I'm Dr Matthew Whitford. The headmaster of St James' Academy, Rookswood, East Sussex.'

'My... sister?'

'Sorry, you are Katherine Goodman, are you not? Emma Reynolds has you down as the emergency contact for her children, Max and Isobel. I'm afraid arrangements need to be made for their care. Immediately. Are you able to come and collect them?'

'Collect them?'

It fleetingly crosses my mind that he must think I'm incredibly slow-witted. Should I pretend that's the case? Or plead ignorance? Of having a sister *and* a niece and nephew that I've only seen a handful of times, though they must be teenagers by now. Should I end this call and push the ghosts and shadows back into the corner of my mind along with all the clutter amassed over all the years – the anger, the guilt?

'We can speak more when you get here. I understand your sister will be fine; she just needs some time to get back up to par. More worryingly, though, the children have been on their own for all of half term. It's only come to light today. For their sake, we want to avoid involving social services.'

'Yes. Thank you.' *What the* actual— *is going on?*

'Good. I'll email you the details. They can stay at after-school club until six o'clock. We look forward to seeing you before then.'

The call ends. I hold the receiver in my hand listening to the dull drone. The familiar surroundings: desk, papers, law books, files, half-dead spider plant, swim before my eyes, morphing into something frightening and unfamiliar.

Someone knocks on the doorframe. When I look up, it takes

me half a second to recognise Kevin. 'You're up, Kate. Conference room three. They were brutal – went over my billings with a fine-toothed comb. Seriously, I felt guilty for not charging my time when I go to the loo.'

'You don't?' My voice is hollow, mechanical, like a ventriloquist's dummy. 'I thought everyone did that.'

He shrugs. 'You'll be fine, then. And I'm sure they'd rather give it to a woman. To get the stats up and all.'

Suddenly, all the hours, the billings, the ball-busting, the satisfied clients – all the statistics and key performance indicators that have been so important for so long swell and burst like a soap bubble. Leaving behind all those other statistics and 'life performance indicators' I've tried so hard to avoid. I'm thirty-five years old, unmarried, no kids. I live in a flat with the same IKEA furniture I've had since uni. I've spent the last ten years climbing the greasy pole as a project finance solicitor in the renewables sector, and now have a shot at making equity partner. I've made choices – some good, some less so. All of that, I can own. But there is one statistic that I wish I could surgically excise from my life. I have a sister, and I have not spoken to her in years. Of course, that's her fault. All of it is *her* fault. It must be—

I put my head in my hands.

'Are you OK, Kate? Really, I'm exaggerating. It's not that bad. You'll do great.'

Manufacturing a smile, I look up. Kevin's a good lawyer, and he's not a bad guy either. He's got a wife, two kids, a house in St Albans, a plug-in-hybrid Range Rover. The other candidate, Dave, just bought a riverside flat in Butlers Wharf with his surgeon partner, Simon. Settled, happy, normal. Everything I'm not.

They deserve equity partnership.

I don't deserve anything.

'I'm fine.' Standing up, I grab my handbag and briefcase and move past him. 'Just a bit light-headed.'

'Well, they've got sandwiches and fruit. Not that I could eat in front of the selection committee—'

'It's not that. It's just... something's come up.' I go over to Carrie's desk. She looks up worriedly from her screen, closing down Facebook.

'I need to go,' I announce – to Carrie, to Kevin, and to the head of the partnership committee who's just poked his head out of the conference room looking for me. I'm aware of all the other PAs and trainees in the open-plan room looking in my direction. 'Family emergency,' I add.

Jaws drop. Most of them would never associate either of those words with me, especially both together.

Ignoring them all, I focus on Carrie. 'I need a train ticket to—' Where had he said? Suffolk? Sussex?

'East Sussex?' Carrie supplies. 'I know St James' Academy. It's near Lewes, where I grew up.'

'Sounds right.' I have no idea if it's right or not.

'You'll need a rental car from the station. I'll sort it, and the rest.' She nods her head towards the glass wall where the five men in suits are seated along one side of the table. 'Don't worry about a thing.'

I am suddenly worried about a great many things. Still, for the first time in what seems a long while, I smile at her, actually meaning it.

'Thanks, Carrie. I appreciate it.'

Every step feels hard and scary as I leave the safety of my office, moving towards the unknown.

2

Rookswood.

The name says it all. It's the kind of village that's quaint on the surface, but with the dark shimmer of something sinister underneath. I think it was Conan Doyle who said something about the countryside being more frightening than the darkest alleyways of London, but I can't recall the exact words. I know what he means, though. I drive down the narrow high street with its half dozen higgledy-piggledy old buildings slumped every which way, propped up by a few ugly modern ones. It's only five o'clock, but already almost all the shops (the ones that aren't boarded up) are shut. Only the off licence, the betting shop, and the chippy have lights on, a few people milling around outside. The only saving grace is that when I stall the rental car at a zebra crossing, there's no other traffic to honk me.

It feels strange to be driving a car, strange to be here.

It feels wrong.

In seconds flat, the landscape shifts from village to hinterland. Just beyond the mini-roundabout, with roads leading to

Brighton, Lewes, and larger and more appealing-sounding places, the houses give way to woodland. The bare branches of winter trees reach over the road like skeletal fingers. It's probably beautiful and leafy in late spring and summer, but in the midst of a dreary February, the atmosphere is lifeless, dead.

I can do this. I repeat the thought in my head, hoping I'll start to believe it. Because at this moment, it's no more than a lie.

The rental car doesn't have a satnav, and as I drive on, even the electronic voice of the Google Maps navigator falls silent. I drive through a deep puddle, drenching the windscreen, and almost drive off the road in my attempt to find the wipers, hitting the indicator instead. My palms grow clammy on the wheel as an unreasonable sense of panic sweeps through me. If this is a nightmare, I'd really like to wake up now.

I'm here for my sister...

The thought pops in my head like a garish jack-in-the-box. My emotions rise; my gorge rises. All those memories – the good ones and the bad ones – all those lost years, all the lost time. Did I do the right thing in cutting Emma out of my life? It had felt right at the time. But that wound had fed the anger, fed the hurt. What have I created now as a result of all that feeding?

The road bends; I have to brake sharply. Right or wrong, we are where we are, and besides, I need to focus not on Emma, but on her two children, Izzy and Max. Not children, but teenagers. Izzy must be what... fifteen? And Max, about eighteen months younger. That is actually all I know about them. And I am all the more terrible a person for that ignorance.

The school is so elite that I drive right past it. Obviously, the sign, tastefully designed in blue with gold lettering, is only for people in the know. There's no place to turn, but behind me, the road is clear, so I reverse back to the gate. The buildings are suitably impressive: expanses of emerald playing fields, a Georgian façade, tasteful outbuildings. There's not a portable classroom, a swathe of graffiti, or a knackered bicycle in sight. In other words, it's nothing like the state school Emma and I attended in Barking, what seems like donkey's years ago.

I pull into a visitor space, my rental car dwarfed on either side by behemoth SUVs. If Emma can afford to send her kids here then clearly, she's 'arrived'. A murky cocktail of nostalgia, anger, and loss churns in my stomach. We used to talk about things like that. Not the children part, but the 'arriving'. For me, it was a high-flying career with a life in London. For her it was... this. We were yin and yang: two halves of the same coin. We were going to do it together; we *should* have done it together.

So why didn't we?

Anger wins out. I press my nails into my palms, taking heavy, unsatisfying breaths. I know all too well why we didn't. The memories I've tried so hard to suppress regroup for a new assault, threatening to stamp their hobnailed boots down those painful neural pathways of old. It wasn't what she did; it wasn't what I said. It was neither and both of those things. Even after all these years, it's the betrayal that stings. But unexpectedly, the sting prompts curiosity. My sister is living at least part of the life that should have been mine. What is it really like?

It starts to rain as I get out of the car; I dash up the steps to the impressive set of double doors. A matronly looking registrar who introduces herself as Mrs Shipley ushers me into the vestibule: a cosy waiting area with sofas situated around a marble fireplace, portraits of headmasters past (no headmistresses, I note), the school magazine, and shelves of yearbooks and trophies. I'm offered tea and biscuits, and as much as I want to take the moral high ground and refuse, I'm tired, jittery, and could murder a cup of tea. She seems to sense the murderous part, and to her credit, brings it quickly. I pace back and forth and finally perch on the edge of a tweed sofa.

'I'm so glad you came,' she says. 'Those poor children – on their own for so long.'

'Well, surely...' *They were with their dad.* I swallow the words. I know nothing. Best not to flaunt it. 'Yes,' I finish. 'It sounds a right cock-up.'

She raises a grey-flecked eyebrow at my language. 'Can I get you anything else? Dr Whitford will be with you shortly.'

'I'm fine,' I say. 'Thanks for your help.'

I take a sip of the too-sweet tea (I forgot to tell her no sugar) and resist the urge to check my phone. God knows what crises have occurred in my absence – it seems like years ago that I was getting ready to go before the partnership selection committee. In the span of a few short hours, I've gone from top candidate to estranged aunt cum failed human being. How did that happen?

The registrar returns. 'Dr Whitford will see you in his office now, if you'd like to follow me.'

I don't want to follow her. Surely the vestibule is neutral territory, where staff members meet with parents and the PTA holds teas and soirees, or whatever they do at a school like this. The head's office sounds like the naughty step. When Emma and I were at school, I was the one forever getting detentions for running or shouting or pranking or backchat. Emma never got in trouble. Not once. Emma was kind and respectful and diligent; she didn't have a bad bone in her body. I both loved and hated her for it.

As I'm half-expecting the Chokey, I'm pleasantly surprised that instead of dark and dreary, or even traditional, the head's office is light, airy and modern. The walls are painted a pale yellow and even on a rainy day, the double aspect windows flood the room with light. There's an area of sofas and bookcases, but the most striking feature of the room is the beautiful collection of large, framed photographs of birds in flight. The photographs capture perfectly the blur of unfurling wings in counterpoint to the detail of every colourful feather: the weightlessness and freedom of flight in defiance of the Earth's gravity. I wish I could escape into that sensation and be transported far away from this place.

At the back of the room, a man stands up from behind a large desk. I've forgotten his name, and for a second, I forget my own as well. His face is narrow and square-jawed, his hair dark brown with a few streaks of grey. He's wearing small, wire-framed glasses and a neatly pressed shirt and a linen jacket: a picture of dedication and erudition. But in his eyes, I sense a strong under-current – judgement.

'Ms Goodman?'

'Yes.'

We exchange introductions and sit down on opposite sofas. As I've left my cup in the vestibule, Mrs Shipley helpfully brings a silver tea service with delicate China cups. The head pours me a cup of tea, but I don't dare take it for fear of my quavering hands.

Dr Whitford opens his mouth to speak. But suddenly, I can't bear to hear whatever he has to say. 'Are you a photographer?' I say, gesturing to the photos on the walls. 'Did you take these?'

He studies me a moment before answering. 'Yes, I did. It's a passion of mine.'

'They're beautiful,' I say.

'Are you interested in photography?' he asks. 'Because as I'm sure you know, Rookswood House has quite the history where that's concerned.'

'I don't know anything about that. But you've captured something interesting.' I point to a photo of a water bird floating on the surface of a pond amidst jagged silver ripples. 'The light, I think.'

I sneak a sip of tea, burning my throat. When I set down the cup, the tea sloshes into the saucer. I'm sure that's bad manners at a place like this. Dr Whitford's saucer is immaculate.

'I took that photo at Monet's garden at Giverny,' he says. 'A photograph can't do it justice. It can only capture a moment in time. Whereas the garden is always moving. Still,' he shrugs, 'I try. *Carpe diem.*'

'I guess you could always take a video.'

The comment sounds gauche and out of place. Stupid.

'I could,' he says. 'But I'm afraid I'm a little too old fashioned for that. In fact, I use only film, not digital. I like to think we're all entitled to a little anachronism here and there.'

He sounds like a human dictionary. The partnership committee was daunting, but they have nothing on Dr Whitford. And if there's one thing I dislike, it's being daunted by anything or anyone. I need to cut to the chase and get out of here.

Dr Whitford beats me to it. 'But apologies, Ms Goodman, I could talk photography all day. We have other matters to discuss.'

'I suppose we do.'

I can't meet his eyes. Instead, I look towards his desk. There's another lovely, framed photograph, this one of him alongside an elfin-looking blonde woman and a smiling, blue-eyed child. His family.

He sees where I'm looking. 'Do you have children, Ms Goodman?'

The question puts me off guard, and I almost blurt out the truth. But I catch myself, the lawyer in me coming to the fore.

'What does that have to do with anything?' I say. It's clear from the family photo that it has everything to do with every-thing – in his mind, at least.

'Nothing. And I didn't mean to offend. It's just, I wondered if your niece and nephew had cousins.'

'No cousins.' I cross my arms defensively.

'I see. Well, it's very nice of you to come down on such short notice. I'm sure Isobel and Max will be glad to see you.' He shakes his head. 'It's such an unfortunate business, is it not?'

'Look.' I perch forward. 'Let me make a couple of things clear. I'm not "in touch" with my sister.' I mime air quotes. 'And I haven't seen her children since they were toddlers, at my mother's funeral. It's a long story, and I won't bore you. We have other matters to discuss.'

'Of course.' He looks at me steadily. 'Occam's razor. I should have guessed.'

'Occam what?'

'William of Ockham?' He sits back, steepling his long fingers. 'He was a fourteenth-century Franciscan friar. Occam's razor states that when considering the hypothetical, if you have two competing ideas to explain the same phenomenon, you should prefer the simpler one. Ergo, I should have realised you and Emma aren't close. If you were, she would have called you herself.'

This man is positively doing my head in, *ergo*, I find myself disliking him. Did I really come all this way only to discover that my first-class degree in law was deficient in failing to cover William of Ockham? Apparently.

'Great,' I say. 'That's all very... "hypothetical". But I need to know the current situation. What exactly has happened?'

'I don't know the details, of course. But I understand that your sister fell down some stairs and hurt her back. She was in a lot of pain, and apparently had a bad reaction to the medication they gave her.'

'When was this?'

'The fall happened just after Christmas, we believe. The hospitalisation occurred just before half term, which was last week. Their father is abroad, and the children were on their own for all that time. We only learned of the situation earlier today when the children returned to school. You were listed as next of kin, so that's when we rang you.'

I can't take it in. My sister: kind, respectful, diligent... perfect. According to Occam's razor, her life, therefore, must be perfect.

'Is she OK?' I ask.

'I understand she's in a stable condition, but not ready to be discharged yet.'

'God.' I put my head in my hands. 'I didn't know.'

'Families are difficult,' he says. 'In this job, I see all sorts. The important thing is that you're here now. There's no reason to be ashamed.'

'I'm not ashamed.' I stand up. *How dare he?* 'Where are Max and Isobel? I'll stay with them for now, until Emma's better. If you need me to sign any forms, I will.'

'I'm sorry, Ms Goodman, I didn't mean to offend you.'

'Look, call me Kate. And it's fine – forget it. I appreciate you not involving social services. I may not have children myself, but I can assure you that I'm a responsible, professional adult. And if Emma's put me down as her emergency contact, then I suppose I'm that too.'

'Of course.' He stands too, ushering me to the door. 'Having met you, Kate, I'm sure they will be well looked after. Mrs Shipley will show you to the study hall where you can collect them.'

'Good.'

He holds out his hand.

I don't take it.

'And in the meantime, if there is anything else we can do—'

'There isn't.'

I don't meet his eyes as the registrar returns. 'If you want to follow me,' she says, 'I'll take you to see the children.'

As I follow her down the corridor, I'm aware of Dr Whitford leaning against the doorframe, looking at me. I have a strong urge to look back...

Luckily, I manage to resist.

3

I'm half-expecting a tattoo of drums pounding in time with my heart, heralding my way to a place of execution. A judge, jury, hecklers, men hawking tobacco, women throwing tomatoes. Mrs Shipley takes me to yet another poshly decorated room: this one a cosy school library. Sweat beads inside the collar of my suit jacket, a slow drip running down my back. Several teenagers are sitting on sofas around a roaring wood fire. Except for the absence of wands and capes, it could be Hogwarts. A horrible fear snakes through me. My niece and nephew were very little when I saw them last, and they won't know me. What if I don't recognise them?

'Ah, so quiet.' Mrs Shipley leads me past the fireplace towards a large bay window overlooking the lawns. Two teens, a boy and a girl, are seated at a carved antique table playing chess. At first glance, both of them are beautiful. The girl has thick, auburn hair and huge, green eyes. The boy has the same eyes, but his hair is dark and wavy. But it's their shared facial features: the line of a jaw, the curve of a nose, a bow-shaped upper lip, that look achingly *familiar*.

'Izzy? Max?' The registrar sounds like a clucking grandma. 'Look who's here to see you.'

If I'm expecting a firing squad of accusations and repercussions, I'm mistaken. Neither of them looks up. Neither of them shows the slightest interest in my arrival.

'Your knight is toast,' Max says. He makes a swift movement to capture the chess piece.

'Fine, but wave goodbye to your bishop.'

'Izzy? Max?' Mrs Shipley tries again. 'Your aunt is here to collect you.'

Izzy pockets the bishop, then, after what seems like an eternity, she turns towards us.

'Who?'

'Your aunt?' There's an uncertainty in Mrs Shipley's voice. My knees feel wobbly. Time to take charge of this situation.

'Izzy, Max.' I move forward with my best 'lone-woman-walking-into-a-conference room-full-of-men' swagger. 'It's so lovely to see you. I know it's been a long time. Too long.'

The two teens look at each other.

'Your move,' Izzy says to her brother.

The pause seems to last forever, punctuated only by Mrs Shipley taking in a sharp, uncomfortable breath. Max moves a black pawn forward to threaten the white knight.

'Isobel, Max.' Mrs Shipley's voice has a note of desperation. 'That's quite enough. It's time for you to go home.'

'I'll be staying with you until your mum's better,' I say.

That gets their attention. Izzy gives me a murderous look. 'At our house?'

I stare at her, mongoose to cobra. 'Yeah, that's right. So let's get going, OK?'

'OK, sure.' Max gives me a tentative smile, and for a moment, the clouds seem to lift.

'Get your stuff,' I say. 'I'll be out at the car. Grey Hyundai.'

Izzy's face curdles. I suppose my sister has some sort of posh car or SUV that they're used to riding in. A tiny, evil part of me rises to the surface. I'd been planning on returning the rental car, but maybe I'll hang onto it, if only to take my niece down a peg or two.

Not exactly a good start.

Leaving them to gather their things, I stride boldly from the room. My chest is constricting with panic, but I can't let anyone see that. Mrs Shipley follows me out and I hand her my visitor's pass. I feel like I ought to say something devastatingly clever, with a few Latin terms thrown in for good measure, but I can't think of a single thing.

'They're lovely children, really,' she supplies. 'I'm sure it will all be tickety-boo.'

'Tickety-boo.' (God, did I just say that?) 'But just to be clear, this can only be temporary. I have a job and a life back in London.'

'Of course.' Even her smile is efficient. 'And the hospital will have all the details on Emma's condition. I'm sure the three of you will want to go for a visit.'

'I'm sure,' I say. And I am sure of one thing: the kids can visit their mum, but I will not be accompanying them.

'And one more tiny thing,' she says. 'It would be great if you could wash Izzy's sports kit.' She wrinkles her nose. 'I have it on good authority that it needs it.'

I have no words.

'Anyway, good luck,' she says. This time, I think I see a twinkle of sarcasm in her eye. I appreciate that above all else. For all this 'safeguarding' and 'pastoral care' malarkey, she knows I'm up against it.

'Thanks.' I search for a stinging retort. 'Have a nice day,' is all I can muster.

* * *

To say the atmosphere in the car is strained is laughable. All those phrases like 'waves of animosity', 'looks can kill', 'stony silence' may be clichés, but they are definitely apt, for Izzy at least. By the time the two bags of reeking sports kit are loaded in the car, along with their lead-heavy schoolbags, I've already decided that I'm not going to blather on to Izzy and Max or make small talk or say anything at all.

But as I pull out of the posh car park, I feel worn down and desperate. 'So, your school seems nice. It's a nice part of the world. Very... leafy. Compared to London.' I laugh nervously. 'That's where I live. In a place called Putney. Right on the river. And actually, not so far away.'

Shut up. Shut up.

'I mean, it must have been awful seeing your mum in a bad way, but you were very brave to handle things on your own.'

'Yes, Aunt Kate,' Max answers politely. I'm grateful for the acknowledgement that I exist. Izzy, in contrast, stares out of the window in palpable silence. I wonder if Emma has a good connection with her and if Izzy knows how lucky she is. My sister and I were both in our teens when we lost our dad, and Mum passed just over ten years ago. Izzy and Max have both parents.

Don't they? My stomach twists in a knot. If I'm going to survive this, I have to ask the question.

'Where's your dad, anyway?'

'Florida,' Max says.

I breathe a little more easily knowing that Philip is on the other side of an ocean, and therefore is unlikely to be popping in of a weekend. I know little about my sister's life, and even less about his, but I know he's a property developer who made a killing in the Spanish bubble, and now mostly does hotels or something. Perhaps he's expanding into the US market. But it still begs the question: if Emma is in hospital, then why isn't he here?

'Is he working over there?'

'Yeah,' Max replies, more animated. 'It's a big property development in Orlando. Right next to Disneyworld.'

I don't question him further because I have to focus on the directions. Mrs Shipley gave me Emma's address – a place called Rookswood House. On Google Maps, it shows up as a big green patch off the main road. I slow down as we drive alongside a high stone wall. The road widens to a small verge and a set of imposing gates. I pull off the road planning to check the map again.

'Why have we stopped?' Izzy says. 'This is it.'

'Is it? Thanks.' I try to keep my tone light, but I feel twitchy with nerves. Emma must truly have *arrived*, because the gates seem to belong to some sort of stately home. But what sort? The ironwork is twisted and forbidding, the edges twined with brambles. Flanking either side are two stone pillars topped with huge stone birds poised for flight. Their dead eyes glare down, framing wicked-sharp stone beaks.

I pull up alongside the keyed entry pad. 'I hope one of you knows the code,' I say. 'Because this car isn't big enough for all of us to sleep in.'

With a huge sigh like I'm inconveniencing her, Izzy huffs out some numbers. I key them in, my fingers trembling a little. I know those numbers... a birthday.

My birthday.

The huge gates groan as they swing apart. Rookswood House must indeed be stately, as I can't even see it. Beyond the gates, a long, straight, gravel road cuts across a field ('parkland', I suppose) and disappears at the far end into a thick woodland. The only sign of a building is the very tip of some kind of tower visible just above the trees.

I drive through the gate and along the road, my pulse beating arrhythmically in my head. I'm on my sister's home turf, going deep inside enemy lines. I drive as far as the tunnel of trees, which seem to steal the last of the remaining light. At the other side, the headlamps illuminate a looming shadow: a large, higgledy-piggledy, Victorian-era house with a steep, jagged roofline, gabled windows, and a tall cupola extending skywards from the roof.

'We aren't supposed to be here. You need to turn around.'

Izzy's voice startles me. I put my foot on the brake.

'What?'

'You passed our cottage,' she says. 'The gatehouse. Like, obviously, it was back by the gate.'

I fling her an exasperated look over my shoulder. 'Why didn't you say?'

Neither of them responds.

'What is this place, anyway?'

'Rookswood House,' Max says.

The house is dark and forbidding, the windows like glass eyes staring down at me. The back of my neck prickles with goosebumps, as though someone has walked over my grave. I'm unaccountably relieved that Emma does not live here, and thus I have no reason to return.

I do a swift three-point turn (with a couple of extra points and one stall added in) and drive back the way we came. As we near the gate, I have the urge to keep driving back out to the main road and back to my life. But surely, I can do this one little thing.

Before the gate, a smaller gravel lane forks to the right. It leads to another house half-hidden behind a tall hedge and framed by large, bell-shaped yew trees. The gatehouse (*like, obviously*) – though it's larger than a mere cottage. I pull into the drive and park near a detached carport with a Mini Countryman, a lawnmower, and a stacked pile of firewood. The kids get out of the car, but I remain where I am, trying to steady my breathing and take it all in.

The cottage has a steep-pitched roof and gabled windows that resemble those of the larger house. The roofline is decorated with carved wooden trim hanging down like icicles. A gingerbread cottage. It reminds me of the wooden doll's house Emma loved to play with as a child. Or the witch's cottage in *Hansel and Gretel*.

I can't decide if the cottage is creepy or charming, or if I envy my sister or not. The indecision feels odd after so many years of estrangement. Izzy opens the door, switching on a light. By the time I reach the door, the only trace of them is the sound of footsteps going up the stairs and their shoes and stinky sports bags scattered on the floor.

Thus, I step alone into my sister's domain. The hall has an encaustic tile floor in a geometric pattern. The cosy yellow light from two wall sconces is amplified by a mirror hanging opposite the staircase, above an Arts and Crafts coat and umbrella stand. It all seems homely enough, except for the fact that there's something of a smell...

Near the stairs, the door to what I assume is a sitting room is ajar. I push it open, feeling for the light switch.

As the central pendant illuminates, I realise the source of the off-ness – and the smell.

'What the—!' I gasp.

I decide then and there that I don't envy my sister any more. In fact, I actually feel sorry for her.

4

It must have been a lovely Christmas. The tree stands in the bay window at the front of the house. At least seven-foot high, trimmed with red and gold baubles and white lights. It must have been thick and full, and given off a comforting scent of fir. It's exactly how I might decorate a tree for Christmas – if I was the kind of person who actually bothered with a Christmas tree, or any kind of celebration beyond treating myself to Uber Eats from Nobu. But even I can tell that this tree must have been very beautiful and special back in December.

Except last time I checked, it's the middle of February.

Now, things are decidedly worse for wear. The tree is drooped and listing, its branches brown and dead, its trunk wrinkled and bare as a hairless cat. Dry needles and broken glass from fallen baubles are scattered underneath, alongside a few sad-looking presents: food gifts from the look of things, that have been chewed right through by mice. I scan the rest of the room, taking in the tatty sofas, an ash-choked fire grate, and the coffee table scattered with dirty dishes, empty pizza boxes, knocked-over Coke cans, and a plate of soggy chips. The room looks like an unhappy cross between Miss Havisham's parlour and a student flat share. Whatever is happening here, it's been going on for a while.

A mouse runs from a corner of the room along the wall with the fireplace. I let out a shriek. If I wasn't missing my soulless urban flat before, I certainly am now. The countryside as a whole, and this place in particular, fills me with a sense of dread.

The back of the room has been knocked through and an archway leads to the kitchen and conservatory. The detritus continues: the rubbish is overflowing, dishes are piled in the sink, the wood floor is covered with mud, or worse. The kitchen table is cluttered with unopened post, a vase of dead flowers, and a bowl filled with rotten fruit. On a whim, I go to the fridge and open it. Big mistake. There's a mouldy loaf of bread, a bag of liquified salad, at least two dozen cans of Coke and cider, and, oddly, several jumbo packs of crisps.

I can see why Dr Whitford was leaning towards calling social services; I almost feel like calling them myself. Clearly, I am not the right person for this job. I don't do children or mess or smells or dishes by hand. I don't do country cottages. Full stop. I don't want to do... *this*.

Yet, here I am.

'What's for dinner?' Max's voice makes me jump. I round on him, my anger spiralling like a tornado.

'I was going to ask you the same thing,' I say. 'This place is a tip! You should have told me there was no food, and we could have stopped at the supermarket. There is a supermarket nearby, right?'

'There's an offie in the village,' he says, sounding eager to please.

'Yes, well, that explains a lot.'

'It's OK, Aunt Kate. You don't have to look after us. We'll manage.' He goes to the fridge and takes out a packet of crisps.

'Oh no you don't.' I stand firm. 'That is not supper. Don't you have a number for takeaway or something?'

'Pizza?'

'Fine, you do the honours.' I extract my credit card from my phone case. 'You probably need this.'

'Thanks, Aunt Kate.' I'm rewarded with a smile. He may be a teenager, but when he smiles, he looks like a Christmas-card angel. It's almost impossible not to smile back. So I do.

Max orders pizza on an app while I plan a strategy for cleaning up (or getting them to clean up) the mess. When he's finished, I take back my card.

'There's twenty quid in it for each of you if you help get this place cleaned up. You interested?'

This time, his smile is mischievous as he sizes me up. 'Thirty?'

The cheek!

'Twenty-five, but it gets done tonight.'

He shrugs. 'OK, sure.'

'Get your sister and make a start.'

'Mum says we're supposed to do our homework first.'

'This is "home" "work".' I make air quotes. 'So let's get to it.'

I feel more than a little bit proud of myself when he leaves the room to fetch his sister. I've got no cash on me, so I hope they'll think my credit is good. I hear some argy-bargy – clearly, Izzy wants thirty quid, too. Is that really the going rate? When Emma and I were their age, we got a pound a week if we made our beds and did chores around the house. There's no accounting for inflation.

Channelling a little bit of Mary Poppins, a little bit of Fraulein Maria, I marshal the teens into action. I end up doing most of the work, but at least it gets done. By the time the pizza arrives, we've at least got the dishes done and one bag of rubbish taken out. When the kids are at school tomorrow, I'll tackle the Christmas tree.

'So tell me,' I say. 'How did all this happen?'

'What?' Izzy says, talking with her mouth full and not meeting my eyes.

'This mess. I mean, who has a Christmas tree up in nearly March?'

'Well, shouldn't you know? I mean, you're Mum's *sister*,' she accuses. 'Shouldn't you have called her? Found out about how things were going?'

The pepperoni repeats on me.

'Look,' I say, 'it's complicated. I'm sorry to hear about your mum. But can you please tell me what is going on? I get that your dad's working, but shouldn't he be here in an emergency?'

'We were doing fine on our own,' she says.

I sweep my hand around the room. 'I hardly call this fine.'

'Whatever.'

'Plus, Aunt Kate, we wanted to go to Florida,' Max says.

'Yeah, seriously,' Izzy adds. 'Who wouldn't? But Mum said we've "got school".' She uses a snooty, grown-up voice. 'So we're stuck here...' There's an unspoken *with you* at the end.

'OK, fine.' I cross my arms. 'We are where we are. But what even is Rookswood? Is that the big house we saw from the car?'

Izzy shrugs, which I take to mean yes.

'Does anyone live there?' I press. 'Who owns it?'

'We do,' Max says. 'Or technically Mum and Dad.'

'Really? This whole place? How big is it.'

'About forty acres,' he says. 'Give or take.'

I let out a long whistle before catching myself. I can't allow myself to be impressed.

'The council auctioned it off,' Max says. 'Mum and Dad planned to do it up as a venue for weddings and events and stuff.'

'The place is a total dump,' Izzy says. 'You shouldn't go near there. It's dangerous.' She punctuates her warning by getting up from the table and shoving the empty pizza box in the bin bag, but not before a shower of crumbs has gone all over the floor.

'We're not allowed to go there since Mum had her fall,' Max says. 'She tripped on a loose board on the staircase and fell all the way to the bottom.'

Though I've not seen inside the place, the image I conjure makes me shudder. 'That's awful,' I say. 'And don't worry, I've got no intention of going there. There's plenty to get on with here.' I indicate the piles of dishes that still need drying and putting away. 'But at least we've made a start. Now, go up and finish your homework. I need to get my laptop set up and deal with some emails for work. I'll see you in the morning.'

Izzy gets up and stomps off. ''Night,' she says over her shoulder.

Max however, hovers for a moment longer. 'Thanks for coming, Aunt Kate,' he says. 'It's good to see you.'

His eyes are so big, his hair so endearingly unruly; he looks a lot like his dad. I want to hold that against him, but I can't. Of the two kids, I prefer Max by a country mile. Whereas Izzy... I shudder. She reminds me too much of *me*.

'You're very welcome, Max,' I say. 'I look forward to getting to know you and Izzy better.'

'Sure.' He flashes me another charming smile. 'Goodnight, Aunt Kate. Sweet dreams.'

5

My dreams are not sweet. In fact, I barely sleep at all. How can I when I go upstairs and discover that the only place for me to sleep is in the master bedroom, specifically, the queen-sized bed that I presume is normally occupied by my sister and her husband. The thought gives me goosebumps. Earlier today when I made the decision to come on a daring crusade to save Emma's kids, with only a brief stop at my flat to grab a few essentials, I didn't think through the logistics of what it might entail. I put my bag on a chair and open it, but I don't unpack anything. The suitcase contains only a few meagre items, but the weight of what I've carried here seems insurmountable.

At the end of the hallway, I find a linen cupboard with a set of spare sheets. I strip the bed, balling up the old sheets in a corner of the room. Even so, the room *smells* like my sister: dainty and feminine. I stalk around until I find a bowl of potpourri in the ensuite bathroom and throw it in the bin, but I can't escape the feeling of wrongness. Fifteen years ago, I cast Emma out of my life. So how can it be that I'm here now, stepping into hers?

I get into bed and turn out the light, but sleep won't come.

Staring into the darkness, my mind wanders all the way back to our childhood. I can picture Emma playing with her doll's house, or dressing up, or some kind of make-believe. Is that what Rookswood is for her? I on the other hand preferred reading books, or building Lego, or riding my bicycle. Time and time again I let her down, telling her I was too busy or her ideas were too babyish, or I was too old, or I just couldn't be bothered. But Emma never got the message. She always wanted to spend time together. If I had appreciated her more, let her get close to me like she wanted, would things have happened differently? Did she build up deep-seated resentment towards me over all the years, which is why it made it easier to do what she did?

Shivering at the coldness of the sheets, I pull the duvet up to my chin. There's so much I don't know about my sister. Maybe it's the passage of time, or seeing her teenage children, but as I close my eyes, I start to wonder – do I want to know more?

Maybe.

* * *

In the morning, the teenagers are groggy and grumpy, which I assume is normal for their ages. I make an effort to engage in cheerful small talk, feeling a little hurt when they don't respond in kind. It strikes me that this must be what motherhood is all about: showing up for your children time and time again, even when it's the last thing they want. The realisation throws me into a moody silence, punctuated only by a few loud sighs over the mess they make, somehow scattering Weetabix all over the table and floor, wasting milk, and not even bothering to take their dirty bowls to the sink.

As we're about to leave the cottage, I realise I forgot to wash the sports kits, which brings on a sense of shame. Mrs Shipley will think I'm not fit to be looking after these kids, which is completely true. I force myself to rekindle a false sense of bonhomie as I herd my niece and nephew out to the car. From Izzy's expression I glean that all I'm managing to do is come across as creepy and annoying.

In the hazy light of morning, the gatehouse looks very quaint, and very Emma. The walls are made of patterned red and yellow bricks, and the gingerbread trim along the roofline is painted dark green with yellow accents. The frosty gravel crunches under the car wheels as I reverse and head to the gate. The rooks on the gateposts are just stone. The black paint on the twisted wrought iron is worn, but still has a sheen in places. Even run-down, it's a lovely spot. A beautiful part of the world.

As we leave the gate, a bus pulls out in front of us, and Max waves to the driver. It's then that I realise I've been duped! Izzy told me they needed a lift to and from school, when it's clear there's a perfectly decent bus. What other surprises do they have in store?

Traffic is backed up well before the school entrance, the country road chocka-block with behemoth Range Rovers and their ilk. I almost suggest to the kids that they get out and walk – it would be faster for them, and I could do a U-turn and get out of here. But when I glance at Izzy in the rearview mirror, she gazes smugly back at me in some kind of silent power struggle. I am beyond annoyed with myself that I don't want to seem deficient and impatient on day one. We sit there, breathing the fumes of the Discovery in front. It takes nearly twenty minutes before we reach the school entrance.

'Can you get the bus home after school?' I say. 'I've got a lot of work to catch up on.'

Izzy gives me a pained look. 'Mrs Shipley said you'd be taking us to see Mum. She's your sister – don't you care how she's doing?'

I swallow back a sharp word, trying to quell the notion that I really don't like Izzy.

'We shouldn't bother Aunt Kate,' Max says to his sister. 'She's a lawyer. I'm sure she has more important things to do.'

I smile at him in the mirror, grateful for this small display of solidarity.

'Of course I'm happy to take you to see your mum,' I say to Izzy. 'If you want to go today, then text me. I'll drop you off at the hospital. Otherwise, please get the bus.'

'Fine.' Izzy huffs and rolls her eyes. I get the sense that she's putting on a show for my benefit, and that underneath, she's not all that bothered about visiting her mum. Which makes two of us.

'Have a nice day,' I say as a group of Izzy's friends comes up and surrounds her. She blanks me, but Max gives me a friendly wave before walking away towards the building.

Izzy and her friends are still standing by the kerb looking at something on a phone as I drive off. I make a show of revving the engine and deliberately stalling the car. I'm happy to embarrass myself if I can embarrass her too a little in the process. I have the odd sense that I'm taking to this surrogate motherhood thing like a duck to water. I have no right to feel proud of myself, but I do.

* * *

I'm planning to return to the cottage and spend the morning working, researching the nearest supermarket, dealing with the Christmas tree, and washing the bedding. As I drive through the main gates, however, at the far side of the field, I glimpse the tail lights of a vehicle disappearing into the tunnel of trees. I don't know anything about Rookswood House and what Emma planned to do with it, but I certainly wasn't made aware that anyone might be on site. If the house is dangerous, I ought to investigate.

I drive slowly along the gravel road. The morning is sunny but cold, and silvery waves of haze rise from the frosty grass as the sun crests overhead. It's a magical sight. I can almost imagine Emma and Philip coming here for the first time, walking hand in hand through the parkland, falling in love with the place, and each other, all over again. Happy when their bid was accepted to buy the property. Happy to be raising their family in the quaint little gatehouse while the restoration works take place... I brace myself for a wave of bitterness, surprised when it doesn't come. Emma and Philip have a family to raise, but they aren't here themselves. Somewhere along the way, things went wrong. But why? Izzy and Max don't seem to have the answers, so I'll have to find them myself.

At the far side of the field, I reach the woodland. The track narrows and roughens, the road damaged by water runoff; I have to slow down to avoid treacherous potholes. The branches of the trees reach skeletally over the road, stealing the light. At ground level, the woods are a dense tangle of laurel and rhododendron, twisting into monstrous shapes. Even inside the car, I can feel the temperature drop.

When I emerge from the woodland, the bright light makes me squint. There's no sign of the other vehicle, but a narrow track forks along the fringe of trees that probably leads to another gate somewhere. The vehicle I saw was probably just a postman or a delivery van cutting through. I park the car in the circular drive and get out. I'm here now, so I might as well have a look around.

Rookswood House is both grand and quirky. The exterior is

decorated in the same high-Victorian style as the cottage, but on a much larger scale. The house stands three storeys high, with gabled roofs rising sharply on either side of the domed glass cupola in the centre. The eaves are lavishly trimmed with wooden gingerbread and the gables are topped with stone finials shaped liked rooks ready to take flight. The house is surrounded by mature formal gardens: topiarised yew trees, tall privet hedges, climbing rose arbours, stone statues and fountains, and two huge palm trees that frame the house on either side. In its heyday, Rookswood must have been an amazing place, created with wonder and imagination.

Now, though...

As I move closer to the house, the truth becomes apparent. The woodwork is rotting, the stonework crumbling, the brickwork scarred green with algae. The many windows of the house stare out like blind eyes, with numerous panes broken or boarded up. Water drips down from leaking gutters like crystal tears. The garden is a rampant wilderness, the hedges unkempt and wild, the palms drooping, the topiarised shapes monstrous and distorted beyond recognition. Yellow plastic tape is stretched over the front porch along with a *Danger, Keep Out* sign. The silence seems unnatural, with no sound of birds or insects; only my own crunching footsteps, the puff of my breath, and my pulse beating behind my ears.

I stand before the rickety wooden porch staring at the intricate patterns of now-rotting spindles and jigsaw work that must have once been the height of fashion and taste. I'm not planning to go inside – absolutely not. But as I reach the entrance, a gust of wind catches the door, which clearly isn't shut properly. It cracks open with a screech that sets my teeth on edge.

'Bloody hell,' I mutter. The place is way too creepy for my liking, and I have the strong urge go back to the car. But first, I should probably try to secure the door. If there is a second gate to the property or a footpath, then someone might come here inadvertently and get injured. I don't want that to happen on my watch. Ducking under the yellow tape, I dodge a rotting plank and go to the door. I try to visualise the house through my sister's eyes. Emma bought the place, so she must have seen untapped potential rather than a latent creepiness. If my sister wasn't spooked, then neither am I.

'Hello, knock, knock,' I call out. 'Anyone home?' I'm not expecting an answer and, fortunately, there isn't one. Curiosity gets the better of me; I push the door open and peer inside.

Even dilapidated, the great hall is impressive. The first thing I notice is the light pouring down from a stained-glass dome set in the cupola high above the triple-high-ceilinged room. The dome illuminates the room like a lantern, casting a kaleidoscope of colourful patterns on the dark oak floor. At the entrance level, the rest of the room is in shadow, the walls covered with the mildewed remains of William Morris wallpaper separated by a dado rail from panelling of hammer-beaten copper that's now green with verdigris. On the far wall opposite the door, a grand oak staircase with turned spindles and rook-shaped newel posts rises up to a mezzanine landing, and from there branches out on either side to the level above: a gallery that surrounds the central hall, held up by large carved arches and columns, the openings protected by an intricate wooden railing. For a second, I picture the room as it might have been: servants wielding trays of Champagne, ladies in ballgowns, dark-suited gentlemen, the scent of hothouse flowers, the sound of a string quartet playing from the gallery above. But as I blink away the image and see instead the dilapidated truth, I'm haunted by another scene – Emma lying in a crumpled heap at the bottom of the staircase.

I shiver. The house is freezing and utterly silent. I stand in the pool of coloured light, but there's no warmth here. Disturbed by my breath and footsteps, dust rises up giving the shafts of light an ethereal form and substance. The house is definitely intriguing, maybe even... inspiring.

I take out my phone and turn on the camera. I'm sure Dr 'I-don't-use-digital' Whitford would find it beneath him, but it's all I have. I take a photo of the staircase, the shafts of coloured lights disappearing into deep, shadowy corners. I must have accidently put some sort of filter on, because when I check the camera roll, the photo is sepia in colour, like something from the time the house was built. The photo looks interesting, even artistic, and there's little about my day-to-day life that falls into that category. So... *carpe diem*... I might as well keep going. I proceed onwards, through the oak door in the wall to the left of the staircase.

The door leads down a hallway, the walls of which are covered with bulletin boards full of old council leaflets from years earlier. The corridor dead ends into the most bizarre room I've ever seen. It must have once been a solarium full of rare and exotic plants. But through time and neglect, the plants have taken over, creating an impenetrable jungle. Vines engulf mildewed rattan furniture, snake up the walls and across the dirty panes of glass that compose the roof. The floor is covered with desiccated oranges and shrivelled lemons, dropped from fruit trees growing rampant in cracked terracotta pots. In the centre of the room, a giant palm tree has broken through the panes of glass, poking its head skywards like the unfurled neck of a dinosaur.

A secret, ruined garden. I stand there, awed and dismayed in equal measure. If it could be restored, it would be magnificent. But that seems pretty unlikely—

Something moves.

I gasp. A rat? A bird? A monster? I want to flee, but my limbs won't move. From the heavy gloom of undergrowth, a ginger cat saunters lazily into a patch of green-dappled sunlight.

'Hello, you,' I say. I'm no animal person, but seeing the cat is a relief. It accordions against my leg, and I reach down and pat it. Then, I feel the pain. It snarls, sharp claws cutting through my skin. I wince and swear, and although the cat clearly wasn't scared of me, it jumps to its feet and runs away, disappearing between two cracked stone urns.

'Charming,' I say. 'Same to you.'

My words sound startling in the emptiness. The plants rustle, then fall silent and still. Everything is so still, and yet...

The hairs on the back of my neck prickle. There's no one here other than the cat, but I have a strange feeling that I'm being watched. By a person? A *presence*? Clearly, it's just my imagination running wild. But then I hear another noise – a thump from upstairs. Something that sounds a lot like footsteps.

Run, my mind implores. *Get out of here! It's not safe!* But the bloody-minded part of me refuses to be daunted by a dilapidated old house. It's probably more cats, or maybe a trapped bird. Or it could be someone from the vehicle I followed. A trespasser?

I look down at my phone, as if that will somehow provide an answer. I've no one to call, and there's no reception here anyway. It's probably best that I leave – which is why I feel duty-bound to check it out.

Returning to the main hall, I grip my phone like a talisman and mount the stairs, walking in the unpolished centre where a carpet runner must once have lain. I go up and up. The staircase snakes around past dark spots on the wall where paintings must once have hung. Upstairs, I reach the main gallery from which two corridors branch off leading to opposite sides of the house. I stop walking, debating which way to go. The house is deathly quiet. But as I take a step back towards the stairs, I hear a fluttering sound, like something trying to escape.

The sound is coming from higher up. I go to the end of the right-hand corridor where another staircase leads upwards. On the second floor, a much plainer corridor is lined with doors to what appears to be servants' quarters and a day nursery. A circular metal staircase leads up to an attic level. I hear the sound again, still coming from above me.

Every muscle of my body is telling me to go down, go away, leave this place and never return. But I push the fear way. I've made it this far; I'm almost to the level of the stained-glass dome. I'm curious to see it close up.

The iron stairs are loose and uneven, and rusted away in places. If the whole thing collapsed, it would be curtains for me. I scramble up the last few steps and emerge into a flood of light. I'm at the very top level of the house, on a narrow circular walkway just below the glass dome. Although there's a railing, my stomach somersaults at the sheer height; the ground floor below looks very far away.

I spend a minute admiring the delicate metal tracery of the dome, and marvelling that most of it seems intact. Then I spot another door that leads towards the back of the house. It's partially ajar; I can't not go check it out.

The door creaks when I push on it. Beyond is a vast attic room that must cover the entire footprint of the house minus the cupola. The space is musty and dark, and I can just make out the sharp gables of the roof, crisscrossed with a lattice of wooden beams. The few small windows set low in the wall are covered in black cloth, now partly disintegrated through years of damp, mould, and moths.

As my eyes adjust to the dim light, I note the room seems to be a stage set of some sort. Just inside the door is a sitting area with a velvet-covered chaise longue and two tub chairs placed in front of a Chinese screen flanked by dead potted palms. Beyond the screen, the room is littered with old photographic equipment: antique studio lights, a giant candelabra, several huge sheets of glass, framed and unframed mirrors, rolls of canvas, and an apothecary cabinet full of tins, vats, and bottles of chemicals. I recall Dr Whitford mentioning a photography connection to Rookswood that I 'should have known' about. This must be it.

I return to the other side of the Chinese screen. My eye snags on something on top of one of the side tables. It's an old sepia photograph in an oval frame, the glass dusty and cracked. The photo is of a family: a man and a woman dressed in Victorian black, and a child in a christening gown perched between them, her eyes open, but strangely blank. I turn the frame over. There's no name but a scrawl of blue chalk:

PM photo, sample

I set the frame down again and as an afterthought take a photo of the photograph with my phone. Perhaps it's a portrait of a family who once lived here, or just a sample taken by the photographer who occupied the studio. I'll probably never know.

The sun goes behind a cloud; I shiver at the sudden chill in the room. Above the door, there's a circular window I didn't notice before that must go through to the cupola to bring in natural light. It's covered by the shreds of an old curtain that are allowing in a narrow beam of sunlight. I hear the sound again: a low hum, like the whirring of an old-fashioned film projector.

The cloud moves on. The shaft of light grows broader. As I walk towards the door, dust swirls up into the light, giving it an ethereal substance. Frosty and delicate, almost like lace, almost like it's moving.

My hand trembles as I raise my phone and take a photo of the blurry shaft of light. The dust has taken on a particular shape. Frosty... delicate... a human face.

'What the—'

I blink my eyes. The shaft of light is gone. All that's left is a chilly sense of a presence that's not mine. And, on my phone screen, the photo I took – of the face of a woman staring back at me.

This time, I conquer my paralysis. I run from the room, down the stairs, and out the front door, all in seconds flat.

II

She runs away, leaving only silence and footsteps in the dust. It's so easy to run from your fears nowadays. There are so many places to go, so many places to hide. In my day, we had to learn to stand strong, stare the pain in the face. Take, for example, the couple in the photograph in the oval frame. It was one of the first portraits I ever made, and it hung for years on the walls of my studio.

The camera has captured every detail: the man in his Sunday suit, the woman in prim, black taffeta. They gaze with love at the infant between them, perched on the man's knee. A little girl dressed in a white lace christening gown and cap, yellow curls escaping from underneath. Her eyes are wide and round; a faint smile plays on her bow-shaped lips. Serene, pure, as if the camera has caught her at the edge of a beautiful dream. A tender moment, captured forever.

In fact, the child is dead. Taken by diphtheria at five months old. Outside, a procession of mourners awaits to take her to the churchyard, where a little grave has been dug, the plot watched over by a stone angel. Inside my studio, I press the button, the camera smokes, the light flashes. Afterwards, the mother bursts into tears; the father wails. That moment is not captured. That truth is lost to time.

Do such things seem strange to you? Morbid, macabre? Over many years, I have noted the changing of tastes, fads and fashions. When I was young, 'PM' or 'post-mortem portraits' were the height of fashion. For some families, it was perhaps the only time that all the members came together, captured in a single image. Fire and flash powder, ashes to ashes, dust to dust. A photograph can capture a moment, but it can never bring it back again.

As the woman walked through the house, she took photographs on her telephone. As if every inch was worth observing, every second worth preserving. She lacks a photographer's eye, but I was glad, at least, of her curiosity. I hid in the shadows, watching and waiting; something in her aura reminded me of me. A sense of longing, perhaps, longing and... anger. Feelings to which I can still relate. Feelings from which I can find no release, not even in death.

Now, the curtain rises on a new beginning – the last beginning. I gave the woman something to think about. A reason to come back. It took all my energy to do it, and I couldn't make it last. I am fading, you see, into the final darkness. I must take this one last chance to find the missing piece of myself, to grasp the hand of light to guide me into the shadows.

This woman does not know it yet, but she will help me do it.

I must take this opportunity.

I must succeed at any cost.

6

The front door bangs shut behind me. I rip though the yellow tape and sprint to the car. My breath is ragged, my pulse hammering inside my head as I turn on the engine, and without looking back, screech into reverse, the tyres spitting gravel. Flooring it, I drive forward into the tunnel of trees...

Where I meet a white van coming towards me at speed. Braking hard, I swerve to the side, skidding on a patch of ice. The seatbelt bites my middle as the Hyundai comes to an abrupt stop, the front wheels swallowed by a pothole.

The van skids to a stop, brakes squealing. The driver gets out and rushes over. 'You OK, love?' he says.

'Yeah.' Shaking, I open the door and get out of the car. 'I think so. But you were going too fast.'

We eye each other up – friend or foe? He can best be described as a 'big, strapping bloke': six-foot tall, broad-shouldered, mid-thirties, sandy-blond hair. He's wearing jeans, a black ski jacket, and workman's boots. His face is rugged, just pushing the edge of handsome. I sense him appraising me. What will he conclude?

'Wasn't expecting to see anyone,' he says.

'Nor I.'

'You were going pretty fast yourself,' he says. 'You look like you've seen a ghost.'

I stare at him, gripping my phone tightly. 'Maybe I have.'

He laughs, deep and gruff, but seemingly friendly. 'I seriously doubt that. Though most of your lot comes round at night.'

'My lot?'

'Trespassers. Peeping Toms. People coming round and playing silly buggers. Bottom line is, you shouldn't be here. This is private property and the house is unsafe. Nothing to see here.'

'Then why are you here?' I say. 'Rookswood House belongs to Emma Reynolds, does it not?'

'It does.'

'She's my sister.'

'Your sister?' He looks surprised. If any part of me was concerned that Emma had bad-mouthed me to the locals, I needn't have worried. I've ghosted her all these years, and she's done exactly the same.

'Yes, that's right,' I say. 'And while she's not here, I'm looking after her kids. My niece and nephew. That's me, then. But what about you?'

'Charlie Blackmore.' He holds out his hand; it's so large that I feel like I'm shaking hands with a boxing glove. 'I'm the builder. Emma and Phil had some grand plans. But your sister seems to have lost the taste for it since the accident.' He frowns, his face turning ugly. 'I was the one who found her. When I saw her there, crumpled at the bottom of the stairs, I wanted to kill someone.' He clenches his fists. 'Though some people would say, you can't kill something that's already dead.'

'What?'

'Oh,' he waves a hand. 'You know, it's a spooky old place. Some people think it's haunted, if you believe in that sort of tosh.'

'I don't,' I say after a pause.

'Me either,' he says. 'Anyway, I know Emma's heart was in the right place when she bought it, but here's hoping she sees sense and gets shot of it. Until then, I'm just trying to make sure no one else gets hurt.'

'Well, it's lucky she's got you, then.'

He beams with pride – and a sprinkling of something else. They way he's talking, it sounds like Emma's the one in charge and Philip hasn't been much in the picture. Maybe it's wishful thinking on Charlie's part. My sister does have a way with people. With men...

'Happy to help out,' he says. 'Even run down and derelict, a place like Rookswood attracts its share of attention.'

'From "trespassers and Peeping Toms"?'

'Exactly.' He laughs again with a comforting warmth. 'There's a public right of way that runs through the property along the stream.' He points to the turning I saw earlier, where the other vehicle (if there was another vehicle) must have gone. 'So it's hard to keep people out if they're serious about getting in. And trust me, some are. You'd be surprised how many odd bods have come round here over the years with a camera. On some sort of pilgrimage to see where the "Weird Sisters" lived and whatnot.'

'The "Weird Sisters"?'

'Did Emma tell you nothing about this place?'

'No.'

'Well, it's a long story. Too long to be standing out here freezing. I've got a flask of coffee if you want some. You can sit in the van while I go check that the place is secure, then I'll tow your car out of that pothole.'

'Thanks. That would be good.'

'Back in a minute, then.'

I get into the passenger side of his vehicle. For a builder's van, it's surprisingly tidy. The coffee is hot and sharp, and as I watch him go towards the house, I wonder if I should have told him that I went inside and warned him about what I saw. But what did I see? Something, or nothing? *Some people think it's haunted.* Not me, though. I'm determined to nip the thought in the bud.

I set down the cup and take out my phone, opening the camera roll. In the photos I took on the ground floor, I've managed to capture some interesting angles, all taken with the sepia filter that I didn't turn on, and didn't think of turning off. But as I flip to the photos from upstairs, my heart beats frantically, like a bird battering its wings against a cage. There's the photo I took of the family portrait. And then...

Nothing.

The family portrait photo is the last in the roll; there are no others. I scroll through again. I know I took the photo – I know what I saw. The shaft of light coming through the circular window, illuminating a thin wisp of dust. Dust that became a woman's face and form.

But no... I close the camera roll, take a long sip of coffee, and laugh out loud. The mind is a strange, wonderful creation. The tricks it can play!

Just to prove it to myself, I get out of the van and walk back towards the house. There's no sign of movement, no feeling of 'a presence'. Eventually, Charlie comes back outside, pulling the door shut tightly, locking it with a key that he replaces under a cracked pot with a scraggly palm on the porch. It's not a very good hiding place; if a trespasser was looking to get in, they wouldn't even have to bother with breaking a window. But really, it's not my problem.

Charlie waves a hand and trudges over to me. If he's seen

anything resembling unearthly faces, shafts of light or... ghosts... then he's not letting on. Obviously, we just met and I don't know him from Adam; he could be a saviour of stray dogs, or an axe murderer. But right now, I'm comforted by his presence and the fact that he doesn't seem at all bothered by the place that scared the bejesus out of me.

'I found one set of footprints in the dust,' he says. 'Yours?'

'Guilty.' We walk back to the van. 'The door was open when I got there.'

'Open?' His brows narrow. 'As in unlocked? Shouldn't have been.'

'Open, as in wide open,' I say. 'Maybe you need a better hiding place for the key.'

He smiles at me, a twinkle in his eye. 'Or maybe I need to come round a bit more often.'

For some completely idiotic reason, I flush. 'Sure, whatever. I definitely won't be coming here again.'

'Best you don't. Like I said, we've had a few incidents lately. People getting in, moving tools and materials around, leaving rubbish and debris. Not all the hazards are obvious. Like that loose floorboard Emma tripped on.' He shakes his head. 'I've fixed that one, but there are plenty more I haven't.'

He takes a rope from the back of his van, ties it underneath his bumper and the one on the hire car, and instructs me to put the car in neutral. Then, with the van pulling, the Hyundai inches forward with a screech as the chassis scrapes the edge of the pothole.

'Job done,' he says, returning to me when all four wheels are back on the road. 'And I'm sorry to have startled you. I guess we were both going too fast.' His smile is a little teasing. Almost like he's... flirting with me?

'I guess so.' I watch as he unties the two vehicles. Clearly, I'm rescued and he's going to leave.

'So what's the story?' I say, leaning out of the window. 'Of the Weird Sisters?'

'Oh that.' He comes back over and rests his arm on top of my car. 'I don't know much about them. Just that Rookswood was originally an old Jacobean manor house. It was bought sometime in the 1800s by a London photographer who rebuilt it in the Victorian style. When he died, his two daughters lived there and carried on his work. They were quite notorious, probably because they never got married. People weren't exactly feminists back then.'

'No, they weren't.'

'Anyway, there was some scandal, I think, and the younger sister buggered off. But the older sister lived in the house until she was about ninety. She had no heirs, and the house passed to the council sometime in the late seventies. It was used on and off as a community centre and offices. But people came away saying they got a funny feeling from the place. A few years back, the council auctioned it as surplus property. Emma and Phil were the highest bidders. Much to the annoyance of Matthew Whitford.'

'Matthew Whitford? The headmaster?'

'Yep.' Charlie chuckles. 'He's a posh tosser, if you ask me.'

'I guess I don't have to ask.'

'Sorry.' He shrugs. 'But anyway, posh doesn't always mean rich. So, the rest is history.'

'How fascinating,' I say. 'I'd love to learn more.'

The glimmer returns to his eye. 'I hope I haven't made you too curious. Wouldn't want you to become just another Peeping Tom.'

'No chance.' I shudder. 'I don't believe in ghosts, but that place gave me the creeps.'

'You and me both then. But how about we chat some more another time. Maybe over coffee? Or something stronger?'

My breath catches. Did he just ask me out? I'm here temporarily, and I don't want to become entangled with the locals. Not that there's much chance of that. Charlie's not exactly my usual 'type' – whatever that is. On the other hand...

'I doubt we'll find anything that's much stronger than your coffee,' I say. 'But text me and we'll see.'

He laughs. 'Will do. But actually, I don't think I caught your name, Emma's sister.'

'It's Kate. Kate Goodman.'

'Kate. That's a pretty name for a pretty lady.'

'Oh, save it.' I blush.

I ping my number into his phone, and he gets back in the van. I follow him all the way to the front gates, where I turn off to the gatehouse, and he leaves the estate. By the time I re-enter the cottage, I'm feeling strangely warm and light on my feet. I'm a fish out of water, but at least I've made an ally of sorts.

And who knows? Big, strapping blokes have a way of coming in handy – sometimes in more ways than one.

III

You may wonder how I did it. The illusion, the projection of myself. Over the years, many people have tried to learn my secrets. But I am a magician of light and shadow, and what self-respecting mage gives up her tricks so easily? And back then, they were tricks. Illusions. Smoke and mirrors, literally. Now, however, my tricks are real, and they – and indeed my very existence – are not so easily explained.

Photography is science: physics, chemistry, optics. My father was a pioneer in the field and taught me everything he knew. He told me that 'energy is neither created nor destroyed, it just changes from state to state'. That is the only explanation I can find for why I am here. I doubt even my father could find a better one; and as far as I know, science cannot.

I died alone in the bed upstairs, the bed where the tragedy happened all those years before. I took comfort in the heavy, smoke-scented curtains, pulled close around me, the darkened windows, the hearth cold, the air still and musty. Cradling my half of the torn photograph, feeling the weight of its sorrow in my fingers with the last of my corporeal strength. Finally, it slipped from my grasp. I was prepared for the nothingness as my spirit left my body; prepared for the final freedom, the final peace. But there was no peace, no freedom, only a terrible flood of loneliness. Instead of dissipating into the oneness, my spirit had become trapped in this house. A captive energy signature, a revenant of consciousness.

And here I have remained. Formless, liminal. Outside of time, and yet aware of its glacial passing. Aware when people come and go; at times there have been many, at others, none at all. Over the years, some people have come here out of curiosity, others to seek counsel or refuge, still others out of an intent to do harm or make mischief. Unseen, I observe them. I can see into their hearts, though most of the time, I have no wish to do so. Sometimes, I want them to notice me, and from time to time, certain people have done so. A select few whose energy signature resonates with mine. These are the souls I can sometimes reach, even sometimes communicate with. I draw my energy from theirs and occasionally it is enough to move objects. To them, I can become a poltergeist or 'noisy ghost'. I do not wish to be either noisy or a ghost, but I will do what I must to achieve my end.

The woman is in danger, though she does not yet know it. There are forces at work in this house that have the intent to harm and the means to do it.

Human forces, first and foremost – let's be clear about that.

7

When Charlie's van disappears from sight, I'm hit by a heavy sense of isolation. I'm used to spending day and night in an office, surrounded by colleagues with busy, noisy lives, and as a result, I usually crave time to myself. But right now, I wish I could drown my own thoughts in a sea of other people. I put it down to being in a new place, full of reminders of my sister. Though, it could also be down to the fact that I may have photographed a ghost—

I may have photographed a ghost.

I look again at my camera roll. Photographs of rooms and corridors, shapes and angles, light and shadow. The tension of empty space, holding its breath, waiting to be changed by me, the observer.

No ghost.

I chalk it up to a trick of my own primitive brain. I went inside a derelict old house, my amygdala sensed danger and triggered my fight-or-flight response. It's Occam's razor: the simplest solution is usually the right one. In this case, it's all just brain anatomy.

Back at the cottage, I make myself a coffee and tidy up Emma's conservatory. The white wicker furniture, potted plants, and shabby-chic soft furnishings look homely and comfortable. The polar opposite of my own semi-lived-in, very unloved flat in London. I set up my laptop on her table, review a draft agreement and dial in to a Teams call with a client, but I can't find my usual rhythm. Maybe it's the quiet, broken only by the ticking of a clock and the occasional sound of a bird. Or maybe it's all the things I'm avoiding.

Like – what the heck do I do about Emma?

To distract myself, I Google 'Rookswood House'. Maybe because the house must have once been very grand, or because Charlie described the place as a magnet for trespassers, I'm expecting to find a wealth of information. Instead, I find very little beyond a planning application put in by Emma and Philip Reynolds, a public notice from a few years ago about the property auction, and before that, a few mentions of AA meetings and clubs for old age pensioners held at the house when it was under council ownership.

It's a little disappointing. I was half-hoping for Rookswood to be shrouded in some great mystery. Charlie mentioned the 'Weird Sisters' who carried on their father's photographic work in the house, but he knew almost nothing about them. Whoever the Weird Sisters were, they must have died a long time ago. Maybe Emma knows something more. She must have bought the place more as a labour of love than out of any real hope of turning a profit. My sister always was twee and whimsical that way.

But if I want to ask Emma about Rookswood, that means I'll have to see her. I splutter as a sip of coffee goes down the wrong way.

Or... actually, I don't have to see her. I try this on for size as I put the bed linen in the dryer, gather the dirty dishes from Max and Izzy's bedrooms, and eventually get in the car and drive twenty-five minutes to the nearest supermarket where I spend a bewildering hour trying to figure out what to buy. Rookswood is nothing to me – a house is just a house, and the kids, surely, can handle all communication with their mum. When she's ready to come back, I can vacate the premises without ever having to exchange a 'hello stranger' or a 'so nice to see you, must catch up soon'. Which, surely, is all we have to say to each other.

She's your sister.

Yes, of course she's my sister. I talk back to the voice of my conscience (that sounds a lot like Izzy's). But you choose your friends, not your family. I have a life back in London: a well-paying job, intelligent friends and colleagues, interesting work. One of these days, I might bite the bullet and sign up for an online dating app. Not that I want or expect to 'find someone'. It would be more like a new hobby to try. I'm happy and content with things as they are. I don't need anyone else, and most certainly not my estranged sister.

My good mood slips as I load the shopping into the car and drive back to the cottage. It's nearly four o'clock; the kids can get the bus as agreed. But when I reach the big gates, I drive past and keep going, taking the turning to the school. Surely Izzy and Max will want to see their mum, if only to tell her I'm here and that they're OK. I can engender some goodwill by offering to drive them, and I can always just sit out in the car and wait.

A Tesla honks from behind, whizzing past me. 'Arsehole,' I call out, but my heart isn't in it. I've been crawling along, creating a hazard. Racked with indecision and guilt. I can just sit in the car and wait...

Or, I could confront my demon.

* * *

'Izzy?'

I pull into the loading zone and call out of the open window. Izzy's coming out of the main building amidst a group of other girls, all of them pretty, all of them with their skirts rolled up a good six inches above the knee. Even though I'm a successful professional in my mid-thirties, there's a part of me that still identifies as a scrappy, insecure teenager. Maybe it's because I don't have a husband or children, or maybe there's a part of every woman that's still a frightened girl at heart—

'Oh God, it's my aunt.'

Izzy's words pull me back to reality, and her face says it all. This girl, who is a real teenager, does not see me the way I see myself. She sees me as a fully-fledged grown-up and a pathetic one at that. I must disabuse any ridiculous notion that we can be friends. She doesn't want me here and certainly doesn't want to be seen with me.

'Hi,' I say. 'I was in the neighbourhood, so I thought I'd spare you the bus.'

'It's fine,' she says. 'We're going to study. I'll be home later.'

'I thought I could take you to see your mum. Would you like that?'

'Not really.'

I'm trying really hard to see Izzy as a nice girl, with any indications to the contrary purely a result of her age. But her *mum* is in *hospital*. How could she not want to see her?

Your sister is in hospital... how could you not—?

'Fine.' I don't bother to hide my irritation. 'But just so you know, I'll be busy with work for the next few days and I have to go up to London on Friday. I've cleared today, but I can't guarantee when I'll be free—'

'Hey, look at this.' One of Izzy's friends grabs her arm and waves a phone in her face. Izzy turns, giving me the cold shoulder. My annoyance boils over. My niece is a brat – she's just like I was at her age.

'Suit yourself,' I say, rolling up the window. 'I'll see if your brother wants to go.'

I pull the car forward, looking for Max and practically collide with another Tesla. The same one that honked me? Who cares? I honk back out of pure frustration. The back door handle rattles.

It's Izzy.

I press the unlock button regretting the honk. Clearly, Izzy just needed a minute to get her priorities straight.

'Hi.' (I give the other driver an apologetic little wave.) 'Do you know where your brother is?'

'In the chemistry lab, probably.' She points to a low modern building set apart from the main school. 'You can collect him there. And then drop me off home. It's on the way.'

I drive nearer to the lab and look for a parking space. 'Why don't you want to see your mum, Izzy?'

'Because she tried to kill herself!'

The words, the tone, everything about her statement startles me half out of my wits. The car clunks as I stall it.

'What? No—'

'Yes, she did. She took a whole load of painkillers, washed down with a bottle of her favourite chardonnay. That's no accident.'

'Are you sure?' I try to recall what Matthew Whitford said. Something about Emma having a 'bad reaction to her medication'. He might not have known the truth, but certainly Izzy's version explains a lot.

'Of course I'm sure!' Izzy says. 'I found her. Slumped on the sofa at home, pills on the coffee table, the glass cracked on the floor. If you don't believe me, then ask the doctors. If you can even be bothered. You're like the worst sister ever.'

My mind whirs; I can't begin to process what she's saying. But one thing keeps coming to the fore. One question that hasn't been answered.

'Why isn't your dad here?' I say. 'You said he's in Florida. But surely he must know what's going on, and that he's needed here?'

She half sobs, half laughs.

'You really don't have a clue, do you? I mean, if you're a lawyer, you ought to be clever enough to work it out. Dad left over a year ago. Ran off with his American girlfriend. *Shari*,' she spits. 'The divorce came through just before Mum had her fall.'

Girlfriend? Divorce?

'God,' is all I can say. *How could I not have known?*

Izzy jumps out of the car, her green eyes shimmering with tears. I get out to follow her, just as Max comes out of the building, his blue PE shirt stained with some kind of acid or bleach.

'Hey, Iz – what's up?'

'*She* wants to take us to see Mum.' She jabs a finger at me like a dagger. 'I don't want to go.'

'Come on.' Max tries to grab her shoulders. She ducks but doesn't run away. 'We should see her. You know that.'

'I don't want to.'

I come up to them. 'Look,' I say, 'we can do it today, or another time. If you want to talk about what happened, I'm here for you. I want to help.'

'Why now?' Izzy practically spits. 'Where were you when we needed you?'

'Not here. And I regret that.'

Max holds his sister as she shakes with tears.

'I hate you,' Izzy says to me. 'And Mum too.'

'I get it,' I say. 'But does it help that I went to the supermarket?

Let's just go home and I can cook something. We can all hole up and chill. Watch a film or something.'

'What did you get?' Max asks.

'Pasta, chicken, oven chips, popcorn.' I don't elaborate on the fruit and veg. 'Lots of things. It'll be fun.'

Izzy lets out a deep sigh and pulls away from her brother. 'We should go see Mum,' she says.

Max nods. 'If it's OK with you?'

'Sure.' I smile. 'That's why I'm here.'

8

I'm sick with dread as I follow Izzy and Max down the corridor. Nurses bustle, machines beep, trolleys trundle busily in the wards. I'm barely aware of any of it.

Dad left over a year ago.

Mum tried to kill herself.

It can't be true. Occam's razor. *My Emma* is perfect; she has a perfect life. *My Emma* never would have done that.

Except, *my Emma* doesn't exist outside my memories. Fifteen years of stony silence and animosity tend to do that: they tend to distort the truth. The fact is, I don't know my sister at all. And right now, I'm feeling pretty terrible about it.

I hang back as Max disappears into a room. What am I supposed to say? What am I supposed to do?

'Are you coming in, Aunt Kate?' Izzy says, pausing at the door.

'You and your brother go and see her. I'll say hi when you're done.'

'You sure?'

A rogue tear wells up in my eye. 'You were right, Izzy,' I say.

'I've made some mistakes that I regret. I need to see Emma on my own, but only when you're done. OK?'

Just for a second, the hard teenage mask softens, and I catch a glimpse of something underneath. Not compassion, exactly, but maybe *understanding*.

'OK.'

Izzy goes inside the room. I skulk over to the waiting area and sink down on a hard plastic chair. Everything I've done and achieved in my career and my professional life – things I've hung my hat on for years – suddenly seem irrelevant. Those things were easy. Whereas people, relationships, family... this is where I needed to put in the real work. *All those years...*

Is it too late?

Almost certainly.

I close my eyes as the memories dart from the wings, commandeering the stage. The last time I saw Emma... the way we looked at each other, the things we said. Did I realise then that it would be the end of us? If I had, would I have acted differently?

Probably not.

But it's painful to realise that part of me wishes I had.

'Would you like a hot drink?' A nurse comes over and addresses me. 'Tea? Coffee?'

She's probably worked off her feet, whereas I'm just sitting here in a puddle of misery. The gesture is more than comforting. It's life affirming.

'Tea would be wonderful,' I say. 'Black, no sugar.'

She goes to a machine across the waiting room and brings me tea steaming from a polystyrene cup.

'Thank you so much,' I say. 'For everything you do.'

'Oh, well.' She blushes. 'It's the little things that matter, isn't it?'

'Yes.' I give her a genuine smile that feels unfamiliar. 'You're absolutely right.'

As she goes off on her rounds and I drink the tea, I make a new resolution. I can't change the big things, like the past or the future. All I can do is decide how I want to show up when I see my sister in the here and now. When the time comes to walk into that room.

After half an hour or so, Izzy and Max come out. 'Mum wants to see you,' Max says.

The little things.

'Fine.' I take out my credit card and hold it out to Izzy. 'Go down to the Costa and buy yourself a snack. And maybe something for your mum too.'

Izzy looks at the card, then at me. 'Thanks,' she says. It's the first one of those I've heard from her.

'You're welcome.'

They go off. I take a breath and try to dispel the terror.

It doesn't work.

* * *

Whatever I'm expecting when I walk into that room, it isn't what I see. Emma has always been beautiful, sweet, ethereal. Perfect. But the woman lying in the hospital bed hooked up to an IV and several monitors is not someone I recognise. She's thin and gaunt, all hard lines and sharp edges, except for her lips which look swollen, and skin that seems stretched over bone. Whatever I was planning to say, if I was planning anything at all, goes straight out of my head.

'Emma?' I go to the bed and sit down in the visitor's chair. Should I take her hand? Kiss her on the cheek? Mum was in hospital for almost a month before her death. I was working in

Singapore at the time, and I didn't manage to return in time to see her. I didn't *make* the time for my mum in her last days. Emma was there, however, and made all the arrangements. That was the last time I saw her – a flustered young mum with two toddlers in tow, glaring at me from across the church at the memorial service. I did what I thought was the honourable thing and left before the reception. Emma lived locally and knew Mum's friends; I didn't. I convinced myself that it was right if she stayed and I went.

Nothing was right about any of it. I realise that now.

'Why are you here, Kate?' Her voice is a thin whisper.

A ghost of the old anger rises up; I swallow it down like a piece of gristle. There are a hundred things I could say. A thousand, even. But only one thing that matters.

'Because I love you.'

Weak as she is, my sister manages a laugh.

'Really?'

Surely, it's been too long to play this game; that's my conclusion, anyway. But Emma always had her own mind, which added to the tension between us. I'm two years older, and when we were children, I was the one in charge. I decided what we played, what dolls and toys we each got, what we watched on TV. She followed me around with a quiet sense of awe until she was about eleven. At that point, she started developing her own personality, and it all went downhill from there. I was *supposed* to be in charge, but suddenly I wasn't. We managed to weather our teenage years – barely – and by the time I went off to uni, we were briefly as thick as thieves. After Emma graduated, she stayed with me for a few months in my flat, and once again I was the alpha wolf. But that ended in carnage, and I've been a lone wolf ever since.

'Look, Emma, I'm sorry. For all of it. Is that what you need me to say?'

She laughs again, weaker this time. It's disconcerting to see a little spike on her heartrate monitor.

'I think you're trying to get me to say it. That's what you've wanted all these years.'

'Maybe.' I shrug. 'But for now, I'd like to put all that aside. I'll look after Izzy and Max until you're better. But I'd like to know how it's come to this.'

'*You* want to put it aside, *you'll* do this, *you* want to know that. Nothing's changed, I see.'

Why is she doing this? Why can't she appreciate how hard I'm trying? How much this is costing me?

I'm the big sister. I suppose she learned it from me.

'I'm sorry, Emma,' I say. 'You don't have to do anything or tell me anything. You don't have to apologise or accept my apology. But I'll leave it there, on the table.'

Her drooping eyelids widen for a second. 'Philip left me. I'm sure you heard.'

'Yes, and I can't believe it.'

She huffs. 'I think you can. But anyway, I lost him. You can feel good about that.'

'I don't feel good about any of it.'

She inhales a ragged breath. 'Izzy and Max want to go and live with him and his girlfriend in Orlando. She's called Shari.' She winces. 'I lost you and then I lost him. Now I'm going to lose them too.'

'You're not going to lose them, Emma.'

'What do you know about it?'

'A fair amount, given what happened. But that's ancient history. I'm here now – that's what matters.'

'Does it? If I had to choose between keeping *them* and getting *you* back, I wouldn't choose you.'

'I get it. I wouldn't choose me either.'

She almost smiles. The sight is so familiar that a sob escapes my throat. Then, without warning, she takes my hand. It's so unexpected that I almost jerk away, but she squeezes it with surprising strength. 'Keep them safe, Kate. Whatever you do, keep Izzy and Max safe.'

'What do you mean?' I lean forward, startled.

'Don't let them go near Rookswood. Especially Izzy. She's in danger.'

I feel the pulse in her wrist speed up even before the machine starts beeping.

'In danger? From what?'

'*She* was there, Kate. I felt her. I know you won't believe it, but it's true. I felt her longing. Her rage. She wants something and will stop at nothing to get it. But I couldn't understand what it was. That's when she hurt me.'

'What? Who?' I squeeze her hand. 'Emma, what are you talking about? Izzy didn't hurt you, did she?'

An alarm goes off; her vitals are going off the charts. 'Not Izzy,' she gasps. A nurse rushes in and presses a button on the IV drip. 'Ada.'

My sister closes her eyes. Her grip loosens on my hand. The beeping gradually slows and levels out.

'That's enough for today,' the nurse says. 'She needs to rest.'

I withdraw my hand. 'What exactly is wrong with her?'

The nurse gestures for me to follow her out of the room. 'She overdosed on opioids and white wine. That, on top of being underweight and anaemic. Basically, she wreaked havoc on her own body. It's going to take time for her to withdraw completely from the physical addiction. She's agreed to go into a residential recovery programme that will give her some time away to rest and recover. Some place where there's no stress and no distractions.'

'Sounds sensible,' I say, a little shocked. 'And I'm sorry I didn't know.'

Judgement flashes across the nurse's face; it's probably well deserved.

'Now you do,' she says.

'Yes.' I head towards the waiting area to find Izzy and Max. 'Now I do.'

9

Memories of Emma haunt me long after we leave the hospital. Her gaunt appearance, her self-neglect and intentional harm, her ravings and paranoia, all the things that remain unsaid between us. When we returned home, Max thanked me for driving them. He seemed content that his mum was making progress and that everything would be fine. When I tried to draw Izzy into conversation, asking if she knew anyone called Ada, she answered with a bored 'no', and closeted herself in her room.

I decided to let it be. But three days on, I'm beginning to wonder if once again I've made the easy – and wrong – choice.

On Friday morning, I drop Izzy and Max at school and get the train to London. Despite making Emma's conservatory my unofficial office and keeping up with emails and calls, as the train pulls into London Bridge, I feel utterly topsy-turvy. Torn between my old life, which I've lived for so long, and my temporary new one.

My office colleagues greet me like a prodigal daughter. The PAs want an update; the other partnership candidates ask me when I'm coming back. I, who am never at a loss for words, don't have the first clue how to answer their questions. Perhaps I've made a mistake by rarely, if ever, taking a holiday. If I had, surely it wouldn't be a big deal and I'd know how to respond. I feel secretly worried that, as the Buddhists say, 'you can't step twice into the same river'. How did I manage to step out of my river in the first place? I'm desperate to dive back in, and yet, my feet are rooted to the bank.

'Ah Kate, you're here. Great.' The managing partner comes out of the conference room where he and some of the other equity partners are holed up. 'I understand you're still dealing with your *family emergency*,' (I sense incredulity in his voice) 'but maybe we can have a preliminary chat?'

'I'm here for a full chat,' I say, finding my sea legs. 'This firm is my home and my family. The other... thing... is just temporary.'

I mean every word, but it doesn't quite land. Most of the partners are family men (*men* being the operative word), and while my commitment ticks a box in the plus column, the fact that I'm different is a big red minus. I was born too late; thirty years ago, my child-free, workaholic proclivities would have been viewed much more favourably. As it is, I need to tread carefully; maybe I can even use this 'family emergency' to my advantage. That's what the old me – the me from last week – would do.

Why, after less than a week, do I no longer feel like that person at all?

'Take all the time you need,' he says. 'You're well overdue a holiday.'

'Maybe, but I don't want to hurt my prospects.'

He leans in: what some women might construe as too close. 'Between you and me, I wouldn't worry. The decision's all but made. Just answer their questions, and if you've got time to come down the pub afterwards, it's all to the good.'

'Thanks.'

Coming from him, that's as good as an assurance. I've officially *arrived*. Equity partnership and all the clout, responsibility and additional compensation that comes with it. Crossing the finish line should put a genuine smile on my face and a spring in my step. I shouldn't feel so oddly flat as I follow him into the conference room and shake hands with each member of the partnership committee.

I've made my choices. This is my life.

* * *

This is my life. I ponder it on the train back to Rookswood, resisting the sensation of being pulled in opposite directions. The interview went well; the boozy pub lunch with my colleagues was pleasant enough. I even found time to visit my flat and grab a suitcase of extra clothes. But all the while, I couldn't stop the whispers in my head. *What do you want? What do you* really *want?*

'I want equity partnership,' I say aloud to my reflection in the train window (drawing a look from two commuters manspreading in the facing seats). 'Nothing has changed.'

But as I get off the train, I'm suffused by a strange sense of urgency. Izzy and Max need me. Emma needs me. For now, I decide, it's OK to want this.

* * *

But what exactly is *this*? The answer eludes me as I lie in bed late that night, turning over the events of the day. At dinner, Max politely asked me about my day, and Izzy was as uncommunicative as ever. Max seems happy and well-adjusted, but when I looked at Izzy, Emma's words came back to haunt me. *Keep them safe.* From what? I'm not aware of any danger other than the usual pitfalls that exist for teenagers: online trolls, stalkers, phishing scams, vaping, regretful selfies, Snapchat—

A noise from the hall renders me fully alert. A door opens and closes. Izzy's door.

At first, I think she's just going to the loo, but I hear footsteps going downstairs. A midnight snack? A late-night Netflix binge? It could be anything. I close my eyes, determined to get to sleep, when I hear the front door open and close. Throwing off the blanket and shivering in the cold, I get out of bed and walk barefoot to the window.

Condensation has frozen in whorls on the inside of the glass, and it must be even colder outside. Beyond the drive, a thin layer of frost shimmers on the ground, and in the light of a half-moon, I see Izzy, diaphanous and insubstantial, like a girl from a Gothic novel. Except for the hoodie and pyjama bottoms, she could be Jane Eyre, Catherine Earnshaw, the Woman in White. There's a dreamlike quality about her movement. Could she be sleepwalking? Should I open the window and call out to her?

No. I vaguely recall reading that you're not supposed to wake a sleepwalker. It could be dangerous for her, and for me. Shivering, I pull on a pair of tracksuit bottoms, heavy socks, and a woollen jumper. I try to ignore the knot of fear tightening in my stomach. Sleepwalking or not, Izzy's going somewhere...

I've got a fair idea of where.

I put on my heaviest coat and two scarves; Izzy will need something warm. Oh God, what if she gets hypothermia? I am so not cut out for this.

I grab the car keys and go outside. The cold is as heavy and solid as a wall, and I have to scrape ice off the windscreen. By the time I'm done, I can't see Izzy – with all my faffing, I've wasted valuable time. I head towards Rookswood, driving more slowly than I'd like to avoid the car-swallowing potholes and patches of black ice. It feels like I'm moving in slow motion as I reach the tunnel of trees and the darkness engulfs the car.

On the other side, Rookswood lies like a giant, sleeping beast, its roofline jagged and sharp in the hazy moonlight, the cupola rising skyward like a sepulchre. The headlamps illuminate a flash of white at the door. Izzy. I'm beyond relieved that I've found her; beyond anxious that she's going inside.

I call out to her as I park the car, but she's already inside. Every nerve of my body fires with adrenalin as I rush to follow her. If she really is sleepwalking, it's time to wake her up. The front door is ajar; wasn't Charlie supposed to secure it? Not that it makes much difference with the key so badly hidden. Cold dread pools in my limbs as I push it open and cross the threshold.

Even with my phone torch and a thin shaft of moonlight entering through the cupola high above, the darkness is smothering. I stand still and listen, hearing only a scrabbling sound in the walls like mice or rats. Before me, the stairs twist upwards like a gnarled tree. I recall my vision of Emma crumpled at the bottom, relive the fright I had in the attic room. Is that where Izzy went? I shine my light on the stairs, but I see no footprints in the dust. I do see, however, another door set into the panelling below the staircase. I only notice it because it's open a crack. I go over to it and look inside, staring into blackness like a mineshaft. A narrow staircase leads downwards. I hear a faint dripping of water, and the groan of wood. A footstep.

'Izzy?' I call out, breathless. I shine my torch over the wall looking for a light switch, but find nothing.

'Please Izzy, answer me. Are you there?'

My heart beats a tattoo of doom in my chest. I *can't* go down there. I *have to* go down there.

With one final frozen, painful breath, I plunge into the darkness. If Izzy made it down the stairs, I can only hope they won't collapse. I take a few tentative steps. The dripping sound echoes louder. I call out again. Why isn't she answering?

As I continue to descend, the sense of wrongness spreads through my body like a virus. A cold breeze chills my neck from above. Then I hear another sound – a faint click. The air falls still but I'm prickling with goosebumps. There's no handrail and the steps are rickety; I spend precious time testing each one before committing my weight to it. Finally, I reach the bottom, but as my foot contacts the stone floor, I slip on something damp and go sprawling to my knees. My phone clatters to the ground, and I scrabble for it. This is ridiculous; Izzy can't be down here. My hand shakes as I shine the thin beam of light around me. I'm in a storeroom of some kind, surrounded by dusty boxes, rotting crates, broken lights and antique appliances. I take a few steps further to satisfy myself that the place is empty, panning the torch.

That's when I see *her*.

A woman lying prone on the floor.

Missing a head.

10

————

I scream bloody murder; my rational brain flees the scene in advance of my body, which stumbles frantically up the stairs. A part of me knows that the headless woman is not Izzy – unless Izzy miraculously managed to don a fully corseted Victorian gown and sever her own head in a span of about five minutes. As I reach the top of the stairs, however, anything seems possible. Especially when I discover that the door is shut, and it won't open.

'No!' I yell, hammering on the wood. This can't be happening. I recall the air current and the click. Did the door just blow shut? Or did someone close it? Izzy? I hate myself for even considering the possibility. But if not her, then who?

My thoughts murmurate like frightened birds. I'll have to go back down the stairs to that... thing... and try to find another way out. Or...?

Silly. I have my phone. The battery is down to 10 per cent and there's a single tentative bar of reception. Who should I call? Max? Izzy herself? She's a teenager – even sleepwalking, she may have grabbed her phone.

Izzy's phone goes straight to voicemail. Max, the same. 5 per cent. Another recently added contact catches my eye. Charlie. No, I couldn't. Could I? I try the door again. Nothing. Rookswood is derelict, deserted. Who knows when someone might return? I have no choice but to dial the number. Charlie answers sleepily on the fourth ring; breathless, I explain my predicament.

'Hang tight,' he says. 'I'll be right there.'

I sit down on the top step, turning off the torch to save the battery. All my neural pathways are furrowed by fear. A headless woman in the cellar! Who is she? And where is Izzy? (I'm ashamed to admit the latter is only an afterthought.)

Scrabbling, dripping. Me and *it*. My teeth chatter violently for what seems a lifetime. At last, however, I sense someone just outside the door.

'Charlie?' I call out. 'Izzy?'

But it's neither of them. Under the door, the darkness lightens and shifts. It *moves* like the blur I caught in the photo. Charlie and Izzy are not here. And yet, I'm not alone. There's someone – or some*thing* – here, just like Emma said. A presence.

I wrap my arms around myself and shut my eyes, curling inwards. But there's nowhere to hide. Never in my life have I been a religious person. I believe that when people die, their energy disperses and becomes part of the universe. But just because I've chalked it up to the unknowable doesn't mean it's true. Can spirits exist? Ghosts?

'Ada?' I whisper.

A noise startles me, and in an instant, the presence is gone. On the other side of the door, footsteps come towards me.

'Kate?'

I'm not the sort of woman who's happy to be rescued by a man. But as the door opens and I make out Charlie's face behind a wide torch beam, I cry out with relief and fall into his arms, shivering and sobbing – I'm not ashamed to admit it.

Well, maybe a little.

* * *

When I finally stop shaking, babbling and gasping Izzy's name, Charlie leads me outside to his van and covers me with a blanket. I apologise for disturbing him, but he waves it off, saying he's a light sleeper. Moreover, he had the foresight to bring a flask of hot water, and makes me a cup of tea. I give him Izzy's number and he calls her, holding the phone so I can hear. She answers on the third ring.

'What's going on?' she says, clearly half-asleep and fully annoyed. 'Who is this?'

'Izzy!' I cry. 'Where are you?'

'What the hell? Aunt Kate? Where are you calling from?'

'Charlie's phone. We're at Rookswood.'

'Charlie's there? Why?' Her voice holds a note of hostile suspicion.

'It's a long story. I saw you go out, and I was worried for you.'

'Are you like totally nuts? It's what, 2 a.m.? I was asleep in bed. And now, I'm going back to sleep. Goodbye.'

The call ends.

Charlie puts the phone back in his pocket. 'I guess that's settled. Shall I take you home?'

'I'm sure I saw her,' I say. 'She left the house and went towards Rookswood. I thought she was sleepwalking so I went after her.'

'Did you check her room when you left?'

'No, but...' I take a gulp of tea. Could I have just imagined all of it? No. Rookswood is creepy, but it hasn't sent me over the edge. 'I know what I saw,' I say aloud.

'Which was what exactly?'

'A headless woman.'

He stares at me, eyes wide. 'As in, missing a head?'

'Yes,' I say. 'She's in the cellar.'

'OK,' he says. 'A headless woman. That's a new one.'

While perhaps understandable, the note of amused incredulity in his voice puts my hackles up. 'If you're brave enough,' I say, 'I'll show you. It won't take long. If there is a corpse down there, we'd better get the police.'

This gets his attention. 'Look, Kate,' he says, 'I've been down in that cellar before. The electrics are there, plus some old junk that we haven't had a chance to clear. But there was no "headless corpse"; I'm pretty darn sure of that.' He frowns. 'That said, I did think the cellar door was locked, so I'd better check it out. We don't want anyone else getting trapped. But I can do that myself, and I'm sure you've had enough excitement for one night. How about I drive you home so you can get some sleep and then I'll come back and have a look?'

'No,' I say emphatically. 'I saw something. Do you really think I can sleep wondering if there's a body in the cellar of my sister's restoration project?'

'I guess not.' He sighs. 'Come on then.'

When we re-enter the house, my fear is muted, like a half-remembered dream. Charlie leads the way to the cellar door. Just before he reaches it, something clunks under his boot and he stops to pick it up. 'Damn,' he says. 'Someone's cut the lock.' He holds up a broken padlock. 'That's how the door got open.' He beams his torch at the upper hinge. 'As for how it closed on you – look.' The light illuminates a metal spring. 'It makes the door swing shut automatically.'

Though surely I was down there for a few minutes before the door closed, and it wouldn't budge when I tried to open it, I am beginning to doubt my own sensory perceptions. First, a woman's face in a shaft of hazy light, then a *presence* in the darkness? At the time, they seemed so real. But as I follow him down the stairs, I feel embarrassed. Emma used to believe in things like unicorns and fairies, but I'm supposed to be the sensible sister.

'See?' he says, nearing the bottom step. 'Nothing to worry—' His whole body jolts suddenly. 'Jesus wept! You're right!'

He shines his torch on the headless woman. My heart gives a vestigial leap. But when I look again, it's clear that she isn't a corpse, or even a mannequin. She's a photograph – tipped over onto her side. Full length, the height of a woman, and sepia in colour, like the photos I took of the house. Every detail of her dress is in crisp, sharp focus.

'A photograph!' I say. 'It must be the work of the Weird Sisters.'

'I can see why it scared the crap out of you.'

'It's so creepy and weird… unnatural. Why would anyone take a photo like that?' I go over to it and find that stacked behind it are others like it. Headless bodies, ladies and gentlemen dressed in various fashions and costumes.

'Search me.' He shrugs. 'But I'm more interested in the mystery of how they got here. Like I said, I've been down here before to check the electrics – not for a while, mind – but that *thing* wasn't there.'

He flicks his beam over the rest of the room. In addition to the photographs, the room contains broken chairs and rotted wicker furniture, old rugs, garden tools, and rickety shelves bowing under the weight of old tins of paint and chemicals. 'I'll pop back tomorrow and start clearing out all this rubbish,' he says. 'It belongs in the skip.'

I know he's trying to be helpful, but I feel an odd reluctance to agree to his plan.

'Actually,' I say, 'leave it for now. I'd like to go through it. See if I can find out more about the sisters who lived here.'

'Not sure that's a great idea,' he says. 'The chemicals might be dangerous. Some of those containers look rusty; they might be leaking.' He beams the torch for emphasis. 'To be honest, before you came here, Emma wasn't very well. She put the brakes on the works so we're not as far along as I'd like to be. I'm hoping that now you're here, we can get back on track.'

'Well, it is her project,' I say. 'And we can't have the place unsafe. I'm fine if you clear out the chemicals. But keep the photographs for now. I'd like to take a closer look at them.'

'Suit yourself. Though I didn't have you down as the morbid type.'

'Oh? What did you have me down as?'

His smile is distinctly flirtatious; I feel both flattered and alarmed. 'Earlier, it was the damsel in distress,' he says. 'But actually, I think you're pretty brave and adventurous to come back here after being locked in with that.' He flicks the torch at the headless portrait.

'Brave and adventurous,' I say. 'I'll take that.'

'Good.' He reaches out and brushes my arm; I experience a ghostly tingling sensation. Not exactly desire...

But close.

'Thanks for coming.' I head up the stairs before I can overthink anything. 'I didn't know who else to call. Sorry to have ruined your night.'

'You definitely haven't done that,' he says. 'Trust me.'

'OK,' I say, not trusting my own dubious flirting skills to say more.

We reach the top of the stairs. Charlie closes the door.

'But Kate...'

'Yes?'

'The lock has been tampered with, and this isn't the first time someone's got in. So if I were you, I wouldn't go back down there alone. I'll bring that stuff outside if you really want to see it.'

I know he's right, and I'm grateful to him for being friendly and concerned. Nonetheless, it needles me when people – especially men – tell me what to do. 'I promise I won't do anything stupid,' I say. 'I'm in no hurry to be rescued again.'

He laughs; the sound is like a warm, cheerful hug. 'Part of me is glad to hear it,' he says. 'But another part thinks that maybe that's a shame.'

'Oh.'

Unusually, I find myself at a loss for words.

IV

Creepy, weird, unnatural.

Words still have the power to sting and wound, even in my present state. It is, after all, my work that she is rejecting, though at least she is not condoning its destruction.

I wish I could explain it; I wish I could make her understand. That, however, like much else, is beyond my power to influence.

One thing is certain: I have had many years to reflect and ruminate on what I did, and what I should have done differently. Many years to repent of a life sentence that has lasted far beyond its expected duration.

I would like this woman to know me. To know the truth so she can act as a new judge and jury. My final judge and jury. I will draw upon her energy and set her on the path. Create the illusion that she will help me achieve my one, impossible desire. Even now, hope is a comfort, and I, like everyone else, enjoy being fooled.

* * *

Voltaire said that 'illusion is the first of all pleasures', and so it was for me. I was born in the year 1880 into a house of illusions. A house where things – and people – were not always what they seemed.

My father was the ultimate magician: a man full of wit, charm, and infectious laughter so appealing that no one desired to look beyond the façade of joviality. Julian Havelock had a rare ability to make people feel like they were the most important person in the room – a quality which will unlock doors anywhere. In this case, it opened the doors of London townhouses and parlours where my father charmed his way far above his station. In one such parlour, he met Sarah Harding, a rich heiress promised to an older, less charismatic man. Instantly, the young beauty was smitten. In addition to being charming, my father also had a lucky streak, and on this occasion it worked in his favour. Before Miss Harding's father could discover their courtship and disinherit her for disobedience, he had the grace to die. Miss Harding had her charming man, and Julian had her fortune. A proverbial match made in heaven.

With wealth added to his arsenal of charm and luck, Julian worked tirelessly on extending this illusion to the masses. He moved into my mother's London townhouse and made grand plans for renovating a house in the country, as befitting a gentleman of means.

Spared the tedious business of making a living, my father was free to pursue his interest in magic and illusion. As a young man, he had dabbled in painting and sculpture, but had lacked the patience and funds to make something of it. As my mother kept up social appearances, my father opened a small studio in Mayfair where he could pursue his other passions: science, invention, and the occult.

Photography, still a fledgling craft, satisfied all three.

The science of photography comes from the Greek word *photos*, meaning 'light', and *graphein* meaning 'to draw'. The concept of drawing with light can be traced all the way back to Aristotle, though the term for our art was coined in the 1830s, a mere fifty years before my birth. The first true photograph, called the Heliograph, was taken in 1826 by a Frenchman called Niépce who used a sheet of pewter coated with bitumen, and an exposure time of over eight hours. He was joined in his work by another pioneer, Louis-Jacques-Mandé Daguerre, who refined the process by using silver-plated copper sheets and mercury vapor, which vastly reduced the exposure time. By 1839, the 'daguerreotype' was being used commercially for portraits, requiring an exposure time of only a few seconds. Further mid-century developments were made by William Henry Fox Talbot, whose 'calotype' process allowed for the creation of multiple prints from a single negative, and Frederick Scott Archer who introduced the wet plate collodion process that was used well into the 1900s.

My father was born into this exciting new world, and though he was less a scientist than a magician and illusionist, he fully embraced new developments and was forever experimenting with the latest techniques to perfect his art.

Unfortunately, for my mother, Julian's passions did not end with photography – in fact, they rather began there. He soon became less interested in the photographs themselves than with their subjects. The Mayfair studio was perfect for photographing subjects from all walks of life, and his work attracted clients of all sorts as well. And my mother? By then she had me. Not the hoped-for boy, but perhaps he would come in due course given a more wholesome environment and fresh country air. After several tense years of threats involving a tightening of purse strings, my father reluctantly let his Mayfair studio and together, the three of us moved to the country. To the old house they had purchased when they had first married, which my mother had paid to renovate in accordance with my father's plans and the latest taste and fashion.

A house called Rookswood.

* * *

Those were the original good years. Whatever you may think of Rookswood now, back then it was a happy house. My mother took it upon herself to make it a home full of laughter and love. She orchestrated fantastical Christmases, magic lantern shows under the stars, tennis and croquet on the lawn, sleigh rides in the woods. She developed passions of her own: for exotic plants and indoor gardens, flower arranging, and Oriental decorative arts. Her friends came to visit from London, and she threw lavish parties and summer fetes. When not entertaining, she performed charity work in the local community and sang in the church choir. She was beautiful, ethereal, kind, and, in polar opposition to my father, utterly lacking in artifice.

I had a governess and a master to teach me riding, dancing, watercolour painting and other pursuits befitting a young lady. I enjoyed the time spent with my mother, reading aloud, riding through the woods, sewing, and listening to her play the pianoforte. But in hindsight, I didn't appreciate those gentle pursuits as much as they merited.

No, for like everyone else, I was charmed by my father. It was his attention I craved, his love I valued above all else. My father was a magician, an illusionist. And oh, how I wanted to be taken in.

It was no secret that my father wanted a son. What self-respecting Victorian gentleman didn't? But as the years passed and one failed to materialise, he began to notice me. The traits that dismayed my mother – my penchant for climbing trees, tearing my dresses, getting dirty, tangling my hair, going in the sun without a hat – made me less of a daughter in his eyes, and ultimately, opened the doors of his studio for me. At first, I was simply 'there' as he worked, playing with jacks or marbles on the floor. He sent me on occasional errands, and I graduated to cleaning the vats, plates, and equipment. Eventually, I grew brave enough to ask questions, and found him willing to oblige me. I learned the names of the chemicals and their functions: silver salts, mercury, fixer, albumen paper. He showed me how to work the camera, and then how to develop the photographic plates. I worked industriously, watching, learning, listening. The arrangement suited me perfectly. I spent less and less time on 'feminine pursuits' and more and more time with my revered father, learning skills that interested and excited me. He had the satisfaction of teaching an adoring acolyte.

Gradually, without him becoming aware, I made myself indispensable. I was allowed to sit in on his portraiture sessions, though purely as an assistant. I fetched water and tea, adjusted the lighting, and occasionally operated the camera while my father rushed around with his boundless energy, charming the sitters, posing them, and doing his utmost to entertain them so they stayed still during the exposure.

My father took his work seriously; he hated mistakes. Secretly, I was petrified to make one, which is probably why I did.

Only one. But that mistake changed everything.

My father was commissioned by a gentleman called Mr Chesterford to produce his photographic portrait as an anniversary gift for his wife. During the sitting, I was charged with taking the exposed wet collodion plates to the darkroom to begin their development. I shall spare you a lecture on the details of the process, with its difficulties, intricacies, and complex chemistry. Much of our work in those days involved experimentation and trial and error. In this case, the error was severe. For when the image appeared out of the aether, the negative showed Mr Chesterford sitting in the paisley armchair, a lit pipe in his hand. But the man in the photograph would not be smoking that pipe.

The unfortunate gentleman was missing a head.

I expected my father to box my ears or whip me for my error. Or worse still: banish me from both darkroom and studio. Instead, when father saw my creation, he instantly realised its potential. Together, we began a new phase of experimentation – trying to replicate the technique and perfect it. This proved difficult and took many attempts and failures. We experimented with double exposures, over- and under-exposing parts of a negative, and ultimately, a technique called combination printing which allowed us to create an early form of photomontage. We weren't the first to use or discover these techniques; the true pioneers in this field were the likes of Oscar Gustave Rejlander and Henry Peach Robinson. However, my father's skill lay in turning our happy accident into a fashion – a fad – starting with our very next sitter.

A gentleman called Mr Armstrong brought his wife and sons to Rookswood for a family portrait. The family posed standing. Husband, wife and sons lined up in descending order of height. Afterwards, my mother served luncheon on the lawn for the wife and sons. My father whisked Mr Armstrong off for brandy and cigars in his study – he had a knack for discerning which of his patrons might want something different – something 'special'. Mr Armstrong's interest was piqued, and money exchanged hands.

I helped my father develop the plates and print a respectable photo for the family. Then, we used the negatives to create a different print for Mr Armstrong. It took us fourteen attempts, but at last we succeeded.

Perhaps you've seen the photo. It ended up reprinted in a newspaper article about my father, and numerous magazines on early photography, much to the chagrin of Mrs Armstrong and her sons.

For in the photo, the Armstrong clan: father, mother and sons, stand respectably lined up in descending order of height.

The patriarch, however, has his head neatly tucked underneath his arm.

* * *

Nowadays, I've heard it said that we Victorians had no sense of humour. In fact, the opposite was true. After the first headless photo was published in a sensationalist broadsheet, the new fashion spread like wildfire. Soon we had callers and clients at Rookswood nearly every day. To my mother's embarrassment and chagrin, not all of them were respectable, though others were far above even her social circles. Though most of the photomontages were my work, the earliest photos that were reprinted in newspapers and magazines give sole credit to Julian Havelock. That changed later, of course, but not for many years.

You may find it crude and macabre, but is it any more tasteless than the photographs that children take nowadays on their phones – their so-called 'selfies'?

Our most popular 'headless' range involved the sitter holding their own head in their hands, on their lap, or tucked beneath an arm. At first the fad appealed mostly amongst men, but it soon spread to society ladies. As my father's assistant, I attended numerous soirées in which a novelty portrait would be unveiled to shrieks of horror and titters of laughter. It became a sort of parlour game to see who could come up with the most outlandish idea.

Headless, armless, eyeless, dismembered lapdogs – anything was possible. A variation of the range involved placing a sitter's head on a different body. Lady Tarrington became Napoleon, Lord Winston became his own wife. And so it went. I did the work; my father got the credit. They called him a master of illusion, the ultimate magician.

The original 'good days' reached their pinnacle.

I should have known they couldn't last.

11

'Sleepwalking?'

Izzy slams her spoon down into the bowl of Weetabix and looks at me like I've got two heads. 'Are you serious? I was sound asleep all night. At least until your phone call woke me up. You're imagining things, Aunt Kate.'

I look to Max for moral support, but he's not looking at me. Smiling blandly down at his bowl, he swishes the spoon through the sludge of cereal and milk.

'You might not even have known you did it,' I say. 'You could have walked to Rookswood and then come right back.'

'What, and cut a lock, and trapped you in a cellar?' She snorts. 'If I did all that in my sleep it's a shame you didn't capture it on video. I could have gone viral on TikTok.'

Max laughs. I glare at him.

'Well, Max,' I say. 'What do you think? Are you aware of your sister sleepwalking? Or do you think I'm making it all up? I mean, why would I do that?'

'Dunno, Aunt Kate.'

'I've got an idea.' Izzy gives me an evil glance. 'Maybe you wanted to be rescued by Charlie. He has a way of showing up at the right place at the right time.'

I blush – which is just so mortifying. 'What's that supposed to mean?'

'You're single, right?'

'That's irrelevant,' I huff.

'Charlie was the one who rescued Mum when she fell. Did you know that?'

'Yes, as a matter of fact, he did mention it.'

Izzy shrugs. 'Just saying. Like sister, like... sister.'

I slam my coffee cup down on the table and stalk off to the kitchen. I shouldn't let Izzy get to me, but this is just too much.

I count slowly backwards from ten, my cortisol spiking. I'm on three when Max comes in, bringing his bowl to the sink and actually washing it out himself. 'Sorry, Aunt Kate.' He lowers his voice. 'Izzy's just messing with you. She was the one who found Mum at home. With the wine and the pills. She's just upset. We both are.'

'Come here, you.'

I open my arms and give Max a hug. The gesture is completely anathema to my nature, but somehow feels right. After a few seconds, he pulls away.

'Sorry,' I say. 'For all of it.'

'Sure.' He puts his bowl in the drainer without looking at me. 'And I don't know if it makes it better or worse, but I don't think Izzy was sleepwalking.'

'You don't? Then who did I see?'

He shrugs. 'Maybe no one. You could have dreamed it. Or maybe you were the one sleepwalking.'

'Me?'

'I mean, it sort of makes sense. You're in a new place. There's a spooky old house that some people say is haunted.' He gives me a cheeky wink. 'Not that I believe in ghosts. But maybe you do?' He wags his finger in front of my eye like a Mesmer's crystal. 'The power of suggestion and all that.'

He's joking, but the humour doesn't land.

'Nice try,' I say. 'But that's just ridiculous.'

Isn't it?

Max laughs. 'You're right, Aunt Kate. Don't worry, there are no ghosts at Rookswood. It's just an old house. You don't have to be afraid.'

'I'm not afraid.'

Am I?

'Good to know,' he says.

* * *

Izzy and Max leave for the bus and I contemplate my plans for the morning. I could work... Or, I could get to the bottom of what happened last night. It's a no brainer. Determined not to repeat past mistakes, I drive to Rookswood House armed with a screw-driver, a torch, and a cricket bat. The morning is dark and grey with the threat of rain in the air. The house looms, dwarfing my car, the untamed garden seemingly hostile and impenetrable. It occurs to me that I could ring Charlie again and ask him to accompany me. He offered, after all, to bring the items up from the cellar. But no. I still have some self-respect. I don't need a man around to rescue me from anything in the light of day. Rookswood and I might have got off on the wrong foot, but I'm determined to prove to myself that a house is just a house, no matter how spooky and creepy it might seem, and that ghosts don't exist.

As I enter the building, however, my temporary bravery is

replaced by a dull sense of dread. I feel like I've suddenly wandered onto the set of one of those ghost-hunter shows where spooky music plays at a subsonic frequency designed to provoke terror. My nerves tense like a cocked trigger, ready to fire. I force myself to breathe... *a house is just a house...* Rookswood is empty and unloved, and ultimately, innocuous.

The light beaming down from the cupola casts everything in pale silver, like all the surfaces are covered by a sheen of dust. I think again of Miss Havisham and her ruined wedding. Cake eaten by mice, flowers wilted, veil dirty and torn. Not terrifying, just sad. Were the Weird Sisters once happy here? If I'm going to find out more, I have to see this through.

I make my way to the door under the stairs. It's almost indistinguishable from the panelling and clearly was designed that way. A hidden door, a secret cellar – my mind unspools into macabre realms of fantasy. I must keep my wits about me, and, in light of the cellar's strange contents, my head squarely on my shoulders.

The broken padlock is still on the floor. I pick it up; the hasp has clearly been sliced through with bolt cutters. The door opens easily, and I shove the cricket bat underneath to keep it propped open. The darkness yawns like an open mouth. I shine the torch into the belly of the beast and descend the stairs.

At the bottom, I shine the light around and find a cord hanging down from an electric light fitting. With some trepidation, I pull it, and to my surprise, a single bare bulb flickers on. I stare at what's around me: a lot of cobwebs, that's for sure, plus a lot of old equipment and junk. And...

The headless woman.

'Hello there,' I say aloud. 'How's tricks?' I force myself to go closer. As I noticed last night, the headless woman is the first of a number of other full-length portraits shoved against the wall. As

I move her aside, a huge spider scurries away. The next photo is of a woman wearing only a laced corset and drawers. Her shoulders are shapely and swanlike. Unlike the first photo, this woman's head is present and accounted for – it's neatly tucked underneath her arm.

My breakfast repeats on me as I flip through the other photos. More headless men and women; women's heads on men's bodies, and vice versa; Victorian cross dressers; provocative nudes of both genders. Every photo is artful in its skill and detail. Every photo is bizarre and disturbing. If the sisters who lived here took these photos, 'weird' doesn't even begin to cover it. Leaving the photos as I found them, I practically run back up the stairs. The cellar door is open just as I left it. But unlike how I left it, the front door is also open. How did that happen? The wind? Charlie?

'Hello?' I call out.

No answer, no one there.

So why do I feel like someone's watching me?

I go back to the cellar door and fetch the cricket bat. The weight of the willow is comforting in my hand. Something creaks; my heart thumps.

'Who's there?' I say again. I look up to the top of the staircase. A shadow blurs across the landing and disappears. A woman?

'Hey!' Hefting the bat, I run upstairs. Nobody's supposed to be here, and if there are trespassers, or squatters – or sleepwalkers – I need to get rid of them. The place may be structurally sound, but there are clearly a lot of hazards about. I don't want anyone getting hurt. Especially me.

The thought comes too late. At the top of the stairs, I trip. Not over my own two feet, but over a scattering of rocks, nails and shards of glass. I scream as I slide to the floor, cutting the palm of my hand in the process. Is there an intruder living here? Or a trespasser making mischief? One thing's for sure, this time, no one is coming to my rescue.

So I get to my feet and crunch over the debris.

'Come on now,' I say. 'This isn't necessary. I don't mean any harm.'

But someone does. At the far end of the corridor, a thin, grey plume of smoke wafts from underneath a door. My heart skitters. If the house is on fire, I should get the hell out before I end up trapped. But if someone else is here, do I have a duty to save them?

'Look,' I yell. 'Whoever you are, I promise you won't get in trouble! Let's just get out of here.'

I approach the door. There's a thunk from inside. Is the person I saw already overcome by smoke inhalation? I'm not going to let that happen – not on my watch.

My hand quavers as I put it on the wood. It's cool to the touch, as is the knob, which feels like I'm gripping an ice cube. But it turns easily enough, and I push open the door...

Inside, the room is dark, the windows boarded up, with only a few pinpricks of light coming in. The beam of my torch reveals heavy mahogany furniture including a huge four-poster bed hung with the remains of damask curtains, dark and shredded with age, and smelling faintly of smoke. But in the here and now, there's no smoke. No fire. No woman.

But there is something: a piece of paper on the floor, peeking out from beneath the sagging valance at the bottom of the bed. I go over and pick it up. It's a photograph; the sepia image shows a young, light-haired girl in her early twenties. Her face is serene as she smiles at the camera; her arm is outstretched as if she's holding hands with another person. But who that person might have been is lost to time. The photo is torn down the middle.

I kneel down and check under the bed for the other half of

the photograph, but already the air in the room feels so heavy, so melancholy, that I know I won't find it.

'Who is she?' I say aloud.

The sun goes behind a cloud, and there's no one there to answer.

V

In doing this thing, I have given everything. I place all my trust, all my hope in this woman, this stranger. A sister to the other woman who came here and suffered an injury, though not by my doing. The injured woman was a creature of light, and I knew I could not reach her. This woman, this shadow sister, is more like me.

Few things in life are more defining than being a *sister*. This I discovered in my twelfth year, when everything changed at Rookswood.

The year was 1892. Mother fell pregnant and my father resumed part-time operations at his London studio. I didn't know how to feel about the former, but the latter caused me great despair. I begged my father to allow me to accompany him, allow me to be his assistant in a proper studio. But instead, he ruffled my hair fondly and insulted me in the worst way: 'You're a young lady, now, Adaline. It's time you start acting like one.'

A young lady. How could he be so cruel as to remind me? Of course the rapidly approaching end of my girlhood had not escaped my notice. My hips and chest had rounded; my moods had grown tumultuous. I'd begun to experience monthly bloods that at first seemed a harbinger of death, but gradually faded to a worry, then a vexation. Worst of all, I was squeezed into a corset, so tight that I couldn't draw a full breath. I wished fervently that I'd been born a boy, or at least could have continued to be treated like one. Even then I suspected that I was not like other young ladies, though I did not entirely understand the points of difference.

I now know the truth about my father and why I was not allowed to set foot in that London studio. I know the truth about myself, too. Most important of all, I know the truth about truth... It is painful. It hurts more than anything.

As for my mother, to her credit and my shame, she tried to fill the void created by my father's absences. Tried to interest me in the old pursuits, and when that failed, she tried to find common ground. Could I not take some lovely photographs of the garden? The church fete? (The latter suggestion was abandoned when I put the head of a local dowager on the body of the vicar.) I did not appreciate her efforts and masked my growing concern over her health with childish displays of petulance and anger. For instead of blossoming with the new life inside her, my mother became corpulent and immobile. Her alabaster skin took on a sickly yellowish hue, and confined to an invalid's chair, her ankles swelled up like elephant's legs. The doctor was worried, and I knew I should be too. My father treated her with his usual obsequious charm, petting her like a lapdog and bringing her flowers and treats when he deigned to return to the house – which occurred less and less frequently. When I asked him about the work at the London studio, begging once again to be allowed to participate, he waved away both my request and my concerns. 'It's too far to travel here and back every weekend,' he would say. 'And the flat above the shop is quite small and would never do for you.' He chucked me under the chin as if I was a small child.

'But what about our work? The novelty photos?'

'Ah,' he said. 'The truth is, Ada, they have become a little less "novel", so I've taken the work in a slightly different direction, temporarily, to please some important gentleman clients. But I promise, I shall return in the summer and in that month, we shall make novelty portraits to our hearts' content. By cutting off the supply now, we shall create an even greater demand!'

He would say no more on the subject, but I chose to be heartened that he would soon be returning. Of course he would want to be in residence at Rookswood when the baby arrived. He would want to see his... son? The very notion drove the breath from my body. If my mother give birth to a boy, would it drive an even greater wedge between my father and me?

Again I am ashamed to admit that these were my chief concerns, even up to the very night of my mother's lying in. A doctor and a midwife were on hand. My father was not. I stood outside the door and listened to my mother's cries and the worried voices of the medical staff. My own heartbeat pounded in my ears and dark spots clouded my eyes. Through the door, I heard the sound of a smack, and a baby's thin wail. The last sound before I fainted dead away.

A nurse revived me with a bottle of salts. I took a sniff, the smell sharp and acrid in my nose. 'You mother wants to see you,' she said, helping me to her feet. 'She wants to say goodbye.'

I didn't comprehend what was happening as I was led into the room. My mother was lying in the bed, wet and bloodied like a dying whale. In her arms was a tiny creature, rooting like a grub, fists tight and angry.

'Meet your sister,' my mother said. She reached out a hand

for mine. Her grip was weak, her last strength ebbing away. 'She's called Camile.'

My sister: Camile.

'Love her, Ada, and keep her safe. Always.' For a second, her fingers tightened over mine. 'Never let her go.'

And with that, she let *me* go, her fingers loosening as her spirit passed from this world.

* * *

I was determined to hate my sister. She had taken everything from me. My mother, to be sure, but, I reasoned, my father too. If it had not been for the pregnancy, he would not have taken himself off to London. If my mother had not died, he might have found reason to return to Rookswood. As it was, the die was cast. In those days, we had staff: a housekeeper, a cook, a governess, a wet nurse hired in from the village, and numerous other maids, footmen, and stable boys. These, my father determined, were more than sufficient to look after his two daughters, giving him space to 'grieve over the loss of his wife', which he effected by moving himself to London to 'look after the needs' of his clients.

In the early months, I took no interest in the baby. It took all my strength and willpower to wrestle with my own grief, anger, guilt, and poisonous thoughts: *I had lost everything; I had nothing left.* I stopped eating, broke crockery, cried and cursed like a mad girl. When finally I managed to subdue my dark humours, locking them away in the deepest part of my mind, I recalled my mother's dying words. *Love her, Ada, and keep her safe. Never let her go.*

My mother was cleverer than I'd credited. Her last wish was voiced not just for the benefit of the babe, but also for me.

Though I felt lost and abandoned by both of my parents, my mother had left me a way to fill the void. She had left me *someone*.

I had a sister.

Camile.

Following that realisation, I emerged from my room and embarked upon a new mission in life. Already I had decided that I would never marry, for I saw no profit in subjugating myself to a man and risking the loss of my identity and remaining freedoms. Even so, I began to understand the pull of motherhood.

Camile was loud, smelly, and demanding. A helpless and useless creature, totally unworthy of love. And yet, I grew to love her with a fervour that defied all reason. As she grew, first bawling and crawling, then walking and talking, she became my shadow. A shadow of pure light. With her blonde curls and blue eyes, she charmed friends and strangers alike. Camile was luminous; she glowed as bright as a star.

I, in contrast, began more and more to embody the darkness. It was my role to protect her, to preserve her pure, bright flame. Light and dark cannot exist without the other, and I took my role seriously. However you may judge me, do remember that.

12

Maybe I'm losing my marbles – surely, that possibility must be considered. As I drive away from Rookswood, the torn photo in my pocket, all my instincts tell me that I should leave this place and go back to London immediately. Of course, there's the matter of Izzy and Max, but there's a way around that. I could buy them each a plane ticket to Florida. Trade being their aunt for becoming their fairy godmother, and grant them their wish of living with their dad.

My palms are clammy on the wheel as I drive through the main gates, planning to turn towards the village. But as I pull out, I find third gear instead of first, and the car thunks to a halt in the middle of the road. Another vehicle comes round the bend, too fast. The driver leans on the horn, just managing to swerve and miss me. The vehicle slows, bumping to a halt on the verge.

'What the hell are you doing?' a man calls out the window.

Great. All I need is an irate driver to make my day a little worse.

I lift my hand in a little apologetic wave, but for some reason, the car won't start. *Oh God, oh God*. Why is this happening? A light comes on the dashboard. *Battery not charging*.

Oh God. I'm stalled in the middle of the road on a dangerous bend. Do I get out of the car, try to move it?

A tap on the window.

The other driver.

'Sorry, but are you all right?'

That voice. Resisting the urge to put my head in my hands, I look up. Dark hair, blue eyes, a penetrating scowl.

Dr Whitford.

'No, I'm not,' I say, a little frantic. 'The car won't move. I think the alternator's carked it.'

'Can you put it in neutral?' he says.

Neutral. Gear stick. I can do this. Nothing happens.

'Press the clutch down.'

Oh – the clutch. He really is very good looking, in a scary headmaster kind of way. I imagine he's the object of many a schoolgirl crush, like a dark-haired version of Sting in that 'Don't Stand So Close to Me' video. I really don't like him at all.

I press the clutch; the car starts to roll. His hair flops in front of his eyes as he bends down and pushes the car backwards out of the road.

'Steer towards the gate.'

I steer – the wrong way.

'The other way.'

If this is an exam and the universe is the invigilator, I'm failing spectacularly. Unable to drive properly, creating a hazard, requiring a man to rescue me... again. That last one annoys me above all else.

'You were going too fast around that bend,' I say, as we reach the verge in front of the gates.

'I wasn't expecting a stalled car.'

'Don't you teach children these days to "expect the unexpected"?'

'Not last time I checked the national curriculum.' He cocks his head. 'And besides, there are no children here.'

'True.' Something about his expression sends a tremor through me. Of ice, of dislike, of... something else.

'You look pale,' he says, frowning. 'And there's blood all over the wheel. Did you hurt yourself?'

I look down and realise that what I'd taken for clammy is actually blood. Of course – the nails and glass. My fall.

'Oh, that.' I wave my hand, wincing. Now that I've noticed it, the wound smarts. I dig out a crumpled tissue from my pocket and press it against my palm. 'It's nothing. Just a little accident at Rookswood House.'

'Rookswood?' His frown morphs into a glare. 'What were you doing there?'

'Long story.'

He crosses his arms. 'I've been round that place back when it was for sale. It's a lovely old house, but not exactly safe. You should be careful.'

I bristle at yet another warning. Do I look like someone who would recklessly go round a derelict old house and do myself an injury? I stare down at my bloody hands. The cuts are superficial, but the truth hurts.

'Is that on the national curriculum?' I say. 'Though, last I checked, I'm not one of your students.'

He looks amused at my sarcasm, for about half a second. But clearly, he's one of those men who always needs to have the last word. 'True,' he says, 'but speaking of students, my assistant will be giving you a call later today. To arrange a meeting about Max.'

'Max?' I feel instantly defensive. 'What about him?'

A line of cars rounds the corner and whizzes by.

'There's been an incident at school. More than one, actually. Given the circumstances, we're doing our best to avoid remedial action.'

'"Remedial action"?' My anger spikes. 'What the hell does that mean? Max is a good boy. A good egg.'

He raises a hand to fend me off. 'You're right, Ms Goodman. Sorry. This wasn't the right time for me to mention it. I'll have my assistant arrange something. In the meantime, can you call the rental car company? Have them tow the car, or replace it?'

'I'll be fine,' I say through my teeth.

'Good.' Without further ado, he heads across the road to his car, gets in, and drives away.

'Have a nice day...' I mutter under my breath.

Arsehole.

13

The encounter with Dr Whitford is a wave of awfulness in a vast sea of awfulness. But it does have one positive knock-on effect.

It makes me feel protective of Izzy and Max.

That evening, Max is out on a school drama trip, but when Izzy returns home, I sit her down. I don't have anything planned to say, but words come out anyway.

'I've had a pretty rough day,' I say, 'but I wanted to catch up.'

'Why?'

I'm not sure which part she's questioning, but I decide to elaborate. 'I went back to Rookswood House,' I say. 'It's a funny old place. Weird – you know. Creepy.'

She shrugs. 'I like the house. It's interesting.'

'I guess that's a good way to look at it,' I say. 'But anyway, I kind of scared myself thinking I heard noises and saw shadows.'

'Did you see the ghost?'

I swallow hard. 'What?'

'There's supposedly a ghost in the house. One of those sisters. The older one, I think. She's called Adaline. Ada.'

What am I supposed to say to that?

'Um, I don't actually believe in ghosts. But when I asked you the other night if you knew an Ada, you said no. Why did you lie?'

'I didn't lie.' She glares at me. 'I *don't* know anyone called Ada. Just because Mum's gone round the bend doesn't mean I have to follow.'

She's got a point but I don't want to acknowledge it.

We glare at each other, neither of us saying anything. Eventually, she gets bored. Grabbing an apple from the fruit bowl, she turns her back on me with a huff and leaves the kitchen. I want to ask her more about Max and if she knows why Dr Whitford wants a meeting. The assistant rang earlier, but I let the call go to voicemail. Suddenly, I feel ashamed. I'm supposed to be looking after these children while my sister can't. I'm feeding them, doing their laundry, and driving them around, but surely, I should also be making sure they aren't... being haunted?

Safe in the knowledge that Izzy's upstairs in her room, I decide to wait up for Max. The events of the day have put me behind in my work, and I have emails to answer, timesheets to submit and client bills to prepare. But I find myself unable to focus or even make a start. Instead, I stare out of the window. My mind harks back to GCSE English and a novella by Henry James we had to read. *The Turn of the Screw*. Two beautiful children, haunted by ill-intentioned ghosts; a gullible, clueless governess who's too hysterical and sexually repressed to work out what's happening. As the sky darkens my, reflection becomes clearer, and I revisit everything I've experienced at Rookswood: locked doors, scattered glass and debris, strange photos, ghostly apparitions, the phantom smell of smoke. And the name that keeps coming up – Ada.

I take the torn photo out of my pocket and look at it again. Is this a photo of Ada herself, like some kind of early-twentieth-century selfie? I don't know much about fashion, but the beaded dress she's wearing strikes me as something from the teens, maybe as late as 1920. Beyond that, I recognise the paisley curtain and chaise longue from the studio at Rookswood as well as the green and leafy potted palm which is still there, but now long dead.

If this is Ada, then who was in the photo with her and why have they been torn away?

I do a few internet searches, but find only a few passing references to a woman called Adaline Havelock who died intestate. Her house, Rookswood, passed to the local council. One article mentions that she was a photographer, and there are several blogs that mention a Julian Havelock who was apparently a pioneer in early photography. Reading up on him and his contemporaries turns out to be a swift canter through a number of bizarre fads in Victorian photos. Apparently, the Weird Sisters were not alone in their penchant for the sensational and the macabre. I read a little bit about some of the 'Photoshopping' techniques Victorians used in the early days of photography such as double exposures, combination printing, layering plates, and retouching techniques used to create the 'wasp waist' that was fashionable for women. In addition to headless photos, other fads included post-mortem photos and spirit photography. It sounds very creative, albeit extremely creepy.

As I read on, Dr Whitford steals into my mind. He was the one who first mentioned the connection between Rookswood and photography. If he's as 'old school' with his photography as he claims, then he probably knows all about the old-time techniques. Instead of talking about Max, I could commandeer the meeting to ask him what he knows about Rookswood and Adaline.

As I'm musing over the possibilities, Max comes home,

dropped off by a friend's parent. He looks tired, and though he gives me what I take to be a genuine smile, he clearly just wants to go to bed. I ask him about the play he's seen; he gives short but polite answers. Clearly this isn't the right time for a deep and meaningful conversation, but as he is about to head upstairs, I broach the subject that has me concerned.

'By the way,' I say. 'Your headmaster mentioned an incident at school. Is everything OK?'

Something flickers across his face – annoyance, maybe – and in that moment, he looks just like his father. 'Everything's fine, Aunt Kate,' he says. 'Just a little misunderstanding. I'm clearing it up. You don't need to worry.' He punctuates his response with a big yawn.

'OK, then,' I say. He has that innocent, boyish air that makes me want to trust him, just like I'd trusted Philip. At the end of the day, Philip *was* trustworthy. It was my sister who proved otherwise.

'Goodnight, Aunt Kate.'

'Goodnight.'

* * *

According to Max, everything may be fine and I don't need to worry, but as I lie in bed that night, I feel very far from fine and definitely worried. My body is poised on high alert; I listen to every creak of the house, every distant car, every noise that could potentially be a footstep. The house is silent, but somehow, that makes it worse. As the clock downstairs chimes two, I turn on the bedside lamp. At three, I turn on my computer and do an internet search. Not on Rookswood or the Weird Sisters...

On ghosts.

The Wikipedia article is comfortingly bland. In every country, in every period of human history, people have attempted to explain what happens after death. And why not? Death is an immutable, inevitable fact of life that none of us can escape. It's only natural that we try to understand and rationalise it. Ghosts are a very human construct. A way to try and explain the unexplainable, to know the unknowable.

But even if these things are unexplainable and unknowable, surely the truth is out there somewhere? Either ghosts exist or they don't. But which is it? I read numerous accounts that are less comforting, and often very different in their explanations of paranormal phenomena. Some so-called 'experts' hypothesise that paranormal phenomena have to do with energy leaving the body at death, and what happens if it doesn't dissipate completely. Several articles propose that after death, energy can become trapped in a particular place. If so, that place will retain a 'form' or 'energy signature' that occupies a liminal space between matter and energy. A consciousness, of a sort. Some of these revenants are strong enough to draw energy from the living – enough to cause draughts and air currents, and even move objects. These poltergeists or 'noisy ghosts' can get angry when the living occupy their space, and in some notable cases, living people have been physically harmed by the trickery of the dead.

Loose floorboards? Nails and glass? Is there a poltergeist at Rookswood who's fuelled by the energy of women who come onto the premises: Emma, Izzy... me? It's a chilling idea, if far-fetched. But what about the alternative? There are, of course, just as many articles debunking these accounts. In modern times, most hauntings are chalked up to the hysteria, overactive imagination, and attention-seeking behaviour of the *haunted*, and, very occasionally, to mischief – silly buggers – carried out by the living.

A poltergeist or human mischief. Which one is responsible for the shenanigans at Rookswood?

My eyelids grow heavy and I'm about to call it a night when a peer-reviewed article in a prestigious academic journal catches my attention. Not the article itself, but the name of the author. A name that keeps coming up like a bad penny...

Dr Matthew Whitford.

Turns out that the headmaster of St James's Academy is quite the jack of all trades. An expert not only on photography, but also on the paranormal. Who would have thought? His approach is scientific and balanced, speaking of 'limbic system autonomic responses' that make the living believe they can sense the presence of the dead, and the 'motivational triad' of the lesser-evolved amygdala region of the brain that is programmed to seek pleasure, conserve energy, and preserve life. I manage to get the gist of the article (despite my ignorance of the erudite Latin terms he's gleefully included), but I'm more interested in the man himself and what prompted him to become an expert on this particular subject. Near the end of the article, I get my answer.

My own interest in the topic arose from accounts of paranormal experiences in an old house at the edge of the village where I grew up. My grandmother, who was acquainted with the elderly woman who lived and died in the house, claimed on several occasions to have 'felt the energy' of the deceased when visiting the house during the time it served as a local community centre. Following complaints of similar phenomena, the council eventually allowed the premises to become derelict. Although prior to writing this article, I visited the house in an attempt to replicate my grandmother's paranormal experience, I failed to do so. Hence, despite accounts of ghostly sightings both around the world and closer to home, I myself remain a sceptic.

His grandmother saw a ghost? At Rookswood? I peruse the article again. Dr Whitford is careful to toe the line of political correctness, debunking the popular notion that most ghostly sightings are made by women: 'traditionally considered the "weaker, more impressionable sex" [citation].' But despite his attempts to normalise the results through a graph based on age, sex, and socioeconomic status, the results show a clear peak: women see more ghosts than men. Young women around the age of puberty and women aged seventy plus account for the majority of documented paranormal experiences. To me, that makes sense. Women my age are probably too busy and stressed to bother with 'opening themselves up to energy frequencies', or whatever. I am a case in point. While engaged in my normal routine, I certainly never had the time or inclination to give ghosts a first thought, let alone a second. But here in the hinter-lands, far beyond the boundaries of my comfort zone, my brain is using its new-found freedom to play tricks on me. End of story.

My head nods; I turn off my laptop and sink down into the bed closing my eyes. When sleep finds me, it brings frightening and troubled dreams.

14

'Morning!'

A booming voice through the letterbox startles me; coffee sloshes onto my papers from the mug in my hand. I've dropped the kids off at school, and a new deal has come in that I need to get on top of. Although I've been busy with work over the last few days, it's been a challenge to wrest my mind away from spooky old houses, ghosts – and academics specialising in paranormal phenomena – and refocus on the world of legal documents. Black and white, open and shut. Now I'm faced with another distraction.

I go to the front door and open it to Charlie, looking wholesome and substantial in jeans, a fisherman's jumper and a woolly hat.

'Hello,' I say. 'How are you?'

He blows on his large hands, clearly chilly in the still-frosty morning air.

'I just wanted to let you know I'm going up to the house. I've set up a meeting with the planners, and I want to be sure we're ready.'

'The planners?'

'Yes,' he says. 'I went and saw Emma – finally talked her around. We're going to apply for a change of use.'

'You saw Emma?' This is as much as I can grasp. The hospital let me know that Emma's been transferred to a residential facility near London. It's much too far away for regular visits, and neither Izzy nor Max seemed keen to make the trek. So the fact that Charlie went to see her, and that she's the 'we'... Of course, I know there's nothing in it; he's working for her, that's all. There's no reason to feel... jealous.

'Yes.' He gives me a reassuringly broad smile. 'I had to go up to London and happened to be in the neighbourhood. It was easy enough to pop by. She's doing well, and says hello, but she doesn't want to disrupt you or the kids. So she's fine with you not visiting.'

'Oh.' Emma probably said this to make me feel guilty. As usual, she's succeeded.

'Anyway, I've offered to take the planners around and show them the new drawings. I wanted to let you know I'll be up at the big house doing some bits and bobs. So you won't think it's the ghost, or anything.'

'There is no ghost,' I feel compelled to say.

He laughs. 'Of course there isn't. But try telling that to the locals. I didn't mention it the other night, either, because I didn't want to scare you.'

'I wouldn't have been scared.'

'I'm sure *you* wouldn't. But Emma was. When she heard stories about the ghost, she went a bit "woo woo".' He twirls a finger. 'She even thought that floorboard she tripped on might have been loosened by a ghost. Like that could actually happen.' He shakes his head. 'No, if anything, it's teenagers or tramps playing silly buggers. That's what we need to put a stop to.'

'I agree,' I say firmly. My palms smart through the gauze bandages as I recall the glass, nails and rocks – all traditional 'poltergeist' accoutrements. 'I'm in the "silly buggers" camp too. We need to keep the place secure so that no one else gets hurt.'

'I'm glad we're on the same page.' Charlie winks. 'So I'd best get to it. And by the way, your coffee is dripping.'

I look down at a thin dribble of brown pooling onto the encaustic tiles of Emma's doorway.

'Oh, yeah. I was just about to get some more.' Stupid, lame. 'Would you like to join me? Warm up before you go to that cold house.'

As soon as the words are out of my mouth, I regret them. I've got work to do, he's my sister's friend, and I don't need any complications.

'I was hoping you'd ask, Kate.' Maybe it's my imagination, but his smile seems only for me as he bends down to remove his boots.

'Great,' I mumble. 'I'll put on another pot.'

My pulse is thrumming as I go to the kitchen and make more coffee. I hear Charlie moving around the conservatory where my laptop and papers are spread everywhere. What will he think when he sees that I've made myself at home?

When I bring the coffee, Charlie's sitting at the table, his size and presence seeming to shrink the size of Emma's conservatory like a giant in a doll's house. A warm and comforting giant. What ghost would dare to show its 'energy signature' when he's around?

'It's good you're here to hold the fort while my sister's unwell,' I say.

He laughs. 'I could say the same about you. And in truth, I also wanted to drop by to see how you were doing after your ordeal the other night.'

'I'm fine, really.' I bristle at the memory of having to be rescued (even if it did have pleasant aspects). 'Though I'm not convinced I imagined seeing Izzy, or someone else, going to the house that night. And the door was open when I got there. It might have blown open, or maybe someone was round earlier and left it unlatched. Maybe the same person who cut the lock – I don't know.'

'Yep, sure is a mystery.'

Is it? I consider mentioning the key, badly hidden under the pot on the doorstep, but I don't want to sound like I'm criticising his security measures.

'The point is,' I say, 'Rookswood House is what we lawyers call an "attractive nuisance". A place that kids or other people know is off limits, so they want to get in there all the more.'

'An "attractive nuisance".' Charlie looks bemused. 'I like that. Though I think "ugly and dangerous" is closer to the mark.'

'That's for sure.'

'But you haven't seen anyone else about the place, have you?'

I look away, a little sheepish. 'I went back yesterday,' I say. 'I was curious about the headless woman and the Weird Sisters.' I decide not to mention the phantom smoke or the photograph I found. I do, however, tell him about the debris at the top of the stairs, showing him my bandaged palms.

He sets his coffee cup on the table a little too hard. 'Jesus, Kate. You shouldn't have gone back. Not on your own. The place really is dangerous.'

'So you said.' I feel irritated, mostly because I know he's right. 'In which case, I think *we* need more security. Unless you're planning on becoming a one-man rescue operation.'

'Maybe I will.' He winks. 'And of course you're right. In fact, I'm going to see about putting up a gate. Just on the other side of the trees as you come towards the house. It will help delineate the new boundary.'

'What new boundary?'

'Like I said, Emma's agreed to a change of tack. Only the façade of the house is listed, not the innards. There's no reason to keep it in its current state. She can gut the house and develop the whole site into a housing estate. Turn a tidy profit. Which she and the kids'll need now that Phil's out of the picture.'

I frown. Philip may be out of the picture, but a housing estate? With my lawyer hat on, I can completely see his point. The site has development potential, and that makes more sense than restoring the house as is. But is Emma really on board with this new plan? I find it hard to believe that my sister who once loved princesses, horses, and fairytale castles would act in such a ruthless way. But that view is based on antiquated impressions that bear no resemblance to my sister as she is now. If Charlie and Emma are on the same page then it's nothing to do with me.

So why do I feel so angry?

I guess it's because Rookswood is spooky and sinister, but it's also a beautiful, historic old house. Also, if there is something – or *someone* – there, even just an 'energy signature', then don't we have a duty to…? I have no idea. Maybe I really am losing my marbles. Certainly, I don't recognise this new version of myself. A version that actually *cares*.

Charlie finishes his coffee and stands up to leave. 'Thanks,' he says. 'I appreciate the winter warmer. And I was thinking that maybe I could return the favour. Do you fancy a drink? The Two Swans is a nice pub in the village. We could do tomorrow night, if you're free.'

'I'm free.' The words are out before I can think them. This new version of me might appreciate Rookswood, but apparently she's not above going to the pub with a nice-looking guy.

'Brilliant.' He goes to the door. 'I'll be looking forward to it, Kate.'

'Yeah, me too.'

15

The day passes; I get very little work done. A drink – that's all it is. Like a coffee, but with a buzz. I go for drinks all the time with colleagues. This is no different.

Do I want it to be?

In the late afternoon, I dutifully go to pick up Izzy after netball (Max has gone over to a friend's house to do homework). Somehow, chauffeuring one or both of my sister's teenage children has become a daily routine. It's easier now that the rental car company has come round and replaced the dead manual Hyundai with a newer automatic Skoda (they offered me a BMW, but I declined). As I enter the scrum of the school car park, unfamiliar emotions swirl inside me – annoyance, anticipation, self-doubt. Things I expect a mother might feel. Why is there so much traffic? Did the children have a good day? Will Izzy like what I'm cooking for dinner?

God. When did I start *doing* family?

Just as I park in front of the school, I get a call from the headmaster's PA. In for a penny, in for a pound, I answer it.

'I'm glad I finally caught you,' the PA says. 'Dr Whitford would like a quick word.'

'How quick?' I say. 'I'm here to collect Izzy.'

'You can meet her in the library. It won't take long.'

'Fine.' My stomach churns like a helter-skelter. It must be those well-trodden neural pathways about naughty students and headteachers' offices. I don't want Max to be in trouble – it's only natural I feel this way. But when I enter the office, with its beautiful photographs of birds and butterflies in flight, I'm more worried for myself than for Max. The glacial blue eyes of the man at the desk draw me in and cause another spark of nerves. Something about him is disconcerting, and I don't like that.

'Ms Goodman,' he says. 'Thanks for coming in.'

I look past him at the photograph of the petite blonde woman and beautiful little boy. What does his wife think of his expertise in the supernatural? With a nice family like that in this world, why is he so interested in the next?

Sitting forward in the chair, I fold my hands in my lap like I'm about to start reciting Latin declensions. 'I recently happened to read a very interesting article,' I say. 'It was written a decade or so ago by a young graduate student. The topic was paranormal phenomena: ghosts, energy signatures, and the like. And here's the funny part. The supposedly "haunted house" sounded a lot like Rookswood.'

His mouth opens and closes; I've taken him by surprise, and probably not many people do that of a day. 'How on earth did you find that?' he says. 'I thought it was only available in scholarly journals.'

'Maybe I'm a scholar – did you consider that? I find it strange that you failed to mention it.'

He rakes a hand through his hair, clearly irritated by my confrontational manner.

'It hasn't exactly come up in conversation before now,' he says.

'You said you spoke to Emma and Philip before they bought the house. Was the ghost disclosed, or is that a "latent defect"?'

He looks at me for a long, tense moment. Then, he laughs.

'I must say, Ms Goodman, you're quite the detective.'

'I said to call me Kate.'

'Kate.' His smile is borderline mischievous.

'To be honest,' he says, 'I'd forgotten about that article. I wrote it a long time ago as part of my thesis on neuropsychology. I didn't know it had been reprinted; I probably ought to have it removed. I'd hate to have it fall into the wrong hands – parents, governors, administrators – pretty much anyone I deal with on a daily basis.'

'I suppose it's not good for your image,' I say. 'Your grandmother seeing a ghost.'

'Actually, she photographed one. She was passionate about photography.' He gestures to the wall. 'She taught me everything she knew. All about light, shadow, and composition, plus the technical nuts and bolts. She learned from the best – from Adaline Havelock. When Gran was a girl, she worked for a short time for Meals on Wheels. She visited Adaline, who was elderly, but Gran showed an interest in her work and they became friends of a sort. So maybe that's why Adaline appeared to her.'

My throat constricts. 'Your grandmother *photographed* the ghost?'

'She photographed a strange blur of light. But if you looked really closely, you could see it was a woman's face.'

'Really?'

'I know it sounds crazy. And believe me, I was the first to question it, even though I saw it with my own eyes.'

I sit forward. 'Where is the photograph now?'

'Gran destroyed it, along with the negatives. She was a little unstable at the end. Rookswood was owned by the council in those days. When her husband died, Gran attended a grief group there. She said that sometimes, Adaline was there too.'

'I'm no maths expert, but I thought Adaline died in the early seventies. Over fifty years ago. So when your Gran said she was "there"...?'

'Adaline's ghost, her spirit. The revenant of her living energy.' He says it with a straight face, like he's giving a lecture on physics or neuropsychology. 'Adaline "told her" to destroy the photo. So she did.'

'Oh.'

'Gran died not long thereafter. That's about all I know.' Absently, he rifles through a stack of paperwork. 'In any case, I'll deal with the article. Thanks for bringing it to my attention.'

'Sure.' I feel like I should say something else. Something... human. But what? Before I can decide, there's a knock at the door and the PA pokes her head inside.

'Dr Whitford, the Smythe-Lyons are here.'

'Thank you, Charlotte,' he says. 'Give me five minutes.'

Five minutes. That's all I'm worth. I feel angry without knowing why.

'Sorry, Kate,' he says. 'I don't want to keep you. But I called you here to talk about Max. There have been some problems with him around the school. Bullying and acting out.'

'Bullying? You mean Max is *being* bullied.'

'Not exactly.' His lips press in a line.

I sit back and cross my arms. 'If you're saying that Max *is* the bully, then I don't believe it. He's a lovely boy – he made me feel welcome, whereas Izzy makes me feel regularly like a bug squashed under her shoe.'

Dr Whitford laughs. 'I can't argue with you there, but Max

does have some issues. Izzy lets her feelings out, but since his dad left, Max has bottled his up. That's not good for anyone. I spoke with Emma about him seeing the school psychologist. And after the incident this week, it's become imperative.'

'OK,' I say through my teeth. 'What's he done? What's so *imperative*?'

'He set a boy on fire.'

'What? You mean, deliberately?'

'We're still investigating,' he says. 'But I thought you'd want to know first thing. We're taking the matter seriously, and I've issued him with a formal warning. The letter will come to Emma by post. If there's another incident, then he'll be suspended. After that... well, let's hope it all ends here.' He checks his watch. 'Now, I'm afraid I have another appointment.'

'Another appointment?' I raise my voice. 'You bring me here, tell me *that*, and you can't even give me the facts? I mean, could it have been an accident?'

'Possibly,' he says. 'Or it could have been a prank gone wrong. Max has been spending a lot of time in the chemistry lab at lunchtime and after school.'

'Isn't that what they do in labs – set fires? With Bunsen burners? In my day, any sort of interest in science would have been seen as a good thing. Or else chalked up to "boys will be boys".'

Just for a second he smiles again, before morphing back into headmaster mode. 'Nowadays, we take safeguarding very seriously,' he says. 'It's all about the welfare of the child. That includes Max, of course.'

'There's nothing wrong with Max,' I say. 'But his parents – now that's another matter. They're the ones who are the bullies. Moving the children to the grounds of a creepy old house that may be haunted. And then splitting up, and Emma trying to...' I swallow back a rogue sob. 'I understand you need to toe the party

line and I'm all for "safeguarding" and acting in the "best interests of the child" – really I am. But to be frank, if you suspend
him, or expel him you'll just be adding to the shit heap, if you'll
pardon my French.'

He cocks his head. 'I believe "shit heap" has an Anglo-Saxon
derivation.'

I sit forward, staring at him. 'Did you just make a joke?'

'Sorry.' Another brief smile, then he stands up. 'I'm sorry,
Kate, if we got off on the wrong foot. I mean no harm to Max –
quite the opposite. He and Izzy are great, and I want the best for
them. As does Emma, and you.'

'I just want my old life back.'

As the words leave my mouth, I question whether or not
they're true. Despite the overall awkwardness of the meeting, that
makes me the most uncomfortable.

'Of course,' he says. 'It must be very difficult for you having
been parachuted into all this. But I thought it best to keep you in
the loop. And to get your permission for Max to see the psychologist. There's usually a waiting list, but under the circumstances,
we can fast track it. Get the ball rolling.'

'Fine,' I agree dumbly, as he ushers me to the door.

'Keep me posted,' he says. 'On all of it.'

'I will.'

Down the corridor, I see the other parents – the 'Smythe-
Lyons' – standing poised and ready for their meeting. She's posh
and perky, he's satisfied and smug. I hate them.

'And Kate...'

I turn. Dr Whitford seems in no hurry to usher them in.

'Yes?'

'Rookswood is a funny old place. It grows on you. When it
went up for auction, I was hoping to buy it, but Emma and Philip
outbid me. I was relieved, however, that Emma seemed

passionate about the place and wanted to do right by it. Drag it into the modern world but keep its character and personality. That's what I was hoping.'

'I'm sensing there's a *but*?'

'Not a "but", just a friendly piece of advice. It's an old house with its own quirks and personality. And not all of its history is happy. You may not believe in ghosts, and most of the time, I'm right there with you. But just be careful, OK?'

I want to tell him where to go. Tell him to mind his own business, and that I don't need any more warnings. Instead, some strange force commandeers my body... and starts spouting Shakespeare.

'"There are more things in heaven and earth, Horatio, than are dreamt of in your philosophy." Is that what you're trying to say?'

He looks a little shocked, even a little impressed.

'Yes,' he says. 'That's it exactly.'

I leave his office and, ignoring the odd look from Mrs Smythe-Lyons, walk off down the corridor laughing my head off.

* * *

I don't mention my meeting with Dr Whitford – not to Izzy that night at dinner, or to Max when he comes home late once again, too tired to talk. I wait up for him, and when he comes into the kitchen, I try to picture him as a boy who might have deliberately tried to set another boy on fire. I can't see it. 'Did you have a good day?' is all I say.

'Yeah, Aunt Kate, I did.' He gives me that Christmas-card smile and any lingering doubts melt away. He grabs a banana and makes to go. I don't know how to broach any of it, but I need to say something. 'You know, Max,' I say. 'If you need to talk about anything, I'm here. Or, if you don't want to talk to me, there are others who can help.'

He stops walking, and for a long second I can't see his face. When he finally does turn towards me, he says, 'I'm fine, Aunt Kate, really.' The smile is just the same as before – I want it to be the same. But his eyes are darker, the pupils dilated. Is there something underneath? Something I'm not seeing?

'Goodnight,' he says, turning away again. 'Sweet dreams.'

16

The next day as I go about my work, I make a concerted effort not to think about Rookswood, Izzy and Max, ghosts, headmasters, *or* my upcoming 'date' with Charlie. The harder I try, the more they stick in my mind like an irritating song. I should cancel Charlie, that much seems clear. At the end of the day, I'm an outsider, an interloper. Here temporarily, inhabiting my estranged sister's territory and trying to manage her problems for as short a time as possible. I'm not here to make friends, let alone 'meet anyone'.

Nonetheless, that evening I order a pizza for the kids and park them on the sofa to watch Netflix, telling them that I'm going out to meet a friend. At precisely two minutes to eight, I walk through the door of the Two Swans pub. It's a warm, friendly-looking place with an understated air of posh gastropub: oak beams, stone floor, soft lighting, chalkboard menus, cloth napkins. About half the tables are occupied by couples, families, older people, and a few well-behaved dogs sprawled underneath. No sign, however, of Charlie.

I use the time to duck off to the loos. The sign points through another room off the main bar. It's a homely space, with shelves filled with books and board games; a fire roars in an inglenook, framed by comfortable sofas.

On a rug in front of the fire, a blond-haired boy of about six or seven is lying on his front playing with a pile of sticks, stones, feathers, and yarn. His focus is intense as he makes a spiral pattern of the twigs, rocks, and string. But when he looks up and sees me watching, he instantly covers his creation, shyly averting his eyes from mine.

'You OK, mate?'

The voice comes from one of the armchairs facing the fire. I can't see the man who's spoken, but his posh accent sounds familiar. From the opposite chair, a pretty woman with light blonde hair stands up.

'It's time to go, Daniel,' she says to the boy. 'Start cleaning up.'

The boy looks at her without making eye contact. There's something unusual about him, almost otherworldly.

'No,' he says. 'It's my dream.'

'Your dream?'

The man gets out of the chair and kneels on the rug next to the boy. 'Tell me about it,' he says.

The woman sighs, clearly annoyed.

'It's the pathway to the stars.' The boy uncovers his work so the man can see it. His father, I presume.

Matthew Whitford.

The boy proceeds to explain the twigs in terms of star clusters, constellations, and celestial reference points. He's clearly very intelligent, but also *different*.

'It's great,' his dad says. 'I'll take a photo of it. So we'll have it forever.'

'I'll get the bill,' the woman says.

I'm still standing there gawking as she walks past me without acknowledgement. She's not same person in the photo on Dr

Whitford's desk; that woman was closer to my age, and had a more angular face, her hair more of a pre-Raphaelite strawberry blonde. This one, in her Ugg boots, skinny jeans, and expensive suede jacket, is a more conventionally attractive, 'yummy mummy' type. Polished, pretty, but also cold. Did Dr Whitford trade in the mother of his child for a younger model? How typical. For all his scholarly erudition, he's obviously just your garden-variety knob.

He gets down on his knees and begins taking photos with a real camera, not a phone, as the boy moves things around on his spiral.

'This is you, Dad,' the boy says, pointing to a blue mallard feather. 'And Mum is here.' He lifts a grey stone. 'The queen.'

'Queen of the stars.' His father ruffles the boy's hair. 'I like that. She's always there watching over us.'

'Like her?' The boy looks up and points at me.

Matthew Whitford looks up at me, frowns. My chest knots with shame. Why am I here, gawking, intruding?

'Um, sorry,' I blurt. 'I was just looking for the loos—'

'Ah Kate, there you are.'

Saved by the bell. Or, in this case, Charlie.

'Oh, hi.' Turning, I duck out of the doorframe. The blonde woman returns with a waitress carrying a card machine. She looks at me, then Charlie. Is she judging me? Does she think I'm less attractive than Charlie? I've already judged her – she may be young and pretty, but she's not a patch on the woman in the photo. What happened to the little boy's mum?

'You OK?' Charlie asks.

And why am I thinking about Matthew Whitford anyway? Surely, I have more important people to focus on.

'Yes, fine.' I smile, trying to ignore my own discomfort as he gives me a once-over. I regret my decision to borrow some clothes from Emma's wardrobe: white jeans, knee-high boots, sage-green cashmere jumper. It's blindingly obvious that I'm trying to be someone I'm not. I should have worn a suit.

'I've got a table in the dining room, OK?'

'Perfect.'

As Charlie steers me towards the main room with a hand on my back, I'm aware of three people watching: a blonde woman, a small boy, and a man who makes my stomach churn with unidentified emotions.

* * *

By the time we're seated and I'm drinking a second glass of red wine, my emotions are becoming clearer. Distrust, annoyance, even... anger.

Charlie sits opposite me nursing a pint of bitter. The table is in a dark corner with discreet recessed lighting from a copper wall sconce. Intimate, romantic. Over the first drink, we made small talk: how Emma's getting on, how the kids are doing in school, his local projects, the new puppy he's thinking of adopting. I could sense myself going through the motions: smiling, laughing, answering questions, and volunteering information, all by rote. My mind kept wandering back to Matthew Whitford and how I can't figure him out. On the one hand, he's a respectable headmaster, but also an authority on ghosts. A caring father, but at the pub with another woman.

'What happened to his wife?' I hear myself saying.

'What?' Charlie looks concerned. 'Who?'

'Dr Whitford. The headmaster.'

'Oh, him.' Charlie looks somewhat annoyed. 'Mr Butter-Wouldn't-Melt.'

I laugh, warming to what seems to be a mutual dislike.

'He's got a thing about Rookswood. He didn't want Emma and Phil to buy the place. I think he had some fancy notion to turn it into a museum or some shite. But then his wife got sick, and he had the boy to look after. He's one of those "idiot-somethings". Like *Rain Man*.'

'You mean the son's autistic? On the spectrum?'

'Yeah, sorry. I'm not too up on the lingo.' He shrugs. 'I'm sure he's a nice lad.'

'So what happened?'

'His wife was called Siobhan. She died, that's all I know. Whitford probably bored her to death with his Latin and his photography.' He laughs. I don't. I'm no fan of Dr Whitford, but Charlie's being downright insensitive.

'Sorry,' he says, realising that I'm not amused. 'I sound like a right bastard, and I don't mean to. Let's not talk about him.'

'OK, fine.'

The rest of the evening passes pleasantly enough. Charlie has a second pint; I have a third glass of wine, which is usually a big mistake. We begin to talk more easily, and I find myself recounting anecdotes about me and Emma from our childhood. I imagine he's curious about what happened between my sister and me, but he's too polite to ask. He does ask if I'm seeing anyone. I say no. I ask him the same question. Same answer.

As we move further into date territory, my mind begins, ever so slightly, to pull back. What's going to happen? What do I want to happen? I'm so rusty with these things. My thoughts return to Dr Whitford, the little boy, and the blonde woman. It must have been a terrible blow when his wife died. On the other hand, he seems to have landed on his feet.

The bell clangs for last orders; I'd no idea we'd been here for so long. Charlie eyes me up from across the table, then reaches out for my hand, engulfing it in his.

'You had enough?' he says. 'Or do you want one for the road?'

The room is positively spinning.

'Not for me, thanks,' I say. 'You?'

'Normally, I'd go for last orders, but I've got an early start tomorrow. That meeting with the planners.'

'Oh, right.' I'm deflated and relieved in equal measure.

'Shall we share a taxi?' Charlie smiles indulgently. 'I don't know about you, but I'm not fit to drive.'

'We could walk back to the gatehouse.'

'Really?'

His eyes light up like a puppy's. Instantly I blush, realising my mistake. The gatehouse isn't far, but I've no idea where he lives. Not walking distance, I'd wager. Is this the part where I'm supposed to invite him over? I can't, surely... not with Izzy and Max in the house. Do I even want to?

'I mean, you could get a taxi from there,' I backpedal.

'Sure. I'll do that.' The spark fizzles out. 'But I'd probably better get home as soon as possible. I need to iron my suit.'

'You own a suit!'

'Two, actually.' (Of all the things he's said, this makes me warm to him the most.)

Charlie pays the bill, refusing my offer to split it. We get a taxi together from the village green opposite the pub.

'I had a good time,' I say, as the cab pulls up beside the big gates of Rookswood. 'Thanks so much.'

He doesn't speak. Instead, he draws me close. Kisses me hard on the lips.

'Me too. And Kate – that's for later. For next time.'

I get out of the taxi, reeling. From the wine, the kiss, the feeling of vertigo. I don't know what the hell I'm doing. And I kind of like it.

'Looking forward to it,' I say.

17

Lying in bed that night, I'm looking forward to nothing. I regret the wine, the kiss, the vertigo. I regret that I don't know what the hell I'm doing – and I don't like it.

And just as I'm drifting off to sleep, I hear a creak of the floorboards, a door opening and closing.

Izzy's door.

Sitting upright, I turn on the bedside lamp; the yellow circle of light dispels the fog in my mind. Footsteps on the stairs. The snap of the front door latch. My fears realised.

Izzy's gone.

I pinch myself to make sure I'm definitely awake, then I jump out of bed, shivering in the cold room. My clothes (or rather, Emma's clothes I was wearing earlier) are crumpled on the floor. I put them on quickly and race down the stairs, scrambling to pull on a coat and boots. By the time I get outside, I've wasted precious seconds. A white blur moves towards Rookswood, disappearing into the tunnel of trees.

'Izzy!' I yell. Last time, I pursued a strategy of not waking her. That proved unsuccessful. The car keys jingle in my pocket, but then I remember that I left the car at the pub. For now, I'm on foot.

The night is dark, the moon pale and sickly. The fog is not just in my head, but all around me, dense and white. If Izzy does wake up and head back to the gatehouse, I might not see her. We will literally be two ships passing in the night.

I reach the tunnel of trees, plunging into the suffocating darkness. By the time I emerge, my heart is pounding double-time. Before me, the house is a menacing monolith, the serrated roofline slicing the sky like a knife. The fronds of monstrous palm trees reach out like many-fingered hands. Dark windows shine like blind eyes. The front door is open. I hear something – voices?

'Izzy!' I call out. 'Are you there?' I'm determined to find her and wake her before she gets hurt or discovers anything else that's too creepy for words.

The wooden stairs creak as I go onto the porch and through the door. Only then do I realise I don't have a torch or my phone. 'Stupid, so stupid,' I mutter.

It should be pitch black – but it's not. As my brain catches up with my senses, I realise that a beam of light is shining down through the cupola, pooling at the top of the stairs.

Izzy is standing in the pool of light on the landing, her white hoodie stark against the darkness beyond. But she's not alone. Behind her is another form, human – or human-shaped. A shimmering, swirling mass of light and shadow, green-tinged and phosphorescent, floating a foot above the ground. *Ada*. The thought bombards me as I stand paralyzed, unable to speak or move.

The... *thing*... reaches out. Clawed fingers encircle Izzy's neck.

'Ada!' I scream. 'No!'

I'm too late. At the sound of my voice, Izzy jerks awake. She stumbles forward as if surprised to be standing up, and topples off balance; one second she's at the top of the staircase, the next, she's bumping down it head first. The dull thudding thunders in my ears as Izzy cries out and I scream.

The beam of light goes out abruptly. The ghost disappears into the blackness, leaving only a faint, phosphoric glow.

I'm shaking all over as I feel, rather than see, Izzy at my feet. She groans in pain – she's alive.

'Izzy!' I bend over her, frantically trying to feel my way in the dark.

'My arm,' she cries. 'It hurts! Oh God. This shouldn't be happening.'

I can see the vague outline of her arm, crumpled beneath her at an impossible angle. I need to get her to a hospital. But I don't have my phone to call an ambulance. Somewhere in the distance, I hear a vague sound of running footsteps, a door slamming. Someone is here inside the house. More footsteps above. Do ghosts have feet? Only then do I notice a vague smell of smoke, and... a presence. Whatever I saw is no longer visible, but there is definitely something here.

Something dangerous.

I sniff the air. 'Do you smell that?' I say. 'Smoke.'

'No. All I smell is old house. How did I get here?'

'If you don't know, then you must have been sleepwalking.'

'Seriously?'

'Yeah. Can you get to your feet?'

'I'm not sure.'

The smell is stronger now, the presence menacing. My pulse is banging against my skull.

'Let's try.' I lean over her torso and very gently try to heft her upwards. She screams in pain, and we only manage a sitting position.

'My arm!' she says again. 'I think it's broken. Should we call 999?'

'We should, but stupidly, I forgot my phone.'

'I've got mine; it's in my pocket.'

'You went sleepwalking with your phone?'

Even in her weakened state, she looks at me like I have two heads. 'Yeah,' she deadpans. 'Of course.'

'Just checking.' It seems my instincts about teens and phones were spot on. I feel a surge of love for my niece as I reach none-too-gently into the pocket of her hoodie, withdraw the phone, and hold it up to unlock with facial recognition. Her face is so contorted with pain that it takes two tries. I manage to explain the situation to the emergency operator – an old house, an injured girl, a whiff of smoke.

Izzy slumps over as I end the call. 'Are they coming?' she gasps.

'Yes, they'll be here soon.' In fact, they didn't say exactly how long they'd be. 'But we need to get you out of the house.'

'My arm hurts. Can't we wait?'

'If something's burning, we can't be in here. Now, come on.'

Clenching my teeth against the sound of her cries, I get an arm around her and help her to her feet. 'You're doing great,' I yell, trying to rally us both. She's a dead weight against me as together, we stagger through the door. Neither of us manages to go any further. Izzy sinks down, prostrate against the rotten spindles of the porch. I put my coat around her to keep her warm.

'The paramedics are coming.' I listen for the sound of sirens, but there's nothing. 'So hang on tight. I'm going back in to make sure no one else is inside.'

'No, Aunt Kate!' Izzy cries. 'Don't leave me!'

'I'll just be a second.'

Before she can protest further, I hurry back into the hall. I stand at the bottom of the stairs and call out, 'Hello, Ada? I don't know what you're playing at, but it's got to stop.'

There's no answer, and the staircase is empty. I can still make out a very faint whiff of smoke, and the back of my neck is crawling with the sensation of something unseen watching me.

'Why did you hurt Izzy?' I say. 'That's just not on. And what's with the smoke?'

A sound coming from somewhere. A skittering of feet.

'Fine,' I say (along with a few unrepeatable other words). 'If you won't answer, then I'll come and take a look for myself.'

I may sound brave, but the trembling beam of light from Izzy's phone torch in my hand betrays the truth. A thin trail of fog-like smoke leads up the second flight of stairs. Something definitely is (or was?) burning. Did Ada try to set fire to the house?

Not on my watch.

I follow the smoke and the smell but feel no heat. It's as if whatever I've seen, smelled, and experienced, is an echo of something that was real.

'By the way,' I call out. 'I don't believe in ghosts.'

There's a loud clatter coming from the top of the house. My heart pole vaults as I mount the final flight of stairs. You don't necessarily have to believe in something to be terrified of it. My feet are weighted down with dread, like in one of those dreams where you're being chased but you can't run. I use the banister to half drag myself up. At the top, I enter the studio.

A noise, a scrabbling, a monstrous shadow, a... meow?

The ginger cat stands just behind a single candle lit at the centre of the room. It growls, hackles raised as I enter. Crisp packets and Coke cans are scattered about like someone was having a party. The cat hisses, then runs off into a dark corner and disappears.

A cat, a candle. Have I got this all wrong? Were there kids here? Did Izzy come to meet some friends, who all left in a hurry when the accident happened? Or was all the noise somehow caused by the cat? That explains a lot, though, it doesn't account for the ghostly apparition. But that can be explained too. Occam's razor...

Maybe a ghost is just a ghost.

In the distance, I hear the sound of a siren; I need to go back downstairs to see to Izzy and the paramedics. I go over to the candle to blow it out and discover that it's resting on a small leather book. A journal or... a photo album. I pick it up and open the flyleaf. There's a name written in sepia ink, the hand thin and spidery.

Property of Adaline Beryl Havelock (Miss)

'Is this your idea of an apology?' I say aloud. 'If so, it had better be good.'

The shadows flicker as the candle gutters; dripping wax drowns the wick. The flame goes out, plunging the room into darkness.

VI

I am powerless to stop them – to stop any of it. How can I who lacks flesh and blood, muscles and limbs, possibly do all that I am suspected of? I may have been born in less enlightened times, but even I would not have been so gullible.

So I must use what strength I have to make her understand. My sole desire, her most important task. The book of photographs I have kept it hidden over all the years. Now, as the end is near, I have used all my strength to bring it into the light.

What will she see when she looks inside? Strangers from another time, people long dead who are nothing to her. But this woman is curious; she will at least look and wonder. She will follow the trail of crumbs... I will gather my energy to leave the next.

* * *

Some indigenous cultures believed that photographic images could trap the soul of a deceased person in this world, or that the flash of a camera could attract evil spirits. Having spent my life taking photographs and trapping moments of light and shadow, I believe that good and evil exist not in the machines and processes themselves, but only in the minds and hearts of humans. Evil is as evil does.

Our father died when Camile was six and I was nineteen. On his last visit to Rookswood, he appeared dull, gaunt and sickly, perhaps from his long years of exposure to darkroom chemicals, or perhaps from other more worldly ailments that can plague a man about town. He went for a ride in the woods and was thrown from his horse, leaving him paralysed from the waist down. For a short while, his spirit was trapped not in a photograph, but in his body. Eventually, he choked to death on a chicken bone.

Camile and I went into mourning, of course. We wreathed the house in black, commissioned clothing in bombazine: dresses for her, trousers for me. When the cat's away (in this case, permanently), the mice will play. All of a sudden, I was my own woman – a woman who, I discovered, preferred wearing trousers, smoking cigars, and keeping her hair cropped short. I still wore dresses for work and company, however, as was expected. Until I built a name for myself, I would keep up appearances.

My father died intestate, and as the eldest child, I inherited. Despite my father's profligate spending in his lifetime, his estate was substantial. It included the Mayfair studio, and I travelled up to London to oversee its closure. There, I discovered the true nature of my father's 'novelty photographs' for his 'gentleman clients'. The images I found shocked even me. If I needed a further incentive not to marry, it was there in those plates, negatives, and photographs. Never would I allow a man to subject my body to such shameful and degrading acts.

While I was there, I could not avoid calls from said 'special clients', who had not heard about my father's untimely demise. With these, I threatened to publish their names in the newspaper unless they returned the photographs for me to destroy. I also suffered visits from a number of Father's models and mistresses: mostly women of a certain class and profession, who had proved themselves more than willing to model for a certain type of photograph. To these, I gave money (much appreciated) and advice (not appreciated at all). I don't blame those women (and men) for what they did or were. For all my father's flaws, I had never lacked for material things; I never had to walk a mile in their shoes.

As soon as I returned from London, I had a solicitor draw up a will in which I left everything to Camile. It was my job to continue to protect my sister and insulate her from the ravages of the world. Camile was all I had, and all I ever needed. And vice versa, or so I thought.

Camile and Ada, Ada and Camile.

* * *

Those were good years – the best years. Do you wonder, therefore, why I didn't want them to end? Camile was my sister, but also so much more. My mother was a bright spot on my memory, my father a dark blur in my past. But Camile was my present, my whole world. Camile was all the family I needed.

Even before my father's death, I made Camile my protégée and taught her everything I knew. About photography, about art, about technology and craft. In my father's absence, I did not give up my pursuits, merely changed their direction.

I was interested in the science of illusion. Finding new and different ways to create the impossible. In the attic studio, I experimented with all manner of techniques and materials. While my father was alive, I had an ample allowance and no supervision, hence I was able to visit local tradesmen and craftsmen to procure what I needed. I experimented with using huge sheets of glass to create life-sized illusions – a theatrical technique called 'Pepper's Ghost'. I developed my own variations using smoke, mirrors, dry ice, and colouring agents to create intricate effects of floating objects and spectral apparitions. Though I had no sitters and no way to publicise or sell my work, I was content. Everything I did in those days was for the delight of my Camile.

Of the two of us, my sister had an artist's eye for form and composition. She was more like my father in these ways, as well as in beauty and charm. Later on, people would call me a 'technical wizard' for my innovations in the craft of photography. But for all my skill as a technician, Camile was the sorceress, the visionary. The creator of true magic.

Although my sister grew and blossomed into her adolescence, her mind and imagination were still those of a young girl. I did anything and everything to indulge her whims and flights of fancy. I devised ways to create photographs of fairies and spirits, strange animals and beautiful goddesses. I used glass, mirrors and cut-outs, I manipulated plates, exposures, and photomontage in ways that had not been done before. When, after our father's death, I made the decision to promote myself as a photographer and began getting paid work, I still spent much of my time and effort on illusions to please my sister.

'I have a client coming,' I might tell her.

'Oh Ada, one more fairy door,' she'd say. 'I do love them so.'

I could never deny Camile anything.

Except the one thing she came to desire most.

* * *

Years passed in the blink of an eye. As Camile grew up, I made a name for us. I sent our best work off to journals and magazines under the name A. C. Havelock, and like my father before me, we started a new fashion, a new fad. In those days, spiritualism was all the rage, with so-called mediums and psychics traveling up and down the country, holding seances and readings. The best drawing rooms of London gullibly flung open their doors, inviting in spirits – or charlatans, depending on what one chose to believe. Influential men like Arthur Conan Doyle were believers and enthusiasts and interest spread like wildfire. Our work provided what people nowadays would call a 'synergy'. Once it became fashionable to attempt to contact spirits, the natural corollary was to photograph them.

Hence, Rookswood opened its doors to a new stream of fashionable visitors. It was Camile's job to interview the client to determine exactly what type of spirit we were expecting. 'In the seance, I saw a bright-white light'; or 'I felt an icy hand brush my cheek'; or 'my mother always loved green – when I saw her ghost, it was wearing green.' There were far fewer variations than you might think. It was not hard for me to listen behind the door and set up the perfect 'spirit' to please the client. While I did so, Camile would set the atmosphere with candles and incense (laced with opium to further cultivate a receptive mind). Then, when I was ready, she would lead them into the studio, dimly lit to hide the huge diagonal pane of glass hung above the chaise longue that I used for our illusions, and the container of dry ice that perfectly evoked the chill of the world beyond. I used projected lights and images: magic lantern and camera-obscura technology, to create realistic-looking ghosts, that I could then further perfect in the darkroom during the development process.

There was no magic involved, and certainly no spirits. But then as now, people believe what they want to believe. Our bank balance grew and our fame spread, as did our notoriety, for not all of our publicity was positive. In those days, there were frequent debates in newspaper editorials about spiritualism, and while the practice had many enthusiasts, there were an equal number of sceptics and debunkers. One newspaper cited A. C. Havelock in an article about charlatans and hoaxers, revealing our real names, and the (shameful) fact that we were women. That same article christened Camile and me 'The Weird Sisters'. I loved the moniker – it suited me down to the ground.

It did not, however, suit Camile.

18

'Seriously, I smelled something burning.'

The firefighter puts her hands on her hips. I feel like a complete idiot, and she clearly concurs.

'We found a blown-out candle in one of the rooms, along with some rubbish. That's it. Most likely it was teenagers making mischief, which is why Isobel went there.'

'Maybe.'

Could the firefighter be right? Is everything down to kids making mischief? I once speculated to Charlie that the house was an 'attractive nuisance'. It's entirely possible that Izzy went there to meet friends who were having a party; a nice, rational explanation that requires no suspension of disbelief. But what about the apparition I saw? Because I did see it. Is Ada trying to scare people away by playing pranks, and did Izzy get on the wrong end of it? And what about the book of photographs? Did the pranksters find it, or did Ada somehow 'leave' it for me?

'We understand, Ms Goodman, that you're in charge of Emma Reynolds' two teenagers. Now, one of them is hurt.' She gestures over to where Izzy is lying on a stretcher, a paramedic on either side monitoring her vitals.

'It's not my fault that Izzy snuck out in the middle of the night.' The cheek of the woman!

'Have you been drinking?'

'I went to the pub. I had a glass of wine or two. What does that have to do with anything?'

'Who was home with the children while you were out?'

'They're fourteen and fifteen. Surely, they don't need a babysitter!'

'It's not for me to say. But obviously, I'll need to report all the facts. As the "responsible adult",' (I detect the implicit air quotes in that statement) 'their safety is your responsibility.'

'I know that, but—'

'We're ready to go.' A paramedic comes up to us. 'Do you want to ride along, Ms Goodman?'

'Yes, I do.' I glare at the firefighter, hoping she doesn't query who'll be staying home with Max. 'If that's OK with you?'

'Fine,' she says, with a look of sheer disdain. If she was police, I'd be under arrest. Which is just so unfair.

'Great.' I turn to the paramedic. 'Just give me a second.'

Leaving the firefighter to her paperwork, I go back to the door of the house and poke my head inside. 'Thanks for dropping me in it,' I whisper loudly.

A chill like the stale air from a grave wraps around me. I shiver, but stand my ground.

'When I come back, you and I are going to have words.'

* * *

The light hurts my eyes. So white, so cold. My earlier buzz is long gone; my head feels heavy and foggy. Even late at night, the ward is busy, with nurses and doctors bustling around, machines groaning and beeping. I'm glad Emma's no longer at this hospital to see what a cock-up I've made of things.

As I wait for Izzy to come out of X-ray, I consider ringing Max to tell him what's happened, but decide to let him sleep. Instead, I open up the book I found. I'm half-expecting it to be blank, like the photo on my phone that 'somehow' got erased. But inside, I find something truly remarkable. A collection of photographs: a snapshot of a forgotten time. Sepia photos with spidery hand-written captions beneath them.

Even though I'm in a bland hospital waiting area, I experience a phantom sense of chill and dread. I look again at the inscription on the flyleaf.

Property of Adaline Beryl Havelock (Miss)

Adaline. The eldest of the Weird Sisters who lived at Rookswood for over ninety years. Died there too, as far as I know. And the sister? I can't recall hearing her name, but for some reason, I think of Emma and myself. If things had happened differently and we had chosen each other instead of the alternative, our lives might be very different. Would Emma be in hospital? Would Izzy and Max even exist? Or would they be... I swallow hard... *mine*?

No. That's a pointless thought if there ever was one. I flip through the first few pages of the book. As I'm half-expecting to see photographs of headless people and dead people, I'm pleasantly surprised to find that the album instead contains intimate family photos and handwritten captions that tell Ada's story. Sunny photographs of Ada on a pony at a village fete; afternoon tea under a spreading plane tree. Her mother, smiling and laughing, wearing an elegant tea gown with white gloves and a huge hat, and carrying a lace parasol. Ada and her father playing croquet, his smile cocky and charming. Then, the mother again, propped on pillows in a huge four-poster bed. Sickly but smiling, her belly swollen with the baby to come. Ada's sister, Camile.

Camile. The child's name is written out with a flourish. A lovely name for a lovely girl. Camile had pale hair, big eyes, and a bow-shaped mouth. There are photos of her playing with a kitten, dancing around a maypole, playing in the sand, hugging a doll. Airy and ethereal, possibly even a little vapid. In contrast, the photos of Ada show a dark-haired girl with a fierce, determined expression. 'Old eyes' sparkling with a keen intelligence – like she's seen and experienced it all. I realise that the torn photo I found was not of Ada, as I'd originally thought, but of Camile.

Two sisters: light and shadow.

Ada's story; my story.

Is that why the book found its way to me?

'Kate?'

I look up, expecting to see the male nurse who took Izzy off to x-ray. Instead, I'm shocked to see Matthew Whitford. My mind naturally jumps to the worst-case scenario. The firefighter called social services, who got Izzy's headmaster out of bed and here at... I check my watch... 4 a.m.!

I quickly shut the book and tuck it away down the chair arm. 'It wasn't my fault,' I blurt. 'I can't lock Izzy in her room, can I? Rookswood House is an "attractive nuisance". If Izzy was going there to meet other kids who were having a party, then I wasn't to know.'

I stop, horrified by my own outburst. Dr Whitford's look of concern morphs to bemusement.

'Sorry, slow down,' he says. 'You lost me at "attractive nuisance". What exactly has happened?'

I cross my arms. 'I'm not saying anything. Not until you promise not to get social services involved.'

His expression hardens. 'You know I can't do that. But let me tell you how I see it. You dropped everything to help Emma out in a tough situation. You're doing the best you can – and that's pretty damn good. Clearly you care about Izzy and Max, and I respect that. In fact, I'd like to help you out. But first I need to know what happened.'

Maybe if he was a little less good looking, I'd keep my mouth shut. Maybe if I hadn't seen him with his son; he'd seemed so caring and loving towards a boy that most people might label as 'different'. But as it is, I find myself telling him about Izzy's sleep-walking and the hold Rookswood seems to have over her. And me. I'm tempted to mention the erstwhile ghost, but I don't want to give it credence by voicing my experience out loud, nor do I want to give Dr Whitford the chance to say, 'I told you so'.

'Wow,' he says, when I've finished. 'That sounds…'

'Far-fetched?' He thinks I'm nuts. And why not?

'…difficult,' he says. 'And I'm wondering where Max was during these paranormal occurrences?'

'Max? He was at home in bed. Asleep. His door was closed and I saw no reason to wake him.' Recalling the firefighter's inter-rogation, I cross my arms defensively. 'I've already had a dressing down for leaving him on his own, but what choice did I have? I can't be in two places at once.'

'Of course,' he says. 'That's not what I mean. But if you want my tuppence worth, I would—'

'Mr Whitford?' A nurse calls out. 'Your son is asking to see you.'

His son. Could I even *be* more rude and unfeeling? I should have asked him why he's here; could I not spare even an iota of curiosity and compassion? He lost his wife, and now, his son is in hospital?

'I'm sorry,' I say. 'Really.'

He shrugs off my apology. 'We can finish this conversation another time,' he says. 'But in the meantime, Kate... do be careful. Please.'

'I will.' I actually mean it.

19

I plan on being careful. I plan on keeping Izzy away from Rookswood and staying away myself. Even if I wanted to, I've no time to do anything else. When Izzy is discharged from hospital, her arm in a cast, we take a taxi back to the gatehouse, at which point my role morphs from that of aunt *in loco parentis* to that of nursemaid. Over the next few days, I turn Emma's sitting room into a sick room, planting Izzy on the couch with the TV remote and all her devices. She's groggy and in pain, but somehow manages to keep up with her Snapchats and social media. Initially, I feel racked with indecision about whether or not to inform Emma about what happened. The programme she's in is all about rest and recovery, and communications are supposed to be limited to 'essential'. I've taken that as carte blanche not to contact her in the last few weeks. But surely, if I had a daughter, I'd want to know about a broken bone, so I ask Izzy what she thinks. I discover then that she's already told her mum a 'porky pie' – that she got a hairline fracture to her wrist playing netball. I know I should correct the falsehood, but somehow, all I manage to do is send Emma a message that

Izzy's recovering and everything is under control, to which I receive no reply.

I also use Izzy's convalescence as an opportunity to get her focused on preparing for GCSEs. Since it's her right arm that's broken, I act as her PA, getting her assignments off Google Classroom and helping her type and hand in her work. It turns into a reasonable bonding opportunity, and I don't mind brushing up on her elective topics: she's doing History, Geography, and Art. I consider showing her the photo album, but in the end, I don't. For the moment, keeping Rookswood 'out of sight, out of mind' seems best for both of us.

As the days go by, my enthusiasm for my own work wanes. One of my transactions closes, another one gets delayed, the volume of Teams calls gradually tapers off. But the biggest demotivating factor is an email from the partnership selection committee, announcing that due to poor results across the firm, the decision has been made not to make up any new equity partners this year. The old me would have been livid. My numbers are solid, and why should I be dragged down by anyone else? The new me goes out for a walk to let off steam, files the email in admin, and watches a *Gossip Girl* marathon with Izzy.

Afterwards, when Izzy's asleep, I continue looking through the little book, trying to find out more about Ada and Camile. After their father died, they took over the family business and became photographers in their own right. There are many photos of Camile; Ada clearly loved her sister and enjoyed photographing her. But around the time of the Great War, the photos of Camile come to an abrupt end. The last few pages of the book are dominated by an unnamed woman I don't recognise from the earlier photos. Tall, thin, and expensive-looking – that's the only way I can describe her. In the first photo, she's wearing a wide-brimmed hat, a tight-fitted dress, smoking a cigarette in a holder, staring at the camera with bold, seductive eyes. There are numerous other images of her taken from all angles. Clearly, she seems to have been a muse of some sort.

Near the end of the book, the paper is discoloured and there are remnants of paste: evidence that several photos have been removed. Did Ada remove them before her death, or were they removed more recently by a flesh-and-blood person? Maybe whoever lit the candle and left the rubbish in the attic? I've got no way of knowing.

But on the last page, there is one final photo: of the two sisters sitting side by side on a bench in the garden at Rookswood. At least, I recognise Ada, sitting next to a figure I believe is Camile. It's hard to tell, though, because the photo has been desecrated with a pen and ink; Camile's face is scored out so deeply that the paper is ripped right through.

It's startling and chilling, and all the more so because it reminds me of what I did to photos of Emma after the 'incident'. Did Ada and Camile have a similar falling out? Did it have something to do with the photos that were removed? Looking from the outside in at someone else's life, it seems tragic and pointless. But I know all too well that awful feeling of desperation, and the need to lash out at the people you love. They, after all, are the only people who can truly hurt you. It's taken me years, but I've finally realised that no matter what the reason is, when two sisters fall out, it's tragic and pointless. Ada and Camile, Emma and me.

I don't know what happened between the Weird Sisters, but as for me and Emma, our estrangement now seems more stupid than tragic. Certainly, the reason seems pointless...

A man.

Kate, can we talk? I... have something to tell you. Words spoken over fifteen years ago echo in my head as if I'm hearing them for the first time. Pain grips my body, a knot that can never be unravelled. The phantom tightening of a golden band with a single diamond solitaire around my finger. I've never worn a ring before or since. I threw it at her; it hit her in the eye. Even now, I hope it hurt.

I met Philip in my first year at uni. He sat a seat away in the lecture hall of Economics 101 and picked up my pen when I accidentally dropped it. When he handed it back to me, he scribbled his number in my notebook. I noted he was gorgeous. We had coffee together, studied together. He was a gentleman; I was cocky and self-assured on the surface, and scared underneath. My dorm room, a single bed...

He was my first.

I thought he would be my last.

In a way, he was. The last time I fell in love. The last time I trusted anyone, including, and especially, myself. That's the ghost that lingers, though my feelings for him are long gone.

It's just... I mean, it was a mistake.

Emma was with me every step of the way, helping me plan the wedding. I wanted to keep things simple; I was more of a registry-office-followed-by-a-meal-at-a-pub kind of bride. But Philip (and his mother) wanted to go whole hog. They wanted the wedding that Emma would have had.

And, in the end... did.

I didn't go, of course. I understand from friends of friends that she had a big, lacy gown that hid her ripening bump.

We both had too much to drink. I just feel so bad.

Let's be honest – she deserved to feel bad. What kind of sister steals her sister's fiancé and gets pregnant?

Who actually does that?

Hurt washes through my veins, fuelling an unnatural rage. I want to get up and punch something, or cut up Emma's clothing, or total her car – or abandon her kids to fend for themselves. I want to not speak to her for another fifteen years. And most of all, I want to confide in her and tell her exactly how I'm feeling right now. Tell her how much I've missed her. How I never should have reacted as I did.

Get out, you stupid slag. I don't know who you are. I no longer have a sister.

Please, Kate, we can get through this. I love you.

You don't know the meaning of the word.

I don't think Emma truly believed I'd cut her out of my life. That's the difference between us. I've always been exactly what you see on the tin, whereas Emma's reality, even her entire personality, was more *fluid*. She saw the best in people, the best in life. She wanted the best.

Clenching my fists, I wander aimlessly into the kitchen, picking up a glass and debating whether or not to shatter it in the sink. The urge now seems like a mere shadow of itself, like a brand new pair of shoes treading down some muddy, overgrown neural pathway. I set the glass down and fill it with wine, swirling the blood-red liquid around the globe.

Do I forgive my sister?

I set the glass down without drinking.

'Izzy?' I call out. 'Can I get you anything? A sandwich? Crisps?'

The volume dips on the TV.

'Can I have an apple cut up?'

'An apple? Sure.'

After all this time, I've actually started to wonder...

Is there really anything to forgive?

VII

We should have been that way forever. The Weird Sisters: delighting our clients, advancing the art and science of illusion, forging our place in the world. Sisters of light and shadow, as we were born to be.

I was happy with our life, so naturally I assumed Camile would be too. Imagine my surprise and shock, therefore, when one day I discovered something upsetting. Something that made me question whether my life was what it seemed, and Camile was who I thought.

When war broke out in Europe, our spirit photography was in particular demand. We had a busy summer, with clients coming and going nearly every day. Many of them were mothers and fathers of young men lost in battle. For obvious reasons, such sessions were emotionally draining, and I spent many hours closeted away in the darkroom developing photos, and experimenting with a new portable Kodak camera model that showed great potential. I'd left Camile to her own devices, and I was sure she had enough to keep her busy running our household, looking after clients, and managing the servants who had not joined the war effort.

As the warm weather turned chill and the leaves on the trees became golden, Camile took to her bed. I assumed it was a bout of melancholy, as our mother had often experienced at the turning of the year. For although Camile had inherited my father's looks and charm, she also displayed on occasion signs of our mother's weaker constitution. I was not particularly concerned; however, our housekeeper took it upon herself to fetch a doctor. Whatever I expected the diagnosis to be, I was gravely mistaken.

My Camile, my jewel of purity and light, was with child.

* * *

To say I reacted badly would be doing an injustice to the word. I was bombarded by a freight train of emotions: rage, fear, disbelief. I found the worst of my father's 'special photographs' and threw them on the bed, accusing her of degeneracy, of debauchery, of betrayal. 'How could you do it?' I shouted. 'And why? With whom?' I fired questions like bullets. 'Am I not enough for you? Do you not appreciate me and this life I've created for us? That you have to do... this?' I shoved a photo at her. 'You disgust me.'

She tried to speak; I wouldn't listen. I raged on, breaking things, throwing things, wrenching open the drawer of her desk and throwing her correspondence on the fire. In the heat of my anger, the icy fingers of fear encircled my heart as she spoke the words I'd been dreading.

'I love him, Ada. We're going to be married.'

'You'll do no such thing,' I yelled back. 'I don't give my permission.'

'I don't need your permission.' When Camile found her voice, it was oxygen to the flames.

'Go then,' I shouted. 'Get out of my sight.'

Tears streamed down her beautiful face. My own words shocked me. They were the very opposite of what I wanted to say. I would have done anything to turn back the clock – five minutes, five months. Whatever was required for this to not be real. For though I was a mistress of light and shadow, I had been hood-winked by the greatest illusion of all. That I could order my life, control every aspect of my destiny. Jean Paul Sartre once wrote that 'Hell is— other people'. I learned a variation that day. 'Hell is trying to control other people'. But I simply could not let Camile live her life on her own terms. I simply could not lose her.

I developed a photo of the two of us, the last photo of us ever taken together. I smashed the glass plate, cutting my hand in the process. Holding it up so she could see, I ripped the photograph down the middle, severing us in two. Then, I dropped the pieces on the floor and trod on them as I left the room.

* * *

Judge me as you wish, but as it was, Camile lost the baby. Miscarried on a cold October night, a few weeks after our row. Do not think me so cruel as to have desired that outcome. By then, my volcanic anger had cooled, and I was doing all I could to make amends. I learned that her paramour was a local lad from the village. He was a baker's son, and a totally unsuitable match for a young lady of fortune. At first, Camile had spurned his attentions, but a combination of her loneliness and his persistence had won out. They had met in secret in a forest glade next to a swift-flowing stream. A 'fairy glade' she called it. I knew then that Camile's nature: romantic, loving, and, if I were honest, a little simple, would not have stood a chance against the carnal desires of a lusty young man. As Camile convalesced, I went to said lusty young man and gave him a sizeable sum of money to join the Royal Sussex Regiment. Do not think me so cruel as to have wished him dead (though, sadly, six months later he was blown to bits by a mortar in a trench at the Somme). I simply reasoned that having him gone would make things easier for Camile. Easier for me. I was determined to get our lives back to normal. My normal. But whatever my intentions, no matter the strength of my determination, the damage was done. I had wronged my sister, and divine retribution was waiting for me in the wings.

It came in the form of a letter. A cream-coloured envelope, sealed with cursive initials stamped in hot wax. A brief note penned by a woman's hand...

Dear Miss Havelock,

I wish to give my husband a special present for his birthday – a particular photographic joke. See enclosed description. If you believe it is something you can accomplish, please suggest a convenient time for an appointment.

Tatiana B— (Countess)

Such an innocent little communication, similar to others I had received over the years. I experienced no premonition, no creeping sensation on the back of my neck, as if someone was walking over my grave.

The letter enclosed a crude pencil drawing that piqued my interest. I turned my attentions to how it could be done. There were ways and means, though not without some risk to the sitter

– was she really a countess? If I could achieve it, the effect would be outstanding.

I opened my writing desk, took out a paper, and picked up my pen to respond.

Oh yes. It could be done.

20

'Sounds like you've had quite the time of it.'

Charlie's voice is warm and comforting, but also a little loud. I'd just sat down to do some work (the first in a while) when he came round. If he was disappointed to see that I wasn't alone, and that despite the TV, Izzy could probably overhear our conversation, he didn't let on. I've regaled him with most of the gory details about what happened, over a week ago now. Evidence of kids having parties, Izzy's injury. He doesn't seem too surprised, but at least he's sympathetic.

'To be honest, it hasn't been great.'

I pour him a second mug of coffee, splashing in some of Emma's Irish Crème. As I turn to hand it to him, he's standing close enough that I brush against him, practically spilling the coffee. As he takes the mug, he cups his hands over mine. Instantly, I feel both uncomfortable and stirred.

He drops his hands. I turn back to the coffee maker.

'Sorry it's been so hard,' he says. 'But things are looking up. I've been in regular contact with the planner, and he's all in favour of our plans for the development.'

My sip of coffee goes down the wrong way. *Our plans?* He means Emma's.

'Was he?' Turning back, I play it cool. 'I don't think you've actually showed me the plans, so can you remind me again of the specifics?'

'Sure, I don't have them on me, but trust me, it will be a great opportunity for your sister to shore up her finances once and for all. We're going to gut the house and develop the site into affordable housing. Just what the area needs.'

Gut the house? I shouldn't care...

He reaches out and tucks a strand of hair back behind my ears. My breath catches.

'I can see you're not convinced.' He smiles warmly. 'So why don't I show you the site and explain the vision. It won't take long. Fifteen minutes? I'll drive?'

I really don't have time, and something about Charlie's vision makes me nauseous. But having now been through Adaline's photo album, I have the itch to return to Rookswood and see what else I can discover about her life. Before her house is *gutted*...

'Sure.' I shrug offhandedly. 'Why not?'

* * *

The instant the house comes into view, I see it through new eyes. Not as someone who's lived there, but perhaps as one of Adaline's patrons might have seen the place when they arrived by horse and carriage or early automobile. An impressive house, substantial yet whimsical, like an overgrown folly. The perfect residence for an avant-garde, shockingly gauche artist. A house of smoke and mirrors. A house of the imagination.

'Such a shame,' I mutter.

'What?' Charlie turns to me as he parks in front of the house.

'That you want to "gut it".'

He laughs. 'Really, Kate? After all you've been through? I thought by now you'd have come round to my and Emma's way of thinking. She's best shot of the whole thing.'

I get out of the vehicle. The morning is chilly and my breath comes out in a white puff, but I can make out the tentative chirp of birds. Spring has arrived. What would the garden look like if it was restored to its former glory, the exotic plants flowering, the bee- and butterfly-friendly borders displaying a kaleidoscope of colours?

I guess we'll never know.

In any case, the house is Emma's business, not mine. I'm increasingly perplexed, however, why Charlie feels so strongly that it's his business too.

'See those outbuildings over there?' He points to the old stables. 'We'll turn those into a duplex and a barn conversion. It will be its own little cul-de-sac. "Rooks – wood." Maybe we can name each road after birds. Or trees. What do you think?'

My business or not, I can't stop a growing sense of anger. Surely Emma can't be on board to destroy the house – she doesn't have it in her. Or does she? If Philip had stayed, would things be different? I know I should just ask her, but other than the odd 'everything's fine' text between us, neither of us seem keen to start a meaningful conversation.

'I think it's a shame,' I say. 'The house is unique. There are lots of housing estates everywhere. But how many places like this are left? How many places with this kind of history?'

He cocks his head, the smile gone from his face. 'You mean the creepy photos?'

'Yes. They were creepy, but back then, they were the height of fashion. I've been reading up. The Weird Sisters created a unique form of art.'

He raises his eyebrows. Clearly, he thinks Rookswood has addled my brain. Maybe it has. 'You're starting to sound like Matthew "Posh-o" Whitford. Just saying...'

'That's a low blow.' I laugh, but my heart isn't in it.

'You're full of surprises,' he says. 'When I asked her about you, Emma said you were the hard-arse sister. Not a sentimental bone in your body.'

'Emma said *that* about me?'

'Sure,' he says. 'She talked about you a lot. How much she respects you.'

'Oh.'

Absently, I walk up to the big house. For once, the front door is closed. Charlie comes up beside me.

'Since we're here,' he says, 'I might as well go inside and check that everything's secure. It's probably pointless. If kids want to get in, then they will. Especially *those* kids.'

'Those kids?'

'Izzy and Max.'

'What?'

'Well, Izzy has definitely caused her share of trouble, hasn't she? I mean, that night you got locked in, it's like she lured you here. Then, she came back again and got injured herself.'

'Lured?' I stare at him.

'Yeah, and did you know that Izzy was here when Emma fell? They had a row, apparently, and Izzy ran to the house and hid somewhere upstairs. So I'm not saying it was anyone's fault, but if Emma was in the wrong place at the wrong time, that's the reason why.'

Opposing thoughts twist in my mind; I can't make sense of them. But Charlie does have a point. Occam's razor – I've been quick to blame a ghost – a ghost! – for the goings on at the house. But is that really the simplest solution?

'Hey...' He reaches out and brushes my hand. I realise I've fallen silent. 'I don't mean to imply anything. Izzy and Max are good kids. Really. The house is... what did you say? ...an "attractive nuisance". It's nobody's fault.'

'Yeah, sure.' I don't know what else to say. Clearly at least part of it is somebody's fault. But which part, and whose? Izzy's? I just don't want to believe it.

Charlie gets the key from underneath the potted palm and opens the door. As I enter the hall, my usual foreboding is replaced by a heavy sense of sadness. Sunlight floods down from the stained-glass cupola, patterning the dust on the floor with spots of colour. It's such a beautiful, special old house. Soon that beauty will be gone, fading away like the ink on an old photograph.

'You want to wait here?' Charlie says. 'Soak in the atmosphere? Or come with me? I'm going to check all the ground-floor windows and the conservatory.'

I tell him I'm fine to stay put. As Charlie goes towards the back of the house, I go to the staircase and sit down on the bottom step.

'I do understand, you know,' I say aloud. 'You don't want your house occupied by strangers. Or worse, torn down. You want your memory preserved. All of that is reasonable. But you're going about it the wrong way.'

I wait. There's nothing.

'I know it's not only teenagers or trespassers playing pranks. You led me to the torn photo and the book.'

From somewhere overhead, there's a clunk. I brace myself against the powerful urge to flee.

I stay put. 'I just want you to leave Izzy alone. She's only fifteen. Whatever you're playing at, you're only making it worse for yourself.'

Another sound – a yowl. I jump up, my heart pounding, as something darts across the landing.

Not a ghost or a phantom, but the ginger cat. It arches its back when it sees me. Could the cat have caused the noise; did it knock something over? Maybe. But I'm not about to go up those stairs to have a look. Not for all the tea in China.

The cat saunters down the stairs like he owns the place. As he reaches my level, I'm about to step back, but he accordions against my leg. Is he actually being friendly? Could he be lonely? I reach down to pat him; his fur is strangely cold. Just as I notice this, he turns nasty, lashing out with his teeth. I barely get my hand away in time.

'You're a traitor,' I say, puppeting the words I once spoke to Emma. 'You're making me remember why I don't like cats.'

The cat stands still, his ears twitching. A moment later, he streaks out the open front door, just as Charlie returns.

'There was a broken windowpane out the back,' he says. 'I think that's how people are getting in.'

'Don't you think it could be the key under the potted palm?'

He laughs. 'That would be too easy.'

As he stands before me, his bulk casts a long shadow over the floor. 'So, are you enjoying the atmosphere?'

'I saw a cat. He wasn't friendly.'

'Oh, him.' He wrinkles his nose disdainfully. 'That's Bones. He's always underfoot, acting like he owns the place. Emma had a soft spot for him, but he's a fickle bugger. Seems he's decided that one beautiful woman is as good as the next.'

'One beautiful—'

Before I can process this, he puts his hands on my arms and draws me close. His lips are surprisingly soft as he leans down to kiss me. I reach up and encircle his neck with my arms, feeling like I'm hugging a tree. I don't know where this is going or whether I want it. But is there any harm in seeing where it—?

A cold draught, a presence. A rumbling sound that shakes the fabric of the building. An earthquake? A bomb? I pull away from Charlie. A flood of rocks, wood, debris, dirt – and dismembered human body parts – thunders down the stairs.

'What the—?' Charlie says.

I respond with a scream.

He grabs my hand and pulls me towards the door. As the dust cloud engulfs us, I see something at the top of the stairs. The dark silhouette of a woman...

She's laughing.

21

'God, what happened to you?'

Izzy's shocked enough to turn off the TV. Her reaction confirms my suspicions that I look like something the cat dragged in, ate, and regurgitated.

'Rookswood happened,' I say.

'Did something collapse?'

'I couldn't actually say what happened.'

Which is the truth. All I know is that I saw a woman at the top of the stairs wearing a dark, old-fashioned dress and a black veil over her face, and that she managed to unleash an avalanche of stuff. Whether she was dead or alive, how she did it and, more importantly, why, are not questions I can answer.

'Were you alone?'

'No. Charlie was there too.'

'Charlie.' She snorts. 'I wish the place had collapsed.'

'What? That's a little extreme.'

'What do you know about it?'

I'm not sure how this argument started, or whose side I should be on. Charlie as good as accused Izzy of being involved in the goings on at the house. But on this occasion, at least, she's in the clear.

'Nothing,' I say, my eyes tearing up with dust and debris. 'I know nothing. I'm going for a shower.'

'*She* doesn't like Charlie,' Izzy says. 'So you'd better be careful.'

'Who?' I blink rapidly. 'Your mum?'

'No. The ghost.'

'The... *ghost*?' I stare at her, my worst suspicions confirmed. I think again of *The Turn of the Screw* and the two children who were haunted by a couple of creepy dead servants. I don't recall the details (I'm sure Matthew Whitford would know) but it ended badly, I think...

'Her name was Ada. She was that weird photographer who used to live there.'

'You told me before that you'd never seen anything like that.'

'*I* haven't. But Max has. And Mum saw her too. I guess she can't be bothered to show herself to me.' She sounds put out.

I decide not to mention the apparition I saw just before Izzy toppled down the stairs, its phantasmagorical fingers closing around her neck. While no one's actually come out and said it, it seems that at least some of the blame for Izzy's fall is due to my waking her up in an unsafe place. I decide not to mention that either.

'There's no such thing as ghosts, Izzy,' I say instead. 'But Charlie did point out that you've been round Rookswood quite a bit. Sleepwalking? Or were you wide awake?'

She rolls her eyes. 'Why would I go there if I was awake?'

'I don't know – you tell me. I guess it's a good place for a party. Or do you have another agenda?'

'Are you accusing me of something?'

'No. Just saying...'

'Believe what you want, but you've got it all wrong. Grown-ups are so stupid. I mean, Mum should just let me and Max go and live with Dad. That's all we want.'

I try to read between the lines. What exactly is Izzy not telling me? But just then, there's a knock on the front door. It's Charlie. After dropping me off at the cottage, he went back to the house to lock up. He tells me that he'll go back tomorrow or the next day to clear up the debris. In the meantime, he's put some barriers across the road until the gate goes in. A last-ditch effort to keep people out. But I can't help thinking it's a futile gesture. Not if the problem is someone who's already *inside*.

'Did you see anyone when you went back?' I say.

'No. They must have scarpered in all the commotion. Probably just a tramp.'

'Should we call the police?'

'I wouldn't bother,' he says. 'Like I said, people get in all the time.'

I almost ask him why he can't manage to keep people out, if that's his job. But instead, I focus on a more pressing question. 'They weren't real body parts, right?'

For a second, he looks startled, but then, to my relief, he laughs. 'No. On closer inspection, it was bits and bobs from a mannequin, and lots of dirt and debris. It scared the bejesus out of me, but in the end, it was all smoke and mirrors.'

'That's a relief.'

'Anyway, I wanted to check that you're OK.' He gives me a searching look. Now that we're away from Rookswood, the whole experience seems hazy. Especially the part where he kissed me. 'And to tell you I've moved the key.'

He leans in and whispers in my ear that the key is now hidden inside a rotted spindle in the porch. It begs the question: why not just get keys cut for people who need them, or get one of those lock boxes? But I can't voice any of these suggestions because suddenly, he's kissing me again. I lift my hands, but instead of twining my arms around his neck, I push him gently away. 'Izzy's in the front room,' I whisper.

'Sure, sorry.' He lifts his finger and draws a heart shape in the dust on my cheek. 'I'm just sorry we were interrupted before. Can I have a rain check?'

I blush, wondering why I feel so cold and... filthy. Maybe because I've been attacked in a spooky old house by a tramp cum ghost.

'I'll let you know,' I say. 'Once things have calmed down a bit.'

'It'll all be fine, Kate,' he says. 'I promise. We'll clear the buggers out and get the place redeveloped. Rookswood will be our goose that laid the golden egg.'

Our? It sounds like he's talking about me. When did that become a thing?

Something in his eye... He leans in and kisses me again.

Suddenly, I can't wait for him to leave.

* * *

The water is greyish brown with dust as the events of the morning dissolve from my body. Charlie, Izzy, the mysterious woman. Smoke and mirrors, light and shadow. I'm missing something, but I don't know what.

Shivering out of the shower, I dress in clean clothing. The feeling of *wrongness* won't go away. I go downstairs to check on Izzy and am disconcerted to hear yet another male voice. Is Charlie back again? Do I want him to be?

I may be a control freak (no *may* about it) but I feel uncomfortable with Charlie's attempts to run the show at Rookswood. If he's in charge then why isn't he doing a better job of keeping the trespassers out? And what was he implying about Izzy – and Max? I've never seen my nephew show any interest at all in Rookswood. Yet Izzy herself said that Max was one of the few who had seen the ghost.

Max is at school so I can't ask him, but anyway, the question falls by the wayside. As I reach the door of the lounge, I discover the identity of the second voice. Izzy is deep in conversation...

With Matthew Whitford.

Why is he here? My mind jolts with annoyance and concern. Surely, he should have called first, asked my permission. I listen in to their conversation.

'It's important that you keep up with your studies,' Dr Whitford is saying. 'Your GCSEs are really important, as you know.'

'Yeah.' Izzy manages to sound tired even with the single word.

'I don't want you to be distracted by this. You're not your brother. It doesn't have to affect you.'

My hackles rise. It's fine for him to give her a pep talk, but to compare her unfavourably to her brother—

'Kate, is that you?'

He's looking not at me, but at my shadow splayed diagonally from the door across the floorboards.

'Dr Whitford,' I say, coolly, as I step into the room. 'What a surprise.'

He pushes his hair back from his face, a faint smile playing on his lips. Izzy looks past him. The TV is muted, but still on. Clearly, she's not overawed by her headmaster. It's only me who feels like a flustered, overgrown schoolgirl who wishes she'd blow-dried her hair and put on lip gloss.

'Sorry,' he says, 'I should have called. But I was in the neighbourhood, so I thought I'd drop off some revision notes for Izzy.' He gestures to a bag near the sofa. 'Good luck, Izzy.' He turns back to her. 'You're going to do very well.'

He stands up as if to leave; I feel instantly annoyed. Am I not even worth five minutes of his time?

'Thanks for stopping by,' I say. 'You must be very busy.'

His smile fades. 'Actually, I was hoping to have a quick word with you, Kate.'

'Fine.' I make a show of checking my watch. 'What's so urgent that the headmaster is making home visits?'

He moves past me out of the front room and into the hall, closing the door so Izzy can't hear.

'Just a little reminder – it would be great if you could call the office next time Max has a doctor's appointment.'

'A what?'

He gives me a look that's somewhere between incredulous and smug. 'His "therapist" appointments?' He emphasises the word. 'He's been out of school a few times now. Apparently, that's where he's been.'

I cross my arms and lean against the door, staring him down. 'Well, you and I both know that's hogwash.'

He laughs. 'I didn't *know*, but I suspected as much.'

'So you're saying that Max has been bunking off school?'

'This morning was the third time. But don't worry. He's back now. He arrived just before lunch. That's a good sign. Whatever's going on, he's not missing any meals.'

'Such a relief,' I say sarcastically. 'How did he get there?'

'He cycled. At least that's good exercise, since he missed PE.'

What can I say? I let out a long sigh. 'Like mother, like son – I just feel so... betrayed.'

He says nothing. I realise with horror that I've spoken aloud. Aired my dirty laundry in front of Mr 'Butter-Wouldn't-Melt'. I press my lips together. 'Look,' I say, 'I think I need a cup of tea. Join me?'

He smiles; my stomach flips. God damn it.

'Sounds good.'

I direct him into the conservatory and go to put the kettle on. When I come back with the tea, he's sitting at the table where my papers are spread, and the photo book is open next to my laptop. It's clearly caught his attention. I feel suddenly protective of Ada's memories.

'What's that?' he says.

'Something I found.'

'Can I look?'

'I suppose so.'

He takes a pair of wire-rimmed glasses from his shirt pocket and puts them on. Then he flips through the book, clearly rapt.

'Amazing,' he says, peering closer at one of the photos. 'I assume you found this at Rookswood?'

'More accurately, it found me.'

He shuts the book, keeping hold of it. 'That's one reason I stopped by. Rookswood. I know Izzy and Emma were both injured there. But I understand there have been other incidents?'

I take a long sip of tea. 'We've had some problems with trespassers. Par for the course with a derelict house.' I feel the same phantom defensiveness as I did during our first conversation, weeks ago, when he mentioned the 's' words: social services. 'I'm taking care of it,' I add.

'Of that I have no doubt.' There's a note in his voice – amusement, but also... respect? 'And is there any word about Emma?'

'She's gone into a residential programme near London. She should be out in a few weeks.'

'I'm glad she's doing better.'

I search his face. Just how glad is he? Something prickles inside of me. Jealousy? No, absolutely not.

'We'll all be glad when things are back to normal,' I say.

I'm expecting my brisk manner to put him off. Instead, he settles back in the chair.

'Maybe. But I wish I could have done more. For the house, that is.' He glances back at the book. 'I've seen the new planning application. A twelve-acre housing estate and community centre. It makes sense – I mean, with the best will in the world, not many people could afford to preserve the house as is. Not when the planners are keen, and a developer is eager to have his wicked way with it.'

'His wicked way?'

'Charlie Blackmore put in the planning application. I assume he and Emma are partners now? Both their names are on it.'

I cross my arms. 'News to me.' I hate how powerless I feel.

'Yes, well, Charlie's quite the operator. Some people have that way about them.'

'True.' A face floats into my mind. Not Charlie, but Philip.

'Anyway, you might know this already, but Rookswood was owned by Adaline.' He runs his finger over the name on the flyleaf. 'She was in her nineties when she died, which was amazing in itself when you consider her long-term exposure to chemicals like mercury, cyanide, bromine, and ether. She must have had a hell of a strong constitution. When she finally did die, she left everything to her sister, Camile. But no one ever managed to find Camile. She'd been missing for years, and it was as if she'd vanished off the face of the earth. In the end, the house went to the council and became surplus property. When the council auctioned it, there were three bidders. I was one of them, but I was up against Philip. It's no surprise that a swish property developer beat out a starving headmaster.' He smiles wryly. 'Anyway, I talked to Emma after they bought the place. She assured me that they planned on keeping the house intact and making cosmetic changes only. They were going to turn it into a boutique hotel and spa.' He rolls his eyes. 'I asked her if she was interested in including an exhibition on Adaline's work. In certain circles, Adaline was a bit of a legend.'

'Pretty macabre circles.' I eye him askance.

'She was a pioneer in her field. If she lived today, she would be a special-effects wizard. My gran knew Ada, like I told you before. She met Camile only once before she disappeared. There was an incident at the house. A fire. The police investigated, and Camile was in the frame. Which, according to Gran, seemed crazy and out of character. By all accounts, Adaline was the strong, controlling sister, and Camile was the sweet, kind one.'

It's almost like he's describing Emma and me.

'I guess we all act out of character from time to time. Sitting here in my sister's conservatory drinking tea with you, I'm proof of that. But what caused the fire? And did Camile really just disappear?'

'As for the first question, I don't know the answer. As for the second, it was easier to disappear in the days before police databases and home DNA testing kits. I remember at the time of the auction, I saw some of the original papers at the lawyer's office. Letters written by Adaline. She was desperate to find out what happened to Camile. Apparently, it was her dying wish to "be reunited" with her and "make things right".'

I frown. 'What things?'

'I don't know.' He stares down at the book. 'But these photos are kind of heartbreaking. When you take away the smoke and mirrors, headless portraits, spirit photography and special effects, Ada and Camile seem so close. I wonder what happened.'

His concern is oddly touching. 'You can borrow the book if you want,' I say. 'But I would like it back.' I draw a breath. 'Actually, I'm curious too.'

He nods. 'I understand. And speaking of curiosity, will you tell me more about the incidents at Rookswood?'

I shouldn't. Matthew Whitford is here uninvited, the house is none of his business, and unlike Charlie, he hasn't been around to rescue me as needed. Besides, if Izzy and Max are involved, then I need to watch my step. But as I open my mouth to change the subject, the whole story spills out...

The photograph I took.

The headless portraits.

The apparition on the stairs.

The debris and body parts.

The... ghost.

To my own ears, the account is laughable. If he didn't think badly of me already, Dr Whitford will surely conclude that I'm a complete nutter; someone who's unfit to walk the streets without a straightjacket, let alone look after two kids. A few weeks ago, I was an upstanding, no-nonsense lawyer. Now, I'm hysterical.

What the hell is going on?

As I'm ranting on, he stands up and wanders over to the window, looking out at the garden.

'You must think I'm crazy.' I voice my own opinion out loud. 'But unless the tramps, trespassers and teenage hoodlums are wizards with smoke and mirrors, something very odd is going on at Rookswood. But please believe that I am doing my best to look after Izzy and Max and keep them safe—'

'Kate.'

I stop talking, holding my breath as Matthew Whitford comes over to me and puts a hand on my arm. I look down at his hand, then at his face. His eyes look deeply into mine and I can't look away. Something in his expression compels me. Frightens me.

'Will you take me to Rookswood?' he says. 'I'd like to check out these ghostly goings-on for myself.'

VIII

A woman on fire.

Oh yes. It could be done.

The countess arrived at Rookswood at the appointed date and time, in a low, black Bentley motor car. As it came to a stop before the house, the driver's window opened and a puff of smoke escaped into the air. Normally, I would have paid no attention, the cigarette signifying only a chauffeur or a husband at the wheel. But when the driver's door opened, a woman got out. A woman who very much captured my attention.

She was tall and thin, wearing an elegant dress in the latest fashion that daringly bared a slender ankle. Her face was dwarfed by a large hat with a floppy brim. I had seen such attire before, but only in the pages of the Paris fashion catalogues that Camile was fond of collecting. She stubbed out the cigarette onto the drive with a low-heeled shoe, and with a gloved hand pushed back the brim of her hat to better take in the view of the house. I watched her from the window of my studio, and when her eyes met mine, a tremor racked my body. Dark and piercing, in that moment I felt like she *knew* me in a way that I had never known myself. Then, she turned away, back to the car where she withdrew a suitcase from the backseat. Camile was making ready for her visit, preparing tea and cakes. I felt unaccountably dizzy; surely this was a commission Camile could handle herself, and I could go to my bedroom, draw the curtains, and lie down until the faintness passed. Instead, when the housekeeper ushered our new client inside, I sent my sister away.

As soon as the countess entered, she *became* the space. Her perfume, heady and expensive; her gloved hand delicate but firm as it shook mine. She did not look around the room or appear curious. Nonetheless, she seemed to take in everything with those dark, knowing eyes. She appraised me openly, and my usual self-assurance vanished under her scrutiny. I imagined that she could see directly into my soul, with all its false pride, wounded vanity, and desire to be noticed, appreciated... and loved. And when she spoke with her low, accented voice, it struck an invisible chord inside me.

'I am Countess Tatiana Bischoff,' she said. 'But you may call me Tanya. And you, I presume, are Miss Adaline.'

'Ada.' I made an effort to recover my composure. 'Please, My Lady, have a seat. Your commission interests me.'

'Good,' she said. 'I am glad to hear it.'

She lowered herself onto the green, velvet sofa, making it appear dowdy as she sat ramrod straight, her long legs elegantly crossed. Camile had set out the spread of tea, sandwiches and cakes that we reserved for our wealthiest clients, but in the presence of the countess, it looked mean and shabby. I went immediately to my own cabinet where I kept my most expensive equipment as well as a cut crystal decanter of brandy and our elegant glasses. These I brought to the table, and by tacit agreement, both of us eschewed the tea in favour of something stronger. The brandy helped me recover some of my boldness, enough to ask the countess not about the commission, but about herself. She was Hungarian by birth, and her husband, Count Bischoff, was Swiss. They spent summers in their villa on Lake Geneva, winters in Biarritz, spring and autumn in Paris, and from time to time came to London where the count had business interests and a townhouse in Belgravia.

'It sounds like a dream,' was all I could say. Gazing at her as she spoke, my eyes were open to possibilities I had never before considered. I hardly ever left Rookswood; I had not even gone up to London for many years. I was content, or so I thought, with our house, our garden, our clients, our work. Content living a life with my sister, though, in the darkest hours of the night, I was still angry with her. Her dalliance with a man had demonstrated that Camile had not been content with this life, and though years had passed, I had not forgiven her. But now, in the presence of this stranger, I began to doubt my own complacence. Perhaps this world – this *small* world – that I had created, was not in fact big enough. Perhaps *I* was not big enough or good enough. For what, I did not know.

'A dream.' She wrinkled her aquiline nose. 'You make it sound like it is not real.'

'I didn't mean to imply that.'

She laughed then, a little too loud. Taking out a golden cigarette case, she offered one to me; I declined. She lit her own cigarette and let out a long, slender puff of smoke. 'You were right the first time,' she said. 'It is not real. Do not look too closely at a marriage, at a life, for things are not always as they seem. You are an illusionist. Who better to see the truth, no?'

'And what is the truth?'

Her eyes followed the smoke curling up from the cigarette; she tapped the glowing ash into the empty teacup.

'Here are the facts which may shed light on the matter. My husband, the count, is older than me. He was acquainted with your father. *Well* acquainted. One of his best clients, back in the day.'

I poured us each another glass of brandy, considering this most unpleasant of all truths. For I had cleared out my father's London studio; I knew exactly what she meant.

'I see,' I said at last.

'Yes.' Her lips thinned out as she smiled. 'I am certain you do.'

Camile and I had never discussed my father or his clients' *proclivities*. We had never discussed the photographs I had used to shame her at the time of her pregnancy. After that incident, I destroyed the photographs.

Most of them.

The countess's eyes held mine, as if she could guess my own shameful secret. The one I was desperate to hide even from myself.

'And what is it you want from me?' I said, finding my voice at last.

The countess sat forward, blowing smoke in my direction. 'I have followed your work for years, Miss Havelock. And if you don't mind my saying so, it has become quite vulgar. Spirits, phantoms – anyone with two eyes in their head can see it is all trickery.' She waved her cigarette for emphasis. 'I have seen much better illusions in Paris. I am acquainted with the great man Harry Houdini himself.'

'Then what is it you want?' I said through my teeth.

'I want to vex you. Challenge you. I believe that, like me, you are a woman whom society has undervalued. A woman who has undervalued herself.'

'You don't know me!'

'You are a woman who wishes to live life on her own terms, is that not right? A woman who wishes to be free. And yet, are you free, Ada? Are any of us?'

'I am free,' I said. 'I have a house. A beloved sister. A successful business enterprise. I do not need to subjugate myself to a husband, to children, to anyone. I live life on my own terms.'

'Yes.' She clapped her hands. 'And that is what I wish you to do for me. Together, we will create the ultimate illusion. Not of a spirit or a ghost, but of the moment of death. My death.'

'Your... death?'

She stared at me without speaking. I leaned closer, drawn by her dark gravity. 'Now that I have met you and seen how you live...' she swept a hand around the room, 'I choose to trust you.' She lowered her voice. 'You must create something that is beyond mere trickery and illusion. Something that my husband will believe. Only then will I be free of him. All my life, I have been dependent on others. On *men*. First my own father, then my husband. Despite the fact that his tastes lie elsewhere, I am his possession and he will not let me go. Though his title stems from me, my wealth comes solely from him. For years now, I have been preparing. Amassing money in accounts he knows nothing of. Making investments, buying property. I am now ready for the final step. My husband once told me this: "You are a destructive force, Tanya. Bright and dark, as deadly as a fire." I always appreciated that image he conjured, if little else about him. Thus, it is a fitting way, I think, to end our shameful union. I must die, and he must have the proof. A special illusion; a photograph that you will take. Of the moment when the flames consume me.'

My mouth crept open, the possibilities swirling in my brain.

'That is what I want from you. Now tell me, will you do it?'

Lifting her hand, she brushed my cheek with her fingers. A

lightning sensation travelled through my body, kindling every cell alight with flame. I didn't know how to do what she was asking but only one thing was important. That she was here now; that she would come back again. Before she could lower her hand, I caught it in mine. I brought it to my lips and kissed it.

'Yes,' I said. 'Yes, I will.'

22

My nerves spark as Dr Whitford and I walk to Rookswood House. It's partly phantom adrenalin from my previous ordeal, but also intrigue at my companion. While Charlie is friendly, uncomplicated, and exactly what it says on the tin, I sense that Matthew Whitford is a different animal. His brooding, reserved manner intrigues me, and like the depths of an iceberg below the surface, I wonder what might lie beneath.

'Ever since I came here the first time, the house has fascinated me,' he says, as we emerge through the tunnel of trees. 'It has a personality all of its own. One that's entirely unknowable.'

'That's for sure,' I say, recalling my own sentinel first visit. 'But at the end of the day, a house is just a house.'

'Some people believe that houses absorb the energy of their inhabitants.'

'Some people are totally daft.'

'Maybe.' He chuckles. 'But it's a fundamental law of physics that energy is neither created nor destroyed, it only changes state. We may not always be able to detect what form that energy takes, or how it's stored.'

'But do you really think it's possible that ghosts exist?'

'For as long as humans have walked the earth,' he says, 'we've attempted to explain the unexplainable. And the most unexplainable – and inevitable – thing is death. "The undiscovered country from whose bourn no traveller returns," to quote Will Shakespeare.' He glances at me. I roll my eyes. 'But for all those efforts,' he continues, 'science hasn't been able to explain it. Ergo, in every culture, people have created their own belief systems. There's anthropological evidence going back thousands of years that even the earliest humans believed in ghosts and spirits. And they have ever since.'

'Phew,' I say. 'That's quite the lecture. But as you say, what happens after death is unexplainable... ergo... just because humans tell stories about ghosts doesn't make them real.'

He laughs. 'True. But don't forget Occam's razor.'

'How could I possibly? But is a ghost a simpler explanation than a prank? I hope you're not teaching that to your vulnerable young pupils.'

'Even if I was, compared to what they learn every day from the internet, it would be the least of their worries.'

'I suppose.'

'And you're right. At the moment, we can't discount the possibility that trespassers, tramps, or teenage hoodlums could be wizards with smoke and mirrors.' He frowns, considering. I think of the veiled woman I saw. A homeless person? A teenager? A ghost? Which is the most likely explanation?

'So you're saying we should keep an open mind?' I say.

'Bingo.'

We walk to the front of the house. The door is locked, but I find the Charlie's new hiding place for the key and draw it out (along with a dozen woodlice). I unlock the door, swallowing back the vestiges of shock and panic from last time. But although

I'm expecting to feel the weird coldness, stumble over the remnants of rubble and mannequin parts, the stairway is completely clear.

'It was here,' I say, taken aback. 'Rubble, dust, body parts. I swear it.'

Dr Whitford goes to the bottom of the stairs and looks up. 'Someone cleaned up,' he says. 'Do you smell that?' He twitches his nose. 'Wax and linseed oil.'

'Charlie said that he was going to clean it up later, but he wouldn't have had time to do it yet. So it must have been the tramp.'

'Maybe the ghost likes a tidy house?'

'Maybe.' I can't quite believe we're having this conversation. 'But then why mess it up before?'

'The school psychologist would probably label it as attention-seeking behaviour,' he says. 'Your ghost is trying to get your attention.'

'She's definitely got it.'

'So have you asked her what she wants?'

'Now you're having me on!'

'Why? People are people, and they always act according to motive. If you were a ghost inhabiting Rookswood House, what would you want?'

'To keep people out,' I say. 'Especially ones who want to tear it down and build a housing estate.'

'Good idea. What else?'

I feel like he's a professor on my law course inflicting torture by Socratic method. 'I might be lonely,' I say, searching for the right answer. 'I want someone to notice me.'

'So who's your best company? Someone living, or someone dead?'

'I guess that depends. On things science doesn't have the answers to.'

'Fair enough.' He gives me a satisfied smile. 'Now all you have to do is work out which motive *your* ghost has.'

'How do I do that?'

'I don't know. That's why you have to ask her.'

'You *are* having me on.'

'Maybe,' he says. 'But before you go waking the dead, let's have a look around first.'

'Be my guest.'

I feel surprisingly safe being at Rookswood with Matthew Whitford. Maybe it's his clear appreciation of the house, as he goes from room to room taking in the environment with the same awe I did. But it's also because this time, there are no strange draughts, creaking floorboards, or smell of smoke. To my surprise, even a few of the electric lights turn on with barely a flicker. There's no sense of a 'presence'. Which is kind of a shame.

I lead the way down to the cellar and show him the headless portraits.

'Fascinating!' he says. 'I can't believe all this was just left here.'

'I guess no one bothered to clear it out.'

'Maybe.' He wanders over to an old Welsh dresser and pulls open one of the drawers. 'Look at this.'

I go over to where he's standing and see that the drawer is filled with old photos. Matthew flips through them and hands them to me. Most of them look like early or failed attempts at the sisters' signature images. I gawk at headless sitters, girls and boys juggling their own heads, a whole series of photos with flames superimposed over a standing woman.

A woman on fire.

'Is this for real?' I say. I recognise the model; it's the dark-haired woman from the latter pages of Ada's photo book.

'It's such an interesting effect.' Matthew tries to explain the nuts and bolts of wet plate collodion prints, double exposures, combination printing and something called a 'Pepper's Ghost' illusion, using light and reflections in glass. Most of it goes right over my head. The woman in the photo is petite but statuesque, her features are strong and commanding, her complexion pale and bloodless. She stares boldly at the camera, with eyes so cold and penetrating that I flinch under her gaze. Ada was a force of nature, to be sure, but this woman, even long dead...

She frightens me.

'I wonder who she was,' I say.

'Me too.' Dr Whitford puts the photos back in the dresser and I do the same. 'It's a shame that we may never know. But Kate, promise me this. Whatever Emma decides to do with the house, please try and convince her to preserve these things. I'll buy them from her if she's willing to sell. It would be such a shame if all this history was lost.' He stares into the dimness, shaking his head. 'How does the song go? "You don't know what you have until it's gone"?'

I sense he's no longer talking about an old house and a drawer of creepy photographs. Everything points to the fact that he's suffered a loss. The woman in the photo on his desk, his wife. I want to ask him about her, but already he's walking back up the stairs.

I follow behind more slowly, suddenly blindsided by my own loss. My sister. 'I didn't appreciate Emma until she was gone from my life. I pushed her away; I created that hole like I was digging my own grave. Is that what happened to Adaline and Camile?'

'Maybe.'

I look at Dr Whitford in something akin to horror. I'm so used to being alone that I didn't realise I was voicing my thoughts aloud.

'Sorry,' I backpedal. 'I... didn't mean to say anything. I just wonder why they were estranged.'

'Why do sisters fall out?' he says. 'I expect it was the same then as now.'

I frown at him. Does he know something about Emma and me? My skin crawls with shame. And yet, here in this place, with Ada as a potential witness, I have a strong urge to unburden myself. Let her know that I, of all people, understand.

'Love,' I say. 'The age-old reason.'

He nods. 'You're probably right.'

I sigh. 'You may not know this, but I was once engaged to Philip. Emma's husband. I'm not pointing any fingers, but things... happened. I'm sure you can fill in the blanks.'

'Gosh.' He stares at me, his eyes sparking. Not with the sort of pity I hate, but with something more akin to anger. 'That explains a lot.'

'It does and it doesn't. It was a long time ago. Too long ago to justify the pain I feel now.' Saying it aloud, I almost start crying. 'Not for Philip, obviously. But for the fact that I lost Emma. That part was my fault.'

'Hey.' His voice is gentle. 'Don't be so hard on yourself. You're here now. When she needed you, you dropped everything and came running.'

'Yes.' A tear trickles down my cheek. I force myself not to turn away. 'I did. But all those years... they're gone.'

He paces across the floor. It occurs to me vaguely that this man is the last person I should be confiding in. I'm already on thin ice, the kids a mistake away from a one-way ticket to foster care. And yet, as I stand in the pool of light coming inside through the cupola, my mind seems clearer, my feelings more coherent, than they have in years.

'You're right,' he says. 'The past can't be recovered. But that's precisely why you need to plug the leak. Don't lose any more time. Stop hurting and start living.'

I look at him, but his gaze is focused on the patterns of light on the floor. Once again, I have the distinct impression that we're no longer talking about me.

'Have you taken your own advice?' I say softly.

My words break the spell. Dr Whitford turns back to me and laughs. 'Absolutely not.'

Before I can enquire further, his phone rings. Frowning, he takes it from his pocket and checks the screen. 'Sorry,' he says, 'I need to take this. My son's not been too well. That night I saw you in the pub, as soon as we got home, he started complaining of bad stomach pains. It got worse in the night, so I took him to hospital. That's why I was there when they brought Izzy in. Turns out he needed an appendectomy. He's still recovering and is quite weak.'

'Sorry,' I say. *I wish I had asked.*

'It's fine.'

He goes out of the front door. I continue to stand in the kaleidoscopic spattering of light on the dusty tiles, and take a deep breath, ready to speak.

'I suspect you overheard all that, Ada,' I say aloud. 'Do you have any thoughts? Any insight you want to provide?'

The house is silent; there's not even a creaking casement or settling floorboard. No noisy, unruly behaviour. Nothing at all.

Again, I feel oddly disappointed.

'I'm sure you can't be bothered with my problems,' I say. 'Which is fair enough. So let's talk about you. What's your motive then? What do you want?'

Still no response. Of course there isn't. Ghosts can't communicate with the living, because ghosts don't exist.

'Fine then,' I say. 'I'll go. Leave you to it. Haunting or... whatever. Have a nice day.'

A faint current in the air chills the back of my neck. A presence... an energy... that is becoming quite familiar.

'We can keep it between ourselves,' I whisper. 'No one else needs to know.'

The front door bangs open. I jump, startled. The hairs on the back of my neck prickle with goosebumps, but that's not all. The chill breeze blows the dust at the bottom of the stairs. Like soap writing on a steamy mirror, the words appear, just legible, like an invisible finger has written them in the dust.

Find her.

In the blink of an eye, the words disappear. The dust is just dust. The house is just a house.

'Find her,' I whisper.

'Kate?' Dr Whitford's voice; he's standing at the door. 'Oh, sorry, are you on the phone?'

'No,' I mutter. 'Just talking to myself.'

'Unfortunately,' he says, 'duty calls. The toilets are overflowing in the gym and it's all hands on deck. I need to get going. But thanks so much for showing me the house.'

'No worries,' I say.

'If you like, I can do some digging,' he says. 'One of our governors is the head of the local historical society. They may have some records on Adaline and her photographs. Or not. If you're interested to learn more, it might be worth a try.'

'I am interested.' The breeze tickles the back of my neck. 'And not just in Ada, but also in Camile. I'd like to find out what happened to her.' My words echo in the empty hall. 'Maybe we can compare notes.'

'Sounds great.' His smile beams its way into half-forgotten places inside me. I feel suddenly self-conscious, and something else too... like the new-found connection between us is a little less than totally private.

Matthew walks out of the house and down the steps. I follow him out, but remain on the porch, finding the key and putting it in the lock. Just before I pull the front door shut, I whisper inside the silent house.

'I can't promise anything, Ada, but I'll see what I can do.'

My hand trembles as I close the door and turn the key in the lock.

23

Find her.

I don't have the first idea how to do it. But the 'old soul' in me rises up stubbornly, ready to take on the challenge. I walk with Matthew Whitford to his car, and he gives me a lift back to the gatehouse. I don't mention the ghostly writing, figuring that if Ada had chosen to reveal herself to him, she could have done so. For now, it can be our secret. But as I'm getting out of the car, all thoughts of ghostly motives go out of my head.

'Thanks for showing me the house,' Matthew says again. 'I really hope Emma does the right thing and preserves it. But either way, I'm glad I got to know you better.'

There's something in his voice, something in his eye when he looks at me. I may be years too old to be glad of a good word from the headmaster, but not too old to appreciate one from a handsome man.

'Me too,' I say.

'As for comparing notes,' he adds, 'we could do it over dinner. Maybe Saturday? I mean...' he backtracks. 'I'll need to make sure the nanny's free to watch Daniel.'

'The nanny?'

He frowns. 'Yes. I think you met her at the pub?'

'Oh, was that who she was? I did wonder.'

Something sparks inside me like a firework. I've spent a lot of years in London on my own, but suddenly the fresh country air seems rife with possibilities.

'Yes,' he says. 'But it should be fine. Unless you have other plans?'

'No, it sounds good,' I say. 'And in the meantime, I'll try to find out everything I can about what happened to Camile. I don't know what I'm looking for, but hopefully I'll know it when I see it.'

I smile at him; he smiles back.

'That's usually how it works,' he says.

'Yes, I think it does.'

* * *

Ghostly writing, dinner with the headmaster. The rest of the day is a write-off as far as getting any work done. Then there's the niggle I've tried to put out of my mind – Max and his absences from school. He has been spending a lot of time lately with his friends, and also putting in time at the chemistry lab. He's told me that he wants to be a chemist, and that the incident with the fire was a freak accident. When I've asked him about school in general, he's been eager enough to tell me. But now I know that he's also being economical with the truth, and I need to get to the bottom of it. Later...

I turn on my laptop and do some internet searches trying to find out about a woman named Camile who once lived in an old house called Rookswood and had a sister called Adaline. Other than some old parish records confirming dates of birth and Ada's date of death, I find nothing online. I'm about to give up when I get a WhatsApp from Dr Whitford (signed Matthew with an x) telling me he's looking forward to seeing me on Saturday night. I reply to the message (no signature or x, but with a silly grin emoji) confirming.

As the message whooshes off into the aether, my brain automatically conjures as many obstacles as possible. He's a man with a past, and having suffered the ultimate heartbreak of losing his wife, he's now focused on raising his son. I'm a woman who's spent most of her adult life trying to avoid feelings and entanglements. How's that supposed to work? And is the blonde woman *just* the nanny, or have I got things all wrong? And what about Charlie? We may not have a great deal in common, but he's been there when I needed him, and he seems to feel something for me. As uncomplicated romances go, I could do worse. But is that really what I want? Why don't I know?

When Max gets home that night, I question him about his absences. 'I'm so sorry, Aunt Kate,' he says. 'It's just, I went to visit Mum. I didn't tell you, or Iz, because I know you don't get on with her. But I thought someone should visit her. I've only gone during PE, because I didn't think you'd want me to miss a real lesson.'

'You're right, I wouldn't want that.' He looks so boyish, so innocent, that I feel almost guilty for telling him off. 'But you do need to be in school, and I'm happy to drive you to see your mum anytime.'

'OK.' He beams me his Christmas-card smile. 'Thanks.'

'I'm sorry I didn't offer before,' I say. 'It's just you didn't mention it, and you and Izzy have such busy lives. I thought you had enough on your plate. But I should have asked.'

'Don't worry. You've got a lot on your plate too, Aunt Kate. I didn't want to bother you.'

'Really, it's fine,' I say. 'I can take you this weekend. Is that soon enough?'

'Maybe not this weekend,' he says. 'But thanks for the offer.'

'No problem.' I hope he can feel the love in my smile. 'No problem at all.'

* * *

For the rest of the week, I go about my daily routine with a renewed sense of anticipation and purpose. I've sorted things with Max, I'm having dinner with an intriguing man, and I know what the ghost of Rookswood wants me to do. On Thursday morning, Izzy announces that she's ready to go back to school. When I drop her off, she's bombarded by friends. Before Max gets out of the car, I make him promise that he won't do anything else to put me in the doghouse with the headmaster (as much as the idea intrigues). I return to the cottage eager to finish my morning work, hoping I'll have enough time to fit in a trip to the local historical society in the afternoon.

I've barely finished answering my emails, however, when a commotion erupts outside. I go to the kitchen window and look out at the road that leads from the main gate to Rookswood. It's Charlie – he's speeding down the track in his van followed by a procession of two lorries, one carrying a skip and the other with a digger, and two more white vans. Whatever is happening, Charlie hasn't kept me in the loop.

I abandon my work, bundle up, and walk swiftly up the road to Rookswood. By the time I arrive, the skip is being unloaded, and half a dozen workmen are preparing to mobilise. There's no sign of Charlie, but the door to the main house is open. Boldly, I march towards it.

'Oi, luv,' one of the workmen calls out. 'Get back, will ya?'

The skip plunks to the ground. The digger drives down the ramp.

'What are you doing?' I call out.

The workman comes over. 'Demolition works are starting today, so from now on, it's hard hats only.'

'Demolition? I didn't authorise that.'

The man shrugs. 'Talk to Charlie. He's in charge.'

We'll see about that. 'Where is he?'

'Must be inside the house. But like I said, it's off limits.'

Ignoring him, I continue on to the porch. The workman calls after me but I don't stop.

'Charlie!' I call out from the door. 'You need to tell me what's happening.'

No answer from Charlie. But as I proceed into the hallway, I experience a familiar chill that sets my teeth on edge.

'Where is he, Ada?' I whisper.

A door creaks in the direction of the solarium. I forget to be scared, or even to question this occurrence. Occam's razor – the simplest solution is usually right. So be it.

'Thanks,' I say.

Sure enough, I find Charlie in the solarium talking to a man with a sledgehammer.

'What are you doing?' I say in an icy voice.

'Kate.' Charlie breaks off his conversation. 'You shouldn't be here. It's hard hats only.'

'Stand down the troops, Charlie,' I say. 'I didn't authorise any demolition works to be started today. Or ever, for that matter.'

Charlie returns my gaze with equal frostiness. 'I spoke with Emma yesterday. She's authorised everything.'

'Did she really? That's strange, because I was told by her care coordinator that she's not supposed to be bothered by non-essential communications.' Certainly, she rarely responds to any of *my* texts, though I don't tell him that.

'This is essential to her,' he says. 'She wants construction work on the housing estate to start in early summer. On that sort of timeline, we should have started the demolition works last month.'

'She hasn't communicated that to me,' I say, 'and while she's away, I'm in charge. You need to call off the dogs. This house has cultural and historical significance; there are things that need to be preserved. You may have talked some local knob of a planner around, but I'll get English Heritage involved. The works need to be halted until a proper survey can be done to assess the cultural assets.'

Charlie laughs. 'Come on, Kate. There's no point you getting your pretty head involved. We'll have the place pulled down by the time you get anyone out here.'

Pretty head. My fist itches with the urge to smash something. I follow Charlie and sledgehammer man as they leave the solarium and return to the great hall. What was I thinking? I want to scrub the lingering vestiges of his kiss off my lips. And Emma: how could she authorise this *vandalism*? I take out my phone and try to ring her. The call goes straight to voicemail. On behalf of Rookswood and Adaline, I feel betrayed all over again. And yet, my sister is now our only hope.

Inside the great hall, two men are hauling in power tools, buckets, a petrol can, a pneumatic drill, and skip bags. Charlie ignores me and gestures to the man with the sledgehammer. 'You can start there, George.' He points to the wall of the vestibule beside the door. 'Bring it all down.'

'Right, boss.' George hefts his hammer. Everything drifts into slow motion as he cocks it back... swings. With a loud thud, a huge crack appears in the wall.

'You're going to regret this—'

My words are punctuated by a loud, low, rumbling sound. The entire house seems to ripple and vibrate. It could just be the shock waves from the sledgehammer blow against a load-bearing wall, but when I look to the empty landing at the top of the staircase...

Ada is there.

And she's pissed off.

I scream as it all happens in an instant – the stained-glass cupola high above our heads cracks, then shatters. Heavy pieces of coloured glass rain down, as sharp and vicious as knives. I cower at the side of the room. The workman with the sledge-hammer presses himself against the wall, managing to avoid the worst of it. Charlie, however, is in the wrong place at the wrong time. He falls to his knees, covering his head as the shards fall over him, bouncing off his hardhat. Other workmen run into the room. By the time the dust settles, Charlie's clothes are torn and filthy, and he's bleeding from shallow cuts to his cheek and hands. But he manages to get to his feet, staggering over to the staircase and slumping down amid a sea of kaleidoscopic glass. My entire body is trembling, but I manage to dial 999. Some of the workmen scatter of their own accord; a few agree to stay on and look after Charlie and George, who also has some cuts on his hands. The rest of the workmen, I dismiss. Rookswood may have an uncertain future, but it's not going to be demolished.

Not today.

IX

You are a destructive force. Bright and dark, as deadly as a fire.

Those words were said about the countess by her own husband, though she was fond of saying it about me. It was true, of course. I destroyed my relationship with Camile. Drove her away, forced her to vanish without a trace. Then wasted the rest of my own life wishing in vain to recover what I had lost. For some people, the past is a sanctuary. For me, it was a torture. All those years spent wishing – for my own destruction as much as anything else. Even that I could not manage, or I would not be here. The shards rain down around me, the workers injured or frightened. Rookswood is not their house to destroy.

That is down to me alone.

As the glass settles, I think again of my pain, my ecstasy. I think again of Tanya. From that very first meeting, the match was lit, and I breathed oxygen onto the nascent flames. That night, I lied to Camile. Told her I was unwell and took to my bed just after dinner. Before I retired, I recovered a bundle of photos I had taken from my father's studio, which I'd kept hidden under a loose floorboard for years. What they portrayed, as well as why I kept them, was too shameful to admit. At least, that was the case before I met *her*. On that night, I looked on them with a new curiosity, and other feelings too. My father had captured every detail of the act. Not the coupling between women and men that his degenerate photographs usually depicted, and which had never interested me. But of similar acts solely between *women*. Before I'd seen the photos, I hadn't known such things were possible, let alone that such debauched images would explain my own desires. I'd hidden them away, out of sight, out of mind. And so it had proved... until that day.

I bring her hand to my lips and kiss it...

The countess was a woman of the world; I was not. I should have foreseen what was coming, and that she would toy with me like a cat does a mouse. The countess returned a week later to discuss details and logistics. Told me that she'd 'taken a house' nearby to facilitate our work together on the project. And this time, when she brushed my cheek with her finger, I drew her into my arms and kissed her on the lips. She laughed... but she kissed me back.

The time after that, I became her and she me. Tanya was the Woman on Fire. But it was me who was set alight.

* * *

Camile noticed. Of course she did. Though years had passed since her bid for freedom, I had remained angry and resentful towards her. She had become a mere shadow of herself, her pure white light all but extinguished in my eyes. Still Camile knew me better than anyone else. She was aware of my meta-morphosis and had gleaned the reason for it. I could see it in the cold, mocking way she treated the countess when she came for her sittings. I saw the judgement in Camile's hollow, blue eyes when she looked at me across the breakfast table. We had other clients, of course, but most of my time was occupied by my work for the countess. She was very particular in her requirements, but in my vanity, I chose to believe she wanted to prolong our time together. The countess wanted a special illusion, and although, I tried many different methods, none of them reached her exacting standards. The countess wanted something more than a double exposure of flames superimposed above her own image, which she believed would be easily exposed as a fake by her husband. Having seen my efforts, she decided that no illusion would do. I had to make it real.

I threw myself into the task, researching all manner of pyrotechnic effects such as those used in the theatre in the last century. Lycopodium powder, *flammes de Bengale*, strontium nitrate, potassium chlorate, and antimony trisulphide, oxyhydrogen limelight. I even allowed the countess to escort me to the theatre in London so I could view the latest stage effects (spending, afterwards, a most liberating weekend together in her Mayfair townhouse). I became a veritable chemist, experimenting with different fabrics and concoctions, trying to find a way to achieve accuracy and perfection without doing my treasured companion an injury. I, however, did not escape injury in the process, causing myself all manner of heat and chemical burns. The countess showed rare care and concern over my physical injuries, which gave me little incentive either to prioritise safety or to achieve results at speed.

The closer I became to the countess, the further I drifted from Camile. Tanya had made it clear that she viewed my sister as little more than a pampered child: pretty, dull, and ultimately, beneath her notice. Like every woman in love, I wished nothing more than for my secret paramour and my sister to be companionable, but mostly, I chose not to notice the friction in our triangle, and most especially, the friction between Camile and me.

As the summer days faded and autumn drew in, I sensed that the countess was growing restless with my lack of results. 'I cannot abide the English damp,' she told me one day in late September. 'It is imperative that you finish your commission so that I may orchestrate my escape from the count.'

'And then...' The words caught in my throat. 'You will be gone?'

In a rare gesture of affection, she took my hands. 'You can join me, dearest, if you like. A change of air would do you a world of good.'

I squeezed her hands with all the energy of fear in my heart. 'Don't go, Tanya,' I said. 'Please.'

She laughed at me, as she often did. 'You stink of sulphur.' Drawing me close, she kissed me hard on the lips.

24

I get in the shower, washing off more streams of rubble, glass, and dirt. One thing's for sure – even if we get through this, Emma's going to have one hell of a clogged drain. Wrapping myself in a towel, I go to my suitcase and find it empty. The clothes I was wearing earlier are filthy, and everything else I brought with me is in the laundry.

Once again, I raid Emma's closet. When I flip through the hangers of neatly folded jeans and ironed T-shirts, it feels less wrong than before, and more like a wardrobe that some version of me might enjoy experimenting with. I'm not sure if that's a good or bad thing.

Outside, gravel crunches in the drive. Someone is here. I quickly choose an outfit and get dressed. As I'm pulling one of Emma's butter-soft cashmere jumpers over my head, I realise that whoever it is hasn't knocked. Footsteps are coming up the stairs. The bedroom door flings open—

I freeze.

Emma screams.

'You—!' we both say at the same time.

She's looking me up and down, her frown deepening as she takes in my outfit piece by piece.

'Um, hi, Emma.' I try and recover. Should I hug her, offer to make her a cup of tea? Is she going to berate me for the fact that her builder got taken to A & E and her house is now half-collapsed? Or for the fact that I ordered the others off the job to prevent its full collapse?

'Why are you wearing my clothes?'

Of all the questions…

'Oh sorry.' I wave a hand. 'All my stuff's in the wash. You know how it is. There are only three certainties in life: death, taxes, and laundry.' I force a laugh.

Her frown deepens. 'Have you been sleeping in my bed?'

'I've been here for weeks. Where else was I supposed to sleep?'

This is not going well. Whatever I'd rehearsed in my head for this moment of reunion, someone hasn't learned their lines.

'Weeks,' she mutters, going over to the bureau and picking up one of the photos of her and the kids. 'It seems like a lifetime.'

I'm not sure she's talking to me, but I decide to go with it. 'It's not really that long,' I say, 'and in fact, I thought you were supposed to stay at the facility for another month.'

'I left early.' She sets down the photo and turns back to me. Her face is a blank mask that doesn't quite hide the hostility underneath. 'I tried to ring you, but it went to voicemail. So I got a taxi.'

'Sorry.'

She puts her hands on her hips. 'You may be sorry, Kate, but you've got a lot to answer for. Charlie rang me too, this morning. He said he had an accident at the house? Now he's waiting in A & E to be checked over?'

'I hope he's OK,' I say, 'but it was his own fault.'

'Really? He told me you were there getting in the way. He said you countermanded my instructions for him to crack on with the project? You may be a rich lawyer, Kate, without a house and children to look after, but some of us aren't so lucky. Philip left us with nothing but debts. Nothing.'

She goes to the window and leans over the sill. For a split second, I worry she's about to do something stupid. 'Emma,' I say, going to her. I risk placing a hand on her back.

My sister whirls around, throwing me off like I've assaulted her.

'You seem to have settled in well.' She indicates the clothing. 'Why don't you just take over, Kate. You always do everything right. I'm sure you'll be a better mum to Izzy and Max than I am. They should have been yours anyway.'

Her words shock me. She slumps down on the bed and ugly cries; her tears flood through the cracks in my heart. I want to go to her, but I can't risk it.

The floorboards creak outside the door again.

'Emma?'

To my surprise, Charlie enters the room. His cuts have been bandaged and his cheeks stitched, but he's covered with dust, and obviously hasn't been home to shower. Still, he fills the room: big, substantial, and warm, like an over-stuffed chair. He doesn't glance at me as he goes to my sister and sits down on the bed next to her. She's as small as a child as he curls her in his arms. 'Shh, shh.' He stokes her hair. 'I'm here now, and I'm fine. Everything's going to be fine.'

'Oh Charlie,' Emma says. 'I was so worried about you when I heard what happened.'

He nestles her closer, then looks up at me. The look in his eye hollows out my insides like a shovel digging a grave. My mind slips into a half-remembered vertigo: that sickly, terrible feeling of freefall, like I've tumbled off the edge of the earth.

History is repeating itself.

I grip the edge of the wardrobe door to steady myself.

I've got something to tell you, Kate. About last night... I'm so sorry.

I wait for the words to leave my sister's mouth. But instead, she pulls away from Charlie and says something quite different.

'You need to leave, Kate.'

'Emma?'

'Charlie and I can handle things now.' I stare open-mouthed as she turns to him and gazes into his eyes; strokes the stubble on his chin. But he stiffens under my piercing stare, which makes her stiffen too.

'Emma,' I say again. 'We need to talk first. Alone.'

'There's been nothing to say for fifteen years,' my sister says. 'And I don't know why we'd start now. I guess you want me to say sorry – and I am, for sure. Or maybe you want to gloat, I don't know. Either way, I'm grateful that you came to help out with the kids, but we need to get back to normal now.'

'We?'

She takes Charlie's hand and entwines it with hers. History isn't repeating itself, but twisting itself into a state of divine retribution. Charlie and I had one date. Two kisses. I'm far from invested. But Emma... Clearly, when I tell her – and I'm going to have to tell her – it will break her heart.

'Seriously?' I say. Emma looks up, startled; but I'm staring at Charlie. 'You two are a thing? For how long?'

'Well, it's brand new,' he says quickly. 'We just realised—'

'Ever since Philip left, Charlie's been there for me,' Emma says. 'When you weren't.'

I don't take the bait. 'Seems like he's been there for a lot of women who need rescuing.'

'How dare you?' Emma spits.

'Hey, let's just all take it easy,' Charlie says. 'Kate, you heard what your sister said. It's been great having you here to help out. But we're going to be fine.'

I recognise this for what it is. A tightrope, a Rubicon. A choice.

I have something to tell you...

I could say nothing. Walk away quietly. That remains an option, surely. Let Emma and Charlie sail off into the sunset together. Life is short – their 'thing' is brand new and I should be glad they've found each other. I should let them raze Rookswood to the ground and have their new start...

Rookswood. Ada.

That's what swings the balance.

'Did you really think I wouldn't tell her?' I take a menacing step towards Charlie. 'That you asked me out on a date? That you kissed me, not once but twice? That you "wanted a rain check" for more? I mean, I'm fine to walk away from all that, but not without telling my sister the truth.'

Emma gapes at me in horror, but I continue addressing her big, strapping boyfriend.

'What were you playing at, anyway? Were you hedging your bets? Thinking that if Emma didn't pull through, you'd try a different tack to get hold of that property?' The phantom itch of something Matthew Whitford told me suddenly becomes strong enough to scratch. 'Because that's what you really want, isn't it? You were the third bidder. Philip and Emma won out, but now, he's gone and you've got a second bite at the apple.'

'You kissed *her*? My sister?' Emma's face is shrivelled. She's younger than me, but she suddenly looks... old.

'She's lying,' Charlie says. 'I invited her down the pub, thinking it would be harmless enough, but I was wrong. Like I told you before, she constantly needed rescuing. She's jealous of you, and lonely too. I think she saw me as an easy mark. Her bit of rough.'

I sputter a laugh. 'Fine,' I say to Emma. 'Believe what you want.'

My sister stands up and approaches me. Whatever she does or doesn't believe, Charlie has ripped a plaster off a very old, but very unhealed, wound. In the time-honoured way of sisters immemorial, she takes it out, not on him, but on me.

'Is this your revenge?' She clenches her fists at her sides; I take a step back. 'After all this time, you still can't let it go.'

'Actually, I can,' I say. 'Surely *you* don't think that I'm still hankering after Philip after fifteen years. Or that I'd sink so low as to steal your boyfriend. That's your m.o., not mine.'

'Get out of my house, Kate – now! You never wanted to hear my side of the story. You just made up your mind and buggered out of my life. For *fifteen years*.'

'I was hurt. You betrayed me.'

'You never listened to what I had to say. You never let me tell you the truth about what happened that night at your engagement party.'

I put my hands on my hips. 'Which is?'

Her eyes cloud with a storm of memory. 'Philip wanted out, but he didn't know how to tell you. All those people, all those arrangements. He'd been texting me for a few weeks and we'd become friends. I was his confidante,' she says proudly.

'*His* confidante? You're *my* sister.'

'That's how it is with you, Kate. *My, my, my.* You want to own people. But some of us just don't want to play along.'

'Go on.'

'Philip had had a few drinks. He asked me to go outside with him to get some air. We went out to the boathouse and he broke down in tears. Told me he didn't love you, and that he wanted to end it. He said that having me as a friend had opened his eyes to what he *really* wanted.'

'So you swallowed it, hook, line, and sinker.'

'No. That's what you've thought all these years, and that's where you're wrong.'

I roll my eyes. 'Well, please do enlighten me.'

'We were cuddling, but then he started to touch me. Kiss me. I was drunk too, and at first, I thought it was kind of nice. But then, I told him to stop. I said that you were my sister, and that he needed to face up to you and break things off. But he didn't stop.'

I stare at her. 'So what are you saying?'

'Just that.'

'You're saying that he...?'

'I told myself afterwards that I'd wanted it. I think I actually believed it. And when you found out what happened, and we rowed, I had no one else to turn to. And then I discovered I was pregnant. He gave me a big song and dance about how this was the best thing that could have happened, and that we were meant to be. I didn't know what to do.' A fat tear rolls down her cheek. Charlie tries to wipe it away, but she shrugs him off. 'I wanted to ask you for advice, like I'd always done. But you were gone. And I understand why. It was all such a huge mistake.'

'But if what you say is true, then how on earth could you have married him?'

'You cut me out of your life. I had no other choice.'

'There's always a choice.'

'OK.' She lifts her chin defiantly. 'In that case, I made one. I felt alone and scared so I decided to make the best of it. I didn't have you, so I chose to become you. I chose to love him, and trust what he said – that he loved me and we were right for each other. And when I had Izzy, and then Max, it all became much easier. I did love him for a while, and I loved being a family. Such as it was.'

I shake my head, all at once bereft of words. Has Emma twisted the truth in her mind now that Philip has left, making herself the victim? Or am I the twisted one, getting lost in a dark forest of pain and betrayal, refusing to listen or see the light?

Emma turns towards Charlie with a sigh. 'And now, it's happening again, in reverse. I thought I could trust you. That all those things you said to me were true. But now, get the hell out of my house. Both of you.'

'Emma, no. Please.' Charlie stands up, towering over the both of us, somehow managing to look like a schoolboy unjustly chastised by the headmaster. 'I love you. I tried to get to know your sister and help her out because I felt it was the right thing to do. Helping Kate made me feel closer to you.'

'Oh, save it,' I say. 'You're using both of us to manipulate things for your own ends.' I turn back to Emma. 'There were three bidders for Rookswood. You and Philip, Matthew Whitford, and Charlie, here.' I round on him, daring him to deny it. 'You and Philip were the high bidders by a long way. Matthew Whitford wanted to preserve the house. He thought you and Philip wanted that too. But Charlie here wants to raze it to the ground and build his housing estate. He doesn't care about history, or anything else. He's only after you for the property, and the money.'

Emma looks at me, then at him. Then, she laughs. Ugly, sad, maniacal.

I've had enough. I turn and run from the room.

25

A small part of me expects Emma to follow. A larger part wishes she would, but is unsurprised when she doesn't. My breathing is short and painful as I go outside into the spring chill, still wearing Emma's clothes. If this was a normal afternoon, I'd be doing a last hour or two of legal work and a quick tidy up of the house before collecting Max and Izzy from school. That's what I *want* to be doing. How dare my sister come home, now of all times. How dare she march in and try and reclaim... *her* life.

My throat is raw with unshed tears as I get in the car and reverse out of the drive. Are Emma and Charlie watching me from the upstairs window? I doubt it. I should drive to the village, collect the curtains I've taken to the drycleaners, buy a few bits and pieces for Emma to cook the kids for supper. Tie up loose ends, and give Emma time to throw my laundry back in my suitcase and leave it at the front door. But how will I give her back her clothes? Somehow, this little problem elbows its way front and centre into my head, and tears rise to the surface. How will I give Emma back her clothes when mine are dirty?

Somehow, I resolve the dilemma by deciding to skip the trip to the village entirely. I turn instead towards Rookswood. I want to see it one last time. Take some photos of the outside. Photos... I wish I'd taken some of Izzy and Max. Will this be the last time I see them, and my sister?

The first tears roll down my cheeks as I get out of the car and go to the main house. The site is in chaos, with debris piled everywhere except, it seems, inside the skip. But at least all the workmen are gone; no one stayed behind to get on with the demolition. The front door has been left unlocked.

The broken glass on the floor is already covered in a patina of white dust, making it look shrouded and lifeless. Above, the leaden strips that were holding up the cupola slice across the sky and a circular portion of the roof is open to the elements. Clouds hang heavy overhead, grey and forbidding. I sweep the glass off the bottom step with my shoe and plop down, not caring if Emma's jeans get dusty or torn. I fold my head in my hands.

'It wasn't supposed to be this way,' I sob.

Somewhere out of sight, something bangs. A shutter? A door? The wind? I hope not.

'I just feel so sad without her. My sister, Emma. And stupidly, when I came here, I think a part of me was hoping this was a road back to being sisters again. But I've left it too long. I see that.'

A draught rustles the hairs on the back of my neck. I shiver with the memory of ice, but in fact, the current seems warmer than usual. Almost comforting. Almost... friendly.

I lift my head. 'You know how it is, don't you? You lived it too. Died it too, I expect. You grow up with someone. Love them. Think they'll always be in your life. And then suddenly, one of you makes a stupid mistake. It doesn't matter who. It feels so terrible, and yet, so good to be angry. The flow of rage feels powerful against the hurt. And even when it stops feeling good, you hold onto it anyway. You cut off your nose to spite your face.'

The breeze grows stronger. Overhead, clouds shift and for a moment, the room is flooded with light. Someone is listening: someone who understands every word I'm saying. Across the room, amidst the tools left by the workmen, I spy a broom. I stand up and fetch it, sweeping the glass into a pile as I continue to talk.

'Days go by. Then weeks and months. You think to yourself, "I'll just punish her a little longer". But really, you're punishing yourself. Staying stuck in the hurt and the rage, reliving the pain, thinking the same thoughts over and over. It's like going to the well and refilling a bucket with polluted water. Suddenly, you discover that years have gone by.' I sweep harder, sob harder.

'I wish I'd done things differently, Ada. I wish I'd been the big sister, the strong sister. I wish I'd listened; I wish I'd forgiven. I wish Emma and I had been there for each other.'

I stop sweeping and lean against the broom. The clouds shift again. The hallway darkens. The house is silent, but I feel a strong sense of presence. An energy frequency that resonates with mine. With my tears, my pain.

'I don't know what happened between you and Camile, but it turned out the same, didn't it? You loved her more than anything in the world, and yet, you lost her. Or maybe, like me, you threw her away.'

Another sound. The phantom crying of a cat. Bones – another lost soul. So many of us...

'I know that things were different in your day. You didn't have Facebook, or the internet, or WhatsApp. You had no real way to find her if she didn't want to be found. So I'm going to do it for you, Ada, like you asked. I don't have any leads yet, but if there's anything out there, I'll find it, I promise.'

I scan my eyes around the dust-shrouded room with all its elegant, faded splendour. The sledgehammer that George used is still on the floor. Anger and helplessness rise inside my chest. I'm alone here for the moment, but Charlie & Co will be back to do their worst.

'I just hope that when I do find some answers, you'll still be here,' I say. 'Because I'm worried that Rookswood is going to be collateral damage to my rift with Emma. She and Charlie are a thing – you probably knew that already.'

The house practically groans as a floorboard creaks above me. I turn around, expecting to see the spectre of a woman at the top of the stairs. But there's nothing. The energy has changed, however, just as mine has. There's sadness and anger here, a pent-up rage even greater than mine. But it's not directed at me.

'I tried to lift the wool from Emma's eyes,' I continue. 'I told her the truth about Charlie. He's only in it for the house and the money. Then he thought he'd try it on with me in case Emma didn't recover.' I give a mirthless laugh. 'You saw the kiss.' I make a point of wiping my mouth with my hand. 'Yuck. Anyway, I tried to tell her, but I can't make her listen. So now, I don't know what's going to happen.'

I finish sweeping and lean the broom back against the wall. 'I'll keep doing what I can, I promise. But I'm warning you that it may not be much. Nowadays, we call that "managing expectations". And frankly, I don't think your shenanigans are helping. You haven't exactly created a warm, fuzzy home that a family's going to fall in love with, have you?'

From somewhere upstairs, a cat meows faintly. A few drops of rain fall through the open cupola, cool and refreshing. A benediction of sorts.

'You don't have to apologise to me. I'm not scared of you, Ada.

I'm just sad for you – and for me. But I'll keep trying to make things right in this life. For both of us.'

A tendril of icy draught dries the lines of tears on my cheeks. It's strong enough to blow the front door open – a little supernatural kick up the backside to get on with it.

'Point taken,' I say. 'I'll keep you posted if I can.'

X

In my life, I have made bad choices. I chose to love the countess; I chose to send my sister away. At the time, they seemed so inevitable, as if they were predestined rather than made by free will. But as the woman, Kate, confides in me, revealing her pain to me as if I were corporeal flesh, I know in my spirit heart that this time I have chosen right. She is a woman of insight and action, a woman who understands that she must heal her own rift at any cost. A woman who wishes to help others like her; she wishes to help me despite all that I have done.

I made the glass ceiling fall, drawing on air, earth, and metal. Drawing energy and spirit from Kate. Drawing from her will to save Rookswood, for I too desire to spare my prison until the key can be found. Would she still help me if she knew it? Yes, I think so.

Yes, I have chosen right.

* * *

As for my own sorry tale, no more was said between the countess and me on the dreaded topic of her departure. But I feared it all the same for I was reaching the end of my commission. Having sacrificed numerous mannequins to the cause, I had at last devised a most life-like illusion. I demonstrated it to the countess, who was delighted by the effect. 'You truly are a wizard,' she said, as she perused the photographs of a headless mannequin on fire. 'And you shall set me free.'

'I want that of course,' I said. 'But—'

'We must do it now,' she said. 'Tonight. In the bedchamber upstairs. That will be most realistic.'

'The bedchamber?' This I had not expected. 'But it is safer to perform the trick in the studio.' I pointed to the sheets of specially treated canvas that I had draped over walls and floor to retard the flames. 'I can superimpose the image upon another background, if you wish?'

'No, no.' Her tone turned hostile. 'I told you, no photographic tomfoolery. My husband will have experts *much more skilled than you* to debunk any trickery.'

She intended the comment to sting and it did.

'I am tired of waiting,' she added. 'We should have finished months ago. I have booked a passage on the steamer to Calais. I leave in two days' time.'

'Two days!' Anguish seared my soul, along with a burning realisation that should have been clear from the onset. The countess didn't love me. She was using me, pure and simple. The pain was unspeakable; the yawning maw of emptiness that was life without her gaping before me was unthinkable. I loved her with all my heart, soul, and body. I would not let her go.

'Prepare the space and I will change into the dress.' There was nothing soft or loving in her tone; it was purely a command.

'Put the retardant sheets on the bed, and hang them from the canopy. It will have the same effect.'

'But I have not tested it,' I protested. 'It's too dangerous.'

'Have I told you all the things he's done to me? All of the terrible, degrading acts I have had to perform. And not only perform, but watch too. Oh, he likes it when I am forced to watch. He made me come to your father's studio – did I tell you? I saw all the things that went on there. My husband disgusts me, but I believe your father was truly evil. The things he allowed, promoted... orchestrated. Violence, rape, sodomy. I did not see it all, of course, but enough. He had a special album to tempt his clients. Did you not know?'

I hung my head.

'Ah,' she lifted my chin with a sharp fingernail. 'But you did know, Ada, didn't you? You cleared out the studio after his death. And continued to follow in his footsteps. Like father, like daughter.'

'No, Tanya. I am not like him.'

'Debauched. Degenerate. You sicken me, Ada. From the moment I saw your eyes, I knew you. So greedy, so desperate. And I saw the way you acted with your sister. She may be simple, but at least she is not *unnatural*.'

'Stop, Tanya. Do not say such things. You know that I only wish to love you.'

'Turn around while I put on the dress. Then get your camera ready.'

'The camera is ready!' I wailed. 'But could you not just lie on the floor?'

'I shall not lie on the floor,' she hissed. 'We shall do it in the bedchamber. Now. I cannot endure your presence any longer.'

My entire body was racked by hurt, disbelief. Leaving her to put on the flame-retardant dress, I did as she asked and lugged the heavy tarpaulins to the bedchamber. I knew she could be cruel. I confess that I loved her all the more for it. She had eclipsed my soul; without her, I was lost in darkness. I was determined to weather her stormy mood, as I had many times before. But had she really bought a ticket on the steamer? In two days' time? No. I had to believe that our love was more than just trickery: that on those nights when we lay in bed together and she let me see her, uncovered, unguarded, I was seeing the real woman underneath the worldly façade. But could I be sure? I, of all people, was a master of illusion. I had built my life on the premise that people could be fooled, and that things are not always as they seem. Was I the wizard or the dupe? With Tanya, my woman on fire, I could never be sure.

She came to the bedchamber dressed in the old-fashioned gown, complaining all the while of the texture of the fabric and the foul chemical smell. I left her there and went to fetch the remainder of my photographic equipment. When I returned, the countess lay sprawled on the bed, preparing to light a cigarette. 'No!' I cried. 'Don't do that. Every aspect must be controlled. If not, the whole place could go up.'

'Then hurry up.' She glared at me, but put the cigarette back in the case.

Eventually, I was as ready as I could be. The lighting was wrong – for though the studio had been wired for electric lights, the bedroom had not. I placed two candelabras near the bed, but I doubted whether they would provide the necessary levels of light. I took heart in the fact that the illusion would not be performed in the way I had rehearsed with my mannequins; in changing the method, I might fail to achieve her desired results. In that case, surely, she would have to delay her departure until variations could be perfected. She had been so set on her goal for all these months; I counted on the fact that she would not jeopardise it now – not when we were so close.

By the time I announced I was ready, her manner had softened towards me. She went to my mirror and looked at herself in the glass, beckoning me over. 'I'm sorry I said those things,' she said. 'It's just, I envy you, Ada. You do not understand my plight. I am a slave who is desperate to be free, whereas you are your own woman. You defy convention and constraint. You would never allow yourself to be subjugated as I have been subjugated. Oh Ada, how I long to be like you.'

'Tanya,' I said, drawing her close. She melted into my arms. Though we both stank of chemicals and the air in the room felt close and oppressive, I did not care in the slightest. I led her by the hand over to the bed. 'Let me love you, dearest,' I said. 'And tell me you will never leave me.'

We lay down together. I let my mouth and hands wander over her neck, her throat. Her skirts were heavy and unwieldy; if I could remove them, then we could abandon this ridiculous escapade. Delay longer, give me time to prepare properly. Give me time to convince her that this was real. The only thing that could ever be real for either of us—

'Ada, are you in here? What's that smell?'

It all happened in a breath, a heartbeat.

'Are you ill?'

My sister. My beloved Camile. She saw me lying face down in the bed. Without thinking, I moved aside. I can only imagine her shock when she saw two faces peering up at her. For so many years I had told her that we were enough for each other. That I loved her and she loved me, and there was no room for anyone else. That I was hurt by her betrayal but I could forgive. That our love for each other was pure and undebauched. That we would never, ever be apart again. Separated neither in life nor in death.

'Oh!' She inhaled sharply. Her elbow knocked over the nearest candelabra. Flames leapt hungrily onto the flammable edge of the countess's gown. In the span of a single breath, the air was sucked from the room, into a roaring conflagration.

As the bedclothes went up in smoke, Camile's hands went to her face, her scream shattering the air.

* * *

It is no comfort that the house did not burn to the ground. For surely, that would have been exactly what I deserved. I jumped from the bed as flames consumed the countess just as she had commissioned. But this was no illusion, and there was no photograph. Camile and I managed to smother the bed with the tarpaulins and stop the spread of the flames. The dress had protected some of the countess's body, as it was designed to do. But her shoulders, her face, her hair... She screamed in pain, unrecognisable. Camile screamed too: that she had knocked over the candle, that it was all her fault. I slapped her across the face. 'Pull yourself together and have the servants ready the carriage,' I shouted. 'She must be taken to hospital.' I held Tanya's hand as the grip loosened, the pain overwhelming her. 'You're going to be fine,' I said, tears leaving black trails down my cheek.

By the time help arrived, the countess was unconscious from the pain. My sister buried her face against my chest as the carriage drove away. 'It's all my fault. All my fault,' she repeated over and over between sobs.

'It's not,' I finally managed. 'It was an accident.'

'But it wasn't!' she yelled. 'I knew what she was to you. And I hated her for it. I wanted her gone – I wanted her dead.'

'No, Camile...' My voice trembled. 'It was an accident. The candelabra was placed too close. It was not your fault.'

'I'm a murderess,' she said. 'And that's what I shall tell the police. I have taken a life – taken a love. I deserve to hang. Nothing else will do.'

'No.' I held her at arm's length and shook her. 'Do you think that is what I want? You are all I have left, Camile. We must be together, always.'

She pulled away. 'No Ada. You know it isn't true. I heard what she said. I'm "simple". You don't need me. I'm a burden to you. Once, I dared to want something else and tried to make a different life for myself. But I failed, and you dished out the ultimate punishment – you gave your love to another. It was no more than I deserved.'

'Camile.' I tried to pull her to me again, but she drew away.

'I can give myself up to save you, Ada.'

'No! That is not necessary. It was an accident. That is what we shall tell the authorities. And in fact, it is the truth.'

She shook her head. 'The countess is vicious. If she survives, she will need to blame someone. If she does not, then her husband will do so. Let it be me.'

'Camile. Please stop this.'

'If you will not let me take the blame, then at least let me go away until the matter is settled. Then, when it is safe, I will return.'

An idea flickered, a plan taking shape in my mind. 'The countess had a ticket on the steamer. Leaving in two days' time. Do you think you could manage it?'

26

I feel drained and exhausted as I return to the gatehouse. I guess a row with an estranged sister and confiding in a ghost will do that to you. Charlie's van is gone and there is no suitcase on the doorstep. Small mercies. I stand in front of the door for a long time debating – do I ring the bell, or let myself in as usual? In the end, I go for a hybrid option of knocking softly before opening the door. 'Emma,' I call out. 'It's me. Can I come in?'

There's no answer. When I left, my sister, just out of rehab, was in a state. To me, that constitutes probable cause to enter. I can be there for her if she needs someone, even if I'm the last person she'd want to see.

'Emma?'

I make my way towards the kitchen and the conservatory. Empty. Did I make another mistake in leaving her alone here? What if she's made another attempt to harm herself? I rush upstairs to her bedroom. The door is closed.

'Emma? I need to know you're all right. Can I come in?'

I put my ear to the door. One faint sound. A sniffle.

I grab the knob and turn it.

'Go away.'

Her voice is strong, but her body, slumped in a chair by the cold fireplace, looks small and weak like a child's. My heart aches with the desire to comfort her. To take away all the pain, all the hurt between us. Much of it caused by me.

'Oh Emma.' I go over to her, standing close but not too close. 'I love you.'

'No.' She doesn't look up. 'No, Kate, you don't. No one does. And I get it.' A sob erupts almost like a laugh. 'I'm utterly unlovable. I betrayed you, and now, every day, I'm paying the price. Philip, the children, Charlie.' She puts her hands over her face. 'I couldn't even manage to top myself properly.'

Inside me, a long-dormant seam of painful, poisonous emotion rises to the surface. 'That's it, then,' I say. I kneel down and envelop my sister in my arms. She squirms a little, but I hold tighter. No matter what happened in the past, no matter what happens in the future, I am not about to let her go.

Not now.

Not ever again.

* * *

Somehow, the logistics get sorted. I call the school and book the kids in to after-school care. I help Emma downstairs, light a fire, make tea, and find a packet of Hobnobs in the back of a cupboard that Max must have missed. I sit next to Emma on the sofa, holding her hand, marvelling at the feeling of *rightness* that is both so alien and so intimately familiar.

She talks, I listen. We both cry. When the tea is finished, I go to the kitchen to make more, and also to call the school again to book Izzy and Max on the late bus. The receptionist connects me instead to Dr Whitford, who apparently has been trying to reach me.

'Kate,' he says. 'Is everything all right? Izzy said there was another accident at the house?'

It's only been a few days since we toured Rookswood together, and yet, it seems like half a lifetime. 'The short answer is, something did,' I say. 'But can I fill you in later? Emma's back.'

'Already? But I thought—'

'She's come home early and I need to take care of her. Can Izzy and Max get the bus?'

'Why don't I drop them by on my way home? We could talk then?'

Even through the whirlwind of events and emotions, my stomach jolts with anticipation.

'Yes, maybe,' I say. 'Let's play it by ear.'

'Kate?' I hear Emma's voice as I end the call.

'Sorry,' I say, bringing the tea.

'Who was that? The school? Where are Izzy and Max?' She puts her head in her hands again. 'God, I should have collected them. Except, I don't want them to see me like this. I should have stayed at the clinic. I should have done so many things differently.'

I grip her hand again. 'Look Emma, I thought we agreed to stop dwelling on the past.'

A little of the old defiance flickers in her eyes. '*You* agreed that, Kate. For both of us. Like always.'

I'm taken aback, but then, she laughs, and I do too. 'I'm sorry if that's what I've always done.'

'I thought we agreed,' she says, smugly. 'No more dwelling on the past.'

'Touché.' I squeeze her hand. I'm relieved beyond measure that despite appearances, Emma's in there somewhere. For years, my sister and I have been apart, lost in the labyrinth of the past. We're still lost, but right now, I'm daring to hope that we might have found each other in the darkness.

'Anyway, that was the school.' I remove my hand and take a sip of tea. 'Dr Whitford.'

'Dr Whitford.' She blanches. 'God, he's so scary.'

I laugh. 'Umm, about that. There's something I ought to mention.'

'What?'

Her mouth becomes a ring of shock as I come clean. 'Well, I kind of like him. And, I'm hoping it's mutual.'

'But I thought you and Charlie had a thing going.'

'No,' I say. 'Absolutely not.'

'I ended it with him.' She stares into her cup. 'I couldn't stand for history to repeat itself. If you want him, I won't stand in your way.'

'Emma.' I take her hand again. 'I do not have a thing for Charlie. But what I told you was true. He kissed me, not the other way around. I'm not imagining that. So you have some decisions to make, starting with whether you want him in your life and helping you with your project. Things have happened at Rookswood that you need to know about.'

Despite the warmth of the tea and the fire, my sister shivers.

'What things, Kate?'

So I tell her.

27

Emma's face is drained of all colour, her hands shaking as she grips the empty teacup. She tells me she's sorry, but we're way past that.

'And you think Charlie is responsible?' Even after hearing everything, her voice still holds a note of incredulity.

'For some of it,' I say. 'At least indirectly. Charlie was there when the cupola shattered; surely, he ought to have made sure it was secure before starting the works. As for the other incidents, he was best placed to orchestrate most of them. He could have loosened the floorboard that caused your fall, and left the nails and glass that I tripped over. He could have locked me in the cellar too.' Now that I'm warmed up, it all makes a certain sense. 'Charlie was the one who told me about all the incidents,' I add. 'And he was on site more often than anyone else. Thus, according to Occam's razor, he's the most likely candidate.'

'Whose razor?'

'Never mind. Just something Dr Whitford taught me.'

She cocks her head, giving me a knowing look. To keep from blushing, I plough on. 'The other thing you should know, Emma, is that Charlie tried to blame Izzy and Max. He said that Izzy "lured" me to the house.'

'I thought you said she was sleepwalking?'

'I think she was. But he tried to convince me otherwise. And Max wasn't even around for any of the incidents. In fact, during at least one of them, he was visiting you.'

'Visiting me?' She frowns.

'Yes. Earlier this week, I think.'

'Oh.' She looks temporarily confused. 'Right.'

'Anyway, Charlie's good at prevarication. Get you on side, get me on side. Discredit me so he'd have no competition for your affections. That part was easy; all he had to do was convince you that I came on to him in order to get my revenge. And if, in the process, he landed Izzy and Max in it and you sent them to stay with Philip, then he'd have you to himself and be able to pull all the strings.'

'God.' Emma puts her head in her hands. 'He must think I'm so weak. And with good reason. I mean, look at me.'

'You look like my beautiful, smart, brave sister. The person you've always been.'

She gives me a wry look. 'Always?'

'Well, almost always.'

I smile at her and the years melt away. She is my sister. *My sister...* We both reach out at once, and then we're back in each other's arms.

'Kate,' she whispers as we pull apart. 'You can't prove that Charlie was involved in any of this, can you? And I can't afford to keep Rookswood. So what are we going to do?'

'I don't know,' I say. 'But as long as we're a "we", then we'll figure it out.'

'You promise? I just feel so—'

Gravel crunches outside. Only a few seconds later, the door

bangs open – a whirlwind of Izzy and Max. Whatever Emma is or isn't, whatever she's done or hasn't done, I know this. These kids love her. They need her.

'Mum!' The three of them sandwich together, with hugs, kisses, and tears all around. Silently, I slip out of the room. The front door is wide open. Standing outside is Matthew Whitford.

'Kate.' He runs his fingers through his hair, looking flustered – and so damn handsome. 'I don't want to disturb you and Emma.'

'You're not.' I smile. 'I've had my reunion with Emma. Now it's Izzy and Max's turn. They've got a lot of catching up to do, bridges to mend and that sort of thing.'

'So you and Emma are better?'

'Early days, but we might get there in the end.'

'Good.' He seems genuinely pleased.

'Do you want to come in?' I say.

'It's a nice evening,' he says. 'We could take a walk?'

'OK, let's do it.'

I tell Emma I'm going out, put on my outer clothing, and join him outside. The sky is streaked pink at the horizon, darkening to twilit blue. It's almost completely silent except for our footsteps on the gravel drive. By unspoken agreement, we walk in the direction of Rookswood. I fill him in briefly on what transpired with Charlie and his work crew.

'You really think he's committing sabotage?' Matthew asks.

'I can't prove it, but he'll do whatever it takes to get hold of Rookswood. He was the third bidder, wasn't he?'

'Yes, I should have said. I should have told you much earlier.' He stops walking and looks at me. 'I'm sorry if you and he were—'

'We weren't,' I clarify. 'Charlie is not my type at all. He

managed to be at the right place at the right time when I needed rescuing, but that's it.'

'And...' He looks away towards the trees. 'If you don't mind my asking, what is your type?'

I laugh. 'I don't have a type so much as a philosophy. "I'll know it when I see it".'

'Ah,' he says. 'Good to know.'

By the time we reach the door of Rookswood, the sky is completely dark. I unlock the door and we go inside. I flip the light switch; a lone bulb in a wall sconce responds, casting a sickly, flickering glow. The corners of the room are wreathed in cobwebs and shadows. The pile of glass I swept up looks like earth from a grave, and as usual, the temperature inside the house is about four degrees colder than outside.

On the wide bottom step, there's an imprint in the dust from where I sat earlier. I go back and sit down in the same spot.

'You take me to all the best places,' Matthew says as he sits down next to me. Our hips touch. Yes, it's a spooky old house that's inhabited by a ghost. But right now, I feel warm and glowing inside.

'I thought you loved this place,' I say.

'I do. Can you imagine what it would be like if it was done up?' He gestures around us. 'The copper polished, the cupola repaired, the wood oiled, the floor tiles scrubbed. It would be magical.' I glance at him, catching a glimpse of his vision in his eyes.

'I think I can see it,' I say, 'and feel it too. The house as it might be, free from the shackles of the past. It's stood here for a century and a half, and it could easily do twice that. Its walls hold a signature of grief, but that could be changed. It's the *only* thing I would change.'

He answers by reaching out and taking my hand. His touch is

tentative, questioning. I grip his fingers and then take my hand away, resting it on my knee.

'What about you?' I say. 'I've told you everything. Aired my dirty laundry, so to speak. But all I know about you is that you're a dab hand at Latin, you've got a weird interest in ghosts, and a photograph of a lovely family on your desk.'

Next to me, he stiffens. I worry I've misread the situation and been too abrupt.

I really hope not.

'It's a nice photo,' he says. 'Me, Daniel, and Siobhan. But photos don't always tell the whole truth, do they? Just ask your ghost.'

I could ask her if I wanted to. Because at that moment, I feel the temperature in the room change. This time, however, it's not a chill I feel, but a lifting, a warmth. Ada's presence surrounds us like a cat curling up in front of a warm fire. Matthew frowns suddenly, as if he too is aware that we're no longer alone. Then he takes a breath and begins to speak.

'The truth is, Siobhan and I weren't right after Daniel's birth. At first, I thought it was postnatal depression. She had trouble bonding with him. She blamed herself that he wouldn't feed, or sleep, or smile, or hit his milestones according to Gina Ford. It was hard in the early days, and I guess I was frustrated too, with both of them.'

I sit forward and listen. Or rather, *we* do.

'Daniel's autistic – you probably spotted that. He's intelligent and loving, but he's also different. We both struggled with that, but I guess as an educator, I was more familiar with seeing it as a superpower, whereas Siobhan saw it as a disability. I was angry that she seemed so distant. She'd fly into these rages. I tried to be supportive, and even stretched to pay for a full-time nanny with special-needs experience. But nothing helped.'

I open and close my mouth but say nothing.

'Siobhan complained that the baby's crying was giving her headaches. She started staying in bed, only getting up when she had to. The GP gave her medication for migraines but it didn't help. Then, one day as she was driving to the supermarket, a dizzy spell overcame her and she crashed the car into a fence. She wasn't seriously hurt, but they took her to hospital and gave her a brain scan. That's when they found it.' He presses his lips tightly together. 'An aggressive, fast-growing tumour. Within three weeks, she was gone.'

'Oh Matthew.' I reach for his hand, cradling it in mine. It feels *right*.

'That was five years ago,' he says. 'But it doesn't feel like that. Grief plays funny tricks with time. Sometimes, it's as if she never existed. Other times, it's like it was all happening yesterday. Daniel doesn't remember her, except in the abstract. He says that sometimes she visits him in dreams.'

'That's what he was doing at the pub,' I say. 'Making a dream spiral?'

'Yes. To him, it's like a ladder bringing them closer. He doesn't feel unhappy that she's gone, it's more of a curiosity. He's only seven, but he's an old soul. That's why I thought he'd like this house. It's why I bid for it.'

'I wish you'd got it,' I say.

The room seems to sigh, as if in agreement.

'It was bad timing,' he says. 'I was still paying off some private medical bills, and I hadn't yet sold our house. If the auction had been a few months later, then who knows?'

'You might have another bite at the cherry. I can't see Emma keeping the place now, can you?'

Ada's presence seems to shift uncomfortably. The next

moment, the last flickering light in the sconce pops. Matthew and I are plunged into darkness. Ada is gone.

Matthew pulls me closer. 'I don't know what's going to happen in the future,' he says. 'If I've learned one thing, it's that none of us do. I've also learned that it's important to seize the moment.'

I entwine my arms around his neck.

'*Carpe diem*,' I say as he runs a finger down the edge of my cheek.

'We'll make a Latin scholar of you yet,' he says, as his lips find mine.

I lose myself. Years of holding back, doubting myself and others, afraid to love or be loved. All of it melts away in his kiss. Ada is there somewhere, hovering in the shadows. The walls hold memories, and now, it's our turn to add a new one. I let him remove my coat and lay it down on the floor. Fumbling in the dark to remove our clothing, we add laughter as well. And then the joy of two people coming together. Life is full of loss, but it's possible to find each other too.

When we're finished and he cradles me in his arms, I can't remember feeling so full to the brim with all the emotions. I can't remember ever feeling so alive. I don't want it to end, but that's the very essence of being human.

My phone lights with a text message. It's Emma, asking when I'm coming back. Matthew gets up, tackling the logistics of finding our clothing in the dark, and we get dressed. Without the warmth of his body, I shiver in the cold. 'Do you want to come back to the cottage for supper?' I say, suddenly shy. 'Or a drink?'

He brushes a strand of hair back from my cheek. 'I can't,' he says. 'I need to get home. The nanny's shift ends at eight.'

I check the time on my screen. 'And just for the record, that's *all* she is, right?' I say. 'She's certainly young and pretty.'

'Is she?' He pulls me close again. 'I didn't notice. I guess she's not my type.'

'And what is your type?' I tease his lips with my finger.

'I know it when I see it.'

We kiss again. The phone buzzes, the world intrudes, relentless. Using the torches on our phones to light the way, we walk to the door. 'I guess I'll have to find an electrician to come round,' I say. 'As Charlie's off the job.'

'I can text you the name of the chap we use at school. He's used to complicated jobs.'

'As complicated as a ghost blowing a circuit?'

'Well, there's a first time for everything.'

'And I guess it was atmospheric for a first date.'

He smiles. 'That it was. Though, maybe we'll try a different venue if you're still up for it. One that's a little warmer.'

'Sounds good,' I say.

We go out of the door and onto the porch.

'Give Emma my regards,' he says. 'Unless you want to keep this a secret for now.'

From out of the aether, the ghostly presence seems to curl in the air around us like smoke. 'It's a little late for that,' I say. 'There are already "three of us" in this relationship.'

He laughs. 'I think you're right.'

As I'm about to close the door, he pokes his head into the blackness. 'Take care, Ada,' he says aloud.

'Bye,' I add in a whisper. 'See you soon.'

XI

Carpe diem, seize the day. I am happy for Kate, but even after all the years that have slipped by in a whisper, I feel a little jealous. For what meaning does this life have other than love? Love for the self, love for another, love for the world. Kate has time to learn this truth, but for me, it was too late.

In the blink of an eye, I lost my two great loves. My sister left later that day, accompanied by a housemaid, travelling to the port of Dover to await the steamer. I cried as I held her and kissed her goodbye. She would only be away for a short while – weeks, a month at most – but that was longer than we had ever been apart.

To facilitate the journey, I rifled through the countess's luggage, finding her papers, the steamer ticket, and a detailed itinerary including confirmed lodgings at Dover, Calais, and Paris. 'Can you manage being her?' I asked Camile. How could my sister, the baby I had nurtured from birth almost like my own daughter, affect such a masquerade?

'I will do it, sister,' she said. 'Do not underestimate me this time.'

'Oh Camile.' I hung my head. It was true that I had underestimated her for all her life. In so many ways, I was no better than the countess. I had used my love and approval as a weapon, as a means of controlling my sister. She had deserved so much more than that. 'Please say you'll return to Rookswood,' I said. 'That things will be as they were before.'

'I will return, Ada,' she said. 'But I do not wish things to be as they were before. I wish to be your equal. I am my own person, and I must be treated as such. I wish to take my freedom, as you have taken yours. To find love, if that is my fate. To have the child I long for, if I can.'

'Yes.' Her words cut me. 'Yes, I promise. You can have all of those things.'

Tears rolled down her cheeks and she hugged me again. 'I promise you this, Ada. I love you. Now and always. I will return and we shall be together again. Do not give up hope.'

With that, she withdrew from her pocket the photograph I had torn in a rage all those years ago. She had kept both halves safe, and in her pale white hand, the sepia ink seemed to trap the sunlight. 'Here,' she said. 'Take this.' She handed her photo to me, and put the ripped half with my photo back in her pocket.

'Camile?'

'When I am returned to Rookswood, we shall mend it. Then we shall be together forever.'

'Yes, my darling. Together forever.'

At the sound of another vehicle coming up the drive, she boarded the trap that would take her and the maid to the railway station. 'Goodbye dearest,' I said kissing her hand. 'We will be together soon.'

'Yes, Ada,' she said. 'Very soon.'

Camile signalled to the driver and the carriage pulled away

just as a police wagon drew up to the house. As the officers disembarked, I lifted my hand to wave to my sister, to salute her. She put her head out of the window, waving back, until the carriage disappeared into the tunnel of trees and out of sight.

* * *

I never saw my sister again. Whether by chance or design, that is the truth that has haunted me, the haunter, over all these years. The policeman took my statement and left. The coachman returned saying that Camile had been delivered safely to the train station. The maid also returned to Rookswood, having been dismissed by Camile at Dover. From there, my sister vanished. Disappeared into thin air. She did not write, she did not return. Half of a torn photograph and an unfulfilled promise were all that I had left. Over the years, I have waited for her. It was not like Camile to break her promises. Unlike the many people I have known over the years who were not what they seemed, Camile alone lacked guile and artifice. Our love for each other was genuine; even now I believe this. So why did she never return to Rookswood? To me? In life, it was my fate never to know.

And yet, even after all this time, even as I fade away, I still believe that one day a miracle will happen. For miracles do happen; my continued existence in this world is proof of that. Someday, Camile and I will be reunited and pass together to the ever after. I will continue to believe with all the strength of my being, until the moment when it becomes too late.

Although I am dead and hence long past the point where it is necessary to 'tie up loose ends', I will recount the story to the end. The countess survived her injuries, but despite several half-hearted attempts on my part, she did not wish for me to visit her in hospital. I understand that her burns were extensive and painful, and that her disfigurement was enough to achieve her desired result. The count granted her a divorce, and she lived out her remaining days, sadly less than a year, on the continent as she'd planned. When the inspectors returned to further investigate the incident, I told them a version of the truth. The countess was a client who commissioned me to take a photograph of her person using a special pyrotechnic effect. I advised her against it, but she insisted that I carry out the feat. The effect went wrong, and the unfortunate accident occurred. I answered their questions: yes, I alone was responsible for the illusion. At the countess's request, neither my sister nor any servants or assistants were present. I alone carried out her wishes.

I half-expected the countess to enact her revenge, accusing my sister and me of grievous bodily harm and seeing that we were duly punished under the law. She could have done so, and I did not understand her inaction. Not until two years later when a letter arrived from her solicitor enclosing a final missive addressed to me.

It was written on the same heavy paper as her original letter, and sealed with the same red wax. Back then, I had opened the envelope innocently, not knowing what havoc the communication would wreak. This time, replete with the memories of horrors and events I could never unknow, my hands shook as I opened it.

My dearest Ada,

By the time you read this, I will be dead. Though my ending has been painful, my freedom has been all that I hoped for and more. I have you to thank for that. I wish I could have loved you as you deserved. Purely and unconditionally. But it

was never in my nature to do so. I take heart, however, that
you have someone in your life who does. Your sister Camile.
Value her, Ada, and keep her close to your heart. And know
that in my own way, I am sorry.

I remain faithfully yours,
Tanya

I cried. Not for Tanya, as she had made it clear that her
freedom had been its own benediction. My tears were for myself,
and for Camile. Where was she? Why didn't she write? Why
hadn't she returned to me?

The not knowing was the worst, and it was impossible not to
speculate. I wanted to believe that Camile went on to have a
beautiful life full of the things I could not give her: a loving
husband, a child, a normal home life. I hoped she had found
these things, and that they had so thoroughly eclipsed her
former life that she had simply chosen a clean break from me
and her troubled past. But equally, I worried that she had fallen
upon ill fortune, her innocence preyed upon by unsavoury
people, or that she stayed away due to hatred of me, or perhaps
out of a loving concern that I could not forgive her.

I did my best to discover her fate and whereabouts. I
published ads in the newspaper seeking information. I hired a
private detective to trace her last movements. She had boarded
the ship to the continent using the countess's ticket, but she had
not stayed in the booked accommodation in either Calais or
Paris. The trail had gone cold and there was nothing more to be
done.

I rifled through her things left at Rookswood looking for a
clue that might help me find her. I found that she'd taken some
photographs, and I was glad of this small sign that she had

valued the work we had carried out together. As for my half of the torn photograph, I kept her image with me always, and it gave me some comfort to know that she had the half that was me.

No – I have vowed not to lie in this account. The truth is, it gave me no comfort at all.

Camile was lost. I never found her.

28

What a difference a day makes. I have a sister. I have a potential *someone*.

I wake up the next morning with spring sun streaming through the window. When I returned home the night before, Emma and the kids were snuggled up on the sofa together watching a film. Emma took one look at me and blurted out, 'What happened?' But it was not the usual, 'What happened?' that I associate with Rookswood – involving dirt, bruises, ripped clothing, and a broken limb or two. I was glowing like a Christmas tree.

'I'll tell you in the morning,' I'd said. I'd refilled their popcorn bowls, kissed Emma on the cheek, and went to bed on a fold-out cot they'd set up for me in Izzy's room.

Now, Emma's already up and folding laundry by the time I shower and go downstairs in her dressing gown. She hands me a pile of my own clothes, and I experience a brief pang of fear that our reunion was all my imagination, and that she's in fact sending me packing. So I'm relieved when she smiles and gives me a hug (knocking half the pile out of my arms and onto the floor). 'I'm so glad you're here, Kate. I was afraid I'd imagined it, and being home.' She gazes fondly around. 'Though, I guess that must mean I didn't imagine the rest either. The bad stuff.'

'No,' I say, 'but let's worry about that later. Are you sure you're up to being on your feet? If you want to lie down, I can look after you.'

'I'm fine. It's good to be home. But I wouldn't say no to a coffee.'

'Stay put,' I say. 'I'll rustle up some coffee and one of my special fry ups.' I frown at her. 'You're skin and bones.'

'I won't say no.'

'Good.'

It's almost like the old days – the days *before* – when I'd come home from uni at the weekend and make Sunday breakfast for the whole family. As I'm cooking, Izzy and Max come downstairs and for once, they're dressed and ready for school without being harangued or shouted at. When I bring the heaping plates to the table, Max smiles at me.

'Thanks, Aunt Kate,' he says.

'Sure.' I grin back.

'Max,' Emma says, 'don't you have something to say to your aunt?'

'Oh yeah.' His face falls. 'Sorry.'

'For what?' I look to Emma.

'I'm afraid Max was being "economical with the truth",' she says. 'What you said the other day – about him visiting me.'

'Sorry I lied,' Max mutters.

Izzy snorts a laugh.

'What?'

'I wasn't visiting Mum,' he says. 'I was at the library. Doing some research on photography. I want a real dark room.' He looks at his mum. 'It would be so cool.'

'Wait – you didn't go see your mum?'

'Sorry,' Max says again.

'Well... it's fine, I guess.' Somewhere inside the distant recesses of my head, a warning sounds. Max in the chemistry lab, Max lying about his whereabouts. Now, an interest in photography? Where did that come from? And putting it all together... what would William of Ockham say?

'You shouldn't lie, Max,' Emma is saying. 'I'm counting on you. Don't be like your dad.'

Max puts his fork down and looks up, his eyes flashing with an anger I haven't seen before.

'Why not?' he says. 'You're not truthful. You said we could go live with Dad if we wanted. Well, we want to.'

'Yeah,' Izzy chimes in. I recall the very first time I saw them, in the common room at school. It seemed to me that they were two against the world. But since then, I've got to know them as individuals. Or have I?

'Hey, that's enough,' I say. Not the substitute parent or the aunt, but once again the hard-nosed lawyer. 'Your mum's been through it. She's home now, and she loves you, and this is the wrong time to be having this conversation. So give it a rest, OK?'

'Does this mean you're leaving?' Max shovels baked beans into his mouth.

'Do you want her to?' Emma asks.

I look from one to the other, hurt. All the effort I've made to keep Izzy and Max in pizza and Hobnobs, and occasionally even something healthy. All the trips I've made to and from school and sports practise. The love I've allowed myself to feel... the first for a long time. Does that count for nothing?

'No,' Izzy says. 'I don't want her to go. I like her.'

'Well, that's something,' I say.

'Me too.' Max beams me his smile.

And call me a soft touch, but all is forgiven.

'Good,' Emma says. 'Because I'm not supposed to drive for a while. So if Aunt Kate wants to stay...' She gives me a pleading look. 'That'd be great.'

'Fine,' I say. 'Why not? It's not like I've got my *own life* to worry about.' Despite my flippancy, I am worried. Because what *am* I supposed to do now? Go back to the office? Spend another year busting balls and hoping that on the partnership front, third time's lucky?

I haven't told Emma about the email I got (no one even bothered with a follow-up call) deferring my equity partnership. A small part of me wants to protest – and I know I *should* protest – but the vast majority can't be bothered.

And even if I did get back into the swing of office life, what is the rest of the picture going to look like? Now that I've got the hang of it again, I could join a dating app, learn to swipe right and left, and maybe even kiss a few frogs. The thought makes my breakfast settle like a lump in my stomach, and I put down my fork, a little nauseous. Emotions flit through my mind like clouds across the sun. What a difference a day makes. I've got people in my life that I want to keep; I've got things to do here. A sister and her family to support, a house to save, a ghost to help. A date with a very attractive man... and after that, who knows?

'Of course you have your own life, Kate.' Emma is frowning at me. 'Don't feel obliged to do anything. We'll manage. We'll have to.'

I check my watch. 'Right now, the only place I'm going is school. Izzy, Max – get your skates on or we'll be late. And go brush your teeth... No – first rinse off your plate and put it in the dishwasher.'

Emma laughs. 'You've taken to this like a duck to water.'

The ghost of a thought skitters along the old neural pathway:

these children could have been mine. A day makes a difference, but there's still a way to go until the healing is done.

'I try.' Shouting upstairs at the kids to hurry up, I go outside to start the car.

When I drop Izzy and Max at school, my stomach does a silly little flip at the sight of Dr Whitford's car in the space reserved for the headmaster. I'm tempted to go inside and see if I can wrangle an emergency 'parents' meeting' alone with him in his office. But then I think of the photograph. His story, his loss. If our connection is going to blossom into something, then we need to take it slow. Dinner on Saturday. One thing at a time.

I stop off at the local shop and pick up a few bits and bobs, including Emma's favourite foods from childhood. I'll stay here, take my sister to her medical and therapy appointments, and care for her for as long as she needs me. In fact, I'm looking forward to it.

* * *

But when I return to the gatehouse, I'm met by the unwelcome sight of Charlie's van.

'Damn,' I mutter. Leaving the food in the car, I rush inside.

Emma and Charlie are sitting at the table drinking coffee, and, I note with some irritation, Charlie's tucking into an extra portion of egg and beans I made for Max but he didn't have time to eat.

'...it's a good offer, especially under the circumstances.'

'I am very grateful, Charlie.'

'What's going on?' I say icily from the door.

'Oh, Kate.' Emma blushes. *I've got something to tell you.* 'Hi. Were the kids OK?'

'Why is he here?'

Charlie smiles at me, but his eyes are hooded like a snake's. 'Emma says you're staying on for a bit, Kate,' he says. 'I'm glad to hear it. And maybe you can help us. You're a solicitor, right? If you could draw us up a letter of intent and a contract for sale, we could save on legal fees all around.'

I clench my teeth in unbridled annoyance. 'I'm not a high-street solicitor,' I hiss. 'And besides, you won't be signing any contract to buy Rookswood. Not on my watch.'

'Kate, please.' Emma sounds distressed. 'We've discussed this. Charlie knows the situation with Philip, and he's made me a fair offer.'

'We'll talk about this later, but not in front of him.'

Charlie's fork is raised to his mouth as I sweep his plate out from in front of him.

'Breakfast's over,' I say. 'You need to go.'

'Kate?' Emma's voice is laced with the old anger. *You always had to be in control.*

'We'll discuss it *later*.' I fall back into my own familiar role. 'There are other solutions for Rookswood. Hear me out, and if you still want to sell the place to Charlie, then I won't interfere.'

Charlie scrapes his chair back from the table, glaring. 'My offer's going down by ten grand every day you delay, Emma. If your sister can't draw up a simple contract, then I'll get my solicitor to do it. It's not rocket science.'

I snort a laugh. 'Lucky for you.'

He takes a step towards me, menacing. 'Watch yourself, Kate. Everybody was fine before you got here. And we'll be fine again once you're gone.'

'I don't think you could say Emma was fine,' I retort. 'She fell down the stairs and hurt her back. That's what caused every-thing. You were supposed to make the place safe and you failed to do it. And that's far from the only time. You started demolition work when the cupola wasn't safe. As for the other things, I can't prove they were you... yet. But I'm working on it.'

'Kate, please stop,' Emma says.

Charlie guffaws with laughter. 'Good luck,' he says. He goes over to Emma and tries to brush away a strand of her hair. She flinches back.

'So that's how it is?' He has the gall to look hurt. 'Your sister hits on me, and you choose her? I love you, Emma. You know that. We could be together, just like we planned.'

'Save it,' I snap.

Emma stands up. 'Seriously, I've had enough of both of you.' Her voice is tight and strained. 'Charlie. Please go – we'll talk later. And Kate...' It breaks my heart to see the same old hurt look on her face. 'Just leave me alone.'

'Please, Emma,' I say. 'Don't do this.'

My sister shakes her head and runs upstairs. Without looking at me, Charlie makes his way from the kitchen towards the front door.

I stand and watch him, ready to explode with anger. But that will only make things worse. I put all my efforts into maintaining a stony silence.

Just before he goes out, he turns back.

'You've made things a lot worse, Kate. And I promise that you'll be sorry.'

* * *

I am sorry – very, very sorry – as Charlie's van drives away spewing gravel, and I'm left alone with more carnage of my own making. As a peace offering, I make Emma a cup of mint tea. I bring it upstairs, tail between my legs. How can I have taken the fragile shoots that were forming between us and stamped on them already? As much as I want to blame Charlie, a large part of the blame lies with me.

'Emma?' I knock softly on the door. 'Please can I come in? I've brought you some mint tea.'

'I meant it, Kate,' comes the response. 'Leave me alone.'

'I'm sorry I interfered. I just thought we were done with Charlie. I didn't realise—'

'You are so unbelievably arrogant.' Emma flings the door open; tea sloshes onto the carpet. 'You think you can waltz in here and *fix* everything. But you can't.'

'I know.'

She takes the cup of tea with a weary sigh and goes back into her room. The door is left open, which is something. I follow her and sit in the chair opposite her by the fireplace, preparing myself for another argument.

'Charlie's made me a fair offer,' she says. 'If I sell up here, I can take Izzy and Max and move abroad. To... Spain.' Her voice raises like a question. 'Or maybe Scotland. Or America. So they can be near their dad.'

'Why is he not paying child support?'

'Because he's broke.' She sighs. 'His scheme in Spain went wrong, and he's hanging on to the development in America by the skin of his teeth. Once I'm well, I need to go back to work. With the money I get from Charlie, I can buy a little cafe, maybe a bookshop.'

'In Spain or Scotland? Or America?'

'Look.' Her nostrils flare. 'I don't have all the answers, OK? We paid the school fees in advance, so it makes sense to stay here for now. But I need to make a plan. ASAP.'

'Why don't you open up a cafe and bookshop at Rookswood? Just to get the place paying for itself?'

'Do you really think it's that simple?'

'No.'

'Everything comes so easily to you, Kate. Money, work, self-confidence. I didn't care about those things before, but now I do. I'm living the wrong life. You of all people should know what that's like.'

Am I living the wrong life? At this moment, I don't feel that I am. There's water under the bridge, of course. But right now, I'm happy with things as they are.

Happy being here.

'I could buy Rookswood,' I say. 'I can match Charlie's offer.'

'*You?*' She gawks at me like I've sprouted a second head.

'Yeah, me. Why not? You must have loved Rookswood once, and I can see why. It's a beautiful, special old place. I could cover the restoration costs and you could open up a cafe and bookshop. Maybe we could have a little museum on the ground floor. There's lots of interest in the Weird Sisters in certain circles. You might get the odd nut job, but you'd be preserving a slice of local history. *We* would be.' Saying it aloud sounds daft, and yet, it makes perfect sense. 'You, Izzy, and Max could live upstairs at the main house, or stay in the gatehouse. You choose, and I'll live in the other one. I could keep my job working remotely and commuting up to London once a week. Maybe start a side hustle of conveyancing and going after deadbeat dads.' I smile wryly. 'I could even take up photography; Matthew can teach me. What do you think?'

Emma laughs. 'I think Rookswood has addled your brain.'

'That may well be. But at least we'd be saving the house. Because if we don't, then I don't know what's going to happen to her—'

'To her...?' Emma repeats. 'Who do you mean?'

I stare into the blackness of the fireplace. 'Ada. I said I would help her. Though I haven't made much progress. The least I can do is to preserve Rookswood for her.'

'Ada?' Her eyes widen. 'Kate, you don't mean what I think you're saying. I mean, you of all people... you can't believe in—'

'Ghosts?'

'It's not funny. I mean... *you*.'

'It's kind of funny. You seem more bothered about me believing in them than in whether or not they exist. And just for the record, I don't believe in ghosts, or at least not the kind that make spooky noises and make things go bump in the night. But I do believe that energy is neither created nor destroyed. And I know what I've felt and experienced at Rookswood.'

'But is Izzy in danger? Does the ghost "want her"?' She claps a hand to her mouth. 'Oh God, what if that's true?'

'I don't think it is,' I say calmly. 'Ada wasn't a bad person, and she's not a bad ghost. If, hypothetically, her spirit is trapped at Rookswood, then I think she's just trying to be heard and understood. I think that if she "wants" anything from anyone, it's me. I'm a similar energy source. An older sister, just like she was, who also happened to be estranged from my sister – again, just like she was. Her younger sister was called Camile. I don't know what happened or why they had a rift, but Camile disappeared. I'm guessing that Ada cut her out of her life. Sound familiar?' I raise an eyebrow. 'But then Ada spent the rest of her life regretting what happened, and wishing her sister would return so they could be reunited and heal the rift between them.'

'I can't believe I'm hearing this from you.'

'What can I say?' I spread my hands. 'I can't prove any of it, of course, but I've decided to keep an open mind. As far as I can tell, Ada's a sort of energy in the house – a consciousness. She can't control physical things – not directly. But occasionally, when she's worked up, she can create a shockwave, or a strong chill current of air. Sometimes, it's strong enough to make things move, like windows and doors. Or particles of dust. That's how I know what she's seeking. Her sister. She wrote to me in the dust. "Find her".'

'She wrote that in the *dust*? You expect me to believe that?'

'Why would I make it up?'

Emma shakes her head slowly. 'It's been fifteen years. Maybe this ghost has possessed the sister I used to know. Maybe that's why you're still here.'

'I realise you think I'm having a laugh, but I'm not. Ada is certainly more active when I'm in the house. Poltergeists draw energy from people with similar energy signatures. That's why I'm so "aware of her presence".' I make air quotes. 'And also, I can't rule out that she's responsible for some of the things I've seen at the house. The apparition on the stairs, maybe even the cupola falling. It's hard to know what's down to her and what's down to Charlie, but she's definitely present, and she definitely has an agenda. I've thought a lot about it, and if I was Ada, I'd want to rest in peace. But I wouldn't be able to do it – and neither can she – not without healing the rift with her sister. Or at least finding out what happened to her. Ada needs my help, and I want to do it. I'm going to find Camile.'

'Who also happens to be dead?'

'Bingo.'

'Do you know how crazy this sounds?'

'Come with me to Rookswood and let me prove it to you. I think one reason she chose me is that she figured out we were sisters. If we're both there, reconciled, I bet she shows up. If you promise to help me – and promise not to tear down Rookswood – she might stop her antics.'

'She *might*?'

'Well, obviously I can't guarantee anything. She's a ghost. We aren't exactly engaging in repartee on WhatsApp. But I've discovered that when I talk to her directly, she often manages to respond.'

Emma checks her watch. 'I'm sure it's a tempting offer, Kate. But it will need to be later, or tomorrow. I need to check in with the GP and go to my first Narcotics Anonymous meeting. And tonight at the school there's a PTA fundraiser.'

'Fine,' I say. 'I'll drop you off in the village. Ada's not going anywhere.'

She gets up from the chair and goes to the mirror to brush her hair. 'What I don't understand, Kate, is why you'd actually want to buy a haunted house.'

'I don't want to buy a haunted house. But a special, historic old house... that's different. Matthew had a vision for it, and I'm coming round to having one too. Which brings me back to the cafe, bookshop, and museum idea.'

'You and Matthew Whitford.' Pursing her lips at the mirror, Emma seems to mull this over. 'I didn't see that one coming.'

'It's early days. As in, we haven't even been on an official "date" yet. Just a few visits to Rookswood together.'

'You, him, and the ghost.'

I blush thinking of the night under the shattered cupola. 'You're not far off.'

'He has a son, you know,' she says. 'I think he has a learning disability of some kind.'

'He's autistic. I saw them together at the pub.' I tell her what I saw, skilfully avoiding any mention of Charlie.

'And you think looking after a couple of teenagers for a few weeks makes you ready to take that on?'

'Like I said, it's early days. But in these last few weeks, I've become a different person. I don't quite know who yet, but for the first time in a long while, I'm looking forward to finding out.'

Emma nods. Then, she comes over and gives me a hug.

'Whoever you are, Kate, and whoever you're becoming, I'm glad you're here. So glad. I love you so much.'

'Oh Emma.' I hold her tightly, breathing in the warmth and love of my sister. I'm so lucky to have this. And I want it for Ada, too.

29

That night, I give Emma a lift to the school for her PTA event. I return to the gatehouse planning to tidy up and do some work. Earlier, Izzy texted to say she was going to dinner with a friend, and I brought Max home by himself. After dinner, he went up to his room to study, and I see he's left his phone on the table. As I'm about to take it to him, the screen lights up with a text. I can't help but see the message – it's from Izzy.

> I'm here... I thought you said it had to be tonight? Where are you?

A tiny icicle of concern needles the back of my neck as I go upstairs. I knock softly on Max's door but there's no answer. Since I've been living in the house, I've tried to respect Max and Izzy's privacy, but on this occasion, I open the door.

The room is empty.

'Max?' I call out, but other than his school bag next to the bed, there's no sign that he's been here or done any studying. But something on his desk catches my eye. An old sepia photograph. I pick it up and find that it has glue on the back. I hypothesise that it was taken from a photo album – Ada's album. I recognise a particular special effect that Ada was trying to achieve. An illusion that cost her everything.

Oh God. I put the photos back, my heart kindling with panic. Where are Izzy and Max?

Occam's razor.

Do I even need to ask?

I rush downstairs, putting on my coat and grabbing my car keys. In my mind, I've chalked up the mischief at Rookswood to Ada and Charlie and discounted all other theories. Because I wanted it to be true.

As I emerge through the tunnel of trees, I see a light in one of the downstairs windows, dim and faint as if it's coming through a door from somewhere else. The great hall, I assume. After a second or two, the light goes out.

I park the car and go to the door. It's open a crack and I hear voices. Instead of just barging in, I stand at the threshold trying to get the lay of the land.

'Come on, this thing stinks. Just do it.' I recognise Izzy's voice.

'Give me a second,' Max replies. 'And stand still; we're only going to get one shot at this.'

One shot at what? Somehow in the tension of the moment, I stay still, letting them get on with whatever it is they're doing. I barely allow myself to breathe. And when I do...

I smell petrol.

Instantly, I react, pushing the door open. 'Izzy? Max?' I say. 'What's going on?'

I shine the light of my torch at the staircase. A girl dressed in a black Victorian mourning gown is standing at the top of the stairs. It takes me an eternally long second to recognise Izzy.

'Shit,' Izzy says. 'What's she doing here?'

But it's Max that draws my eye. An expression that I've not seen before. Not a Christmas-card angel. More like a fallen one.

'Turn off the torch, Aunt Kate,' he says. 'And get out.'

'What are you doing? Why does it smell like petrol?'

'Do it.'

That menacing edge to his voice. It's so startling, so new. In an instant, I relive all my interactions with Max from the time of my arrival. He was the nice boy; Izzy was the brat. He went out of his way to make me feel welcome and needed. And yet, there were signs that I chose to ignore. Dr Whitford threatening to suspend him, his 'accident' in the chemistry lab, lying about his whereabouts, clearly angry with his mum for not letting him go and live with his dad. Those nights when Izzy was 'sleepwalking' but I didn't check his room. I didn't think I needed to...

'Max?' Izzy sounds tentative. 'Maybe we should stop?'

'Stand still!' he hisses. 'Aunt Kate, turn off that torch.'

'No,' I say. 'I'm not going to.' I shine it directly in his face. His eyes darken, the irises swallowed by dilated pupils.

'Then you're going to be sorry.' He lights a match. Holds it up.

'OK.' I take a step back. 'I'll put down the torch. But only if you blow out that match.'

'You first,' he says.

'Fine.' I have to believe I can trust him. 'But you'd better do it.'

I switch off the torch. The room plunges into darkness, but only for a moment. 'Stop moving!' he calls out to Izzy.

Then, he drops the match.

'No!' I scream as the flames race up the staircase like hungry wolves, tongues licking frantically. In less than a few seconds, they reach Izzy and the bottom of that ridiculous dress.

'Great, Iz!' Max calls out. 'Perfect!' He's got an old-fashioned camera – a camera! – and takes a photograph. A woman on fire. Ada's greatest illusion, except, it's not an illusion at all.

'What are you doing!' I shout. 'You'll kill her.'

'Shut up, Aunt Kate,' Max yells. 'No one's going to be hurt. I'm not stupid, OK? The dress is covered in flame retardant. Izzy's fine; it's all perfectly safe. Just shut up and let us finish.'

But Izzy is not fine. In that moment, she screams. It's not the dress or the flames. From underneath her feet there's a groaning sound, then a snap. The entire staircase shifts, the landing hanging, suspended in time and space, like a child's toy made of matchsticks. And then it crumbles, burning timbers crashing to the ground.

One second, Izzy's there.

The next, she's gone.

'Izzy!' I scream. 'Oh God... Izzy!'

I stumble forward blindly as smoke and flames engulf the room, fuelled by the cold night air rushing in from the hole in the roof. I sense Max beside me, but I turn and shove him hard towards the door. 'Go outside and call for help,' I say, thrusting my phone at him.

'Please, Aunt Kate. I'm so sorry.'

'Shut up and do it!' I scream.

Max goes outside. I leap forward, covering my nose and mouth with my sleeve. I can just make out a shape – a dark figure crumpled underneath the burning staircase, blocked from me by a fallen beam. In that moment, I am single-minded; I am super-human. Ignoring the flames, I hurdle over the beam and go to Izzy, even as over our heads, the fire spreads across the first-floor gallery, and other timbers begin to weaken and fall.

'Izzy!' I jostle my niece hard. She moans – she's alive.

'Oh God,' she says. 'I can't breathe.'

From overhead, sparks shower down just inches from my eyes. Even the air seems like it's burning, shimmering. And then the entire landing crashes down. We're trapped, as the conflagration blows and swirls like a hurricane. We're trapped, and we're going to die.

Unless...

'Ada!' I scream. 'Ada, are you there? Can you help us?'

I'm grasping at straws – or rather, at aether. I didn't feel her presence when I entered the house, but she must be here somewhere.

'Ada?' Izzy says. 'The ghost?'

'Unless you have a better idea?'

Sadly, she doesn't. 'Ada!' she joins in.

The billowing smoke makes me cough and gag. Max... the ringleader... playing silly buggers along with Izzy. How could I have missed it? And Charlie? I still believe he was committing acts of sabotage to further his own agenda. Rookswood, it seems, was haunted not by one ghost, who may well be a figment of my imagination, but by three very real *humans*. I doubt even William of Ockham could have seen that one coming.

Unfortunately, my brilliant hypothesising is of little use in the moment. The flames are nearly upon us. If I don't do something quickly, Ada's going to have some permanent company...

Not on my watch.

'Your dress,' I say to Izzy. Whatever flame retardant Max put on it still seems to be working. I squeeze next to her and lift the voluminous fabric up like a shield, covering both of us. It works, sort of, but all around our bivouac, the smoke and heat are becoming unbearable.

'Come on, Ada,' I mutter under my breath. 'You couldn't make amends in life for whatever you did, but now's your chance. Do the right thing.'

Nothing. I hang my head. I don't know what else to say. What else to—

There's a rushing sound like a freight train, and all of a

sudden, I can't breathe. Fire and air are sucked from around us, spinning like a tornado, and out the hole in the roof. Far above our heads, rain begins to fall through the ruined cupola. I slump against Izzy, sinking back into a liminal oblivion as somewhere in the distance, across the barrier to another world, I imagine that I can hear the sound of sirens. But they're too late. Too far away. A cold, unearthly presence surrounds us, cocoons us. Ice against the fire's heat, a shivering embrace before the gates of hell. Where everything goes black.

30

I float. The sky above me is black, like the inside of a coffin, the inside of a grave. I'm cold, but somehow, I don't feel it; I can't form the thought to feel it, or anything else. Here and nowhere. Liminal. I drift outside of time. I am conscious, and all around me, I'm aware of other conscious- nesses. Some are at peace, becoming drops in an endless ocean. Others restless, the ones who have yet to forget; the ones who have failed to put things right. I want to surrender, to become a part of the infinite whole. But something is pulling at me. Someone won't let me. *Visions swim before my eyes. Blackness and flame. An embrace of ice keeping me safe. Me... and... Izzy?*

Izzy.

My mind slams back into place. My endless form becomes aware of its boundaries. I have a body. I have a purpose. Must go back. Things to do.

She *whispers to me as she guides me back. Through the darkness and into the light. She's one of the restless ones, and I can feel her longing to sink into the oneness. But not alone. I've promised her some- thing. I have to go back. I must move towards the light—*

The light hurts my eyes. White and clinical. Something heavy covering my mouth. A soiled dress? No. I try to suck in a breath. It hurts to breathe, but the air is pure and oxygen-rich. A beeping sound. Voices. I try to sit up but everything hurts. I try to open my mouth and speak, but the breathing mask prevents me.

Ada... Her icy grip loosens. She lets me go, fleeing back into the shadows.

A high-pitched beep. Another hand on me, this one warm and capable. 'Her pulse and breathing seem to be stabilising. That's a good sign.'

A good sign.

It seems I'm alive.

'Oh my God, Kate.' A frantic voice. One that I haven't heard in years, or so it seems. Emma's voice.

'Is Aunt Kate...?' Another smaller, scared voice. Izzy. She's alive too. 'Is she going to make it?'

No thanks to you, I want to say. It's probably just as well that I can't. I want to stand up and jump for joy, hug my niece; give her the telling off of her life.

Emma does the latter for me.

'I just can't believe it!' Emma says. 'That you and Max...' She can't seem to finish the sentence. 'You set the house on fire. What the hell were you thinking? And what the hell do we do now?'

The beeping of my machine speeds up. We are nowhere near being able to answer those questions.

The paramedic motions to her. 'Sorry, but I need you step away,' he says. 'Your sister's not out of the woods yet. We don't want her agitated.'

'Fine,' Emma says, breathless. She's silent for approximately five seconds before going right back to it. 'What I don't under-stand, Izzy, is how you both managed to survive the smoke and the fumes?'

'It was the old dress,' Izzy says. 'Max found all these notes left by that nutty old woman who was a photographer. All her methods for doing illusions and stuff. He wanted to try them out. He created a really cool illusion of a ghost using a big glass plate, with his iPad projected underneath. When I saw that, I said I'd help him do the Woman on Fire. I mean, it was wicked cool. He had all her notes about how to use flame retardant chemicals and stuff. It should have been safe.'

'Well, it wasn't,' Emma says.

'Yeah, I get that.' Izzy sounds in no way remorseful. 'But anyway, the flame retardant worked. We pulled the old dress over us like a tent.'

'That old dress saved their lives,' the paramedic says.

But he's wrong. For a second, I almost drift back to that liminal place... but it's no longer available to me. The old dress did not save our lives. It was that cold, chill hug that saved us, like the great wings of a bird. Cocooning us away from the heat and the fumes.

'Thank you, Ada,' I whisper silently.

But the ambulance is already speeding away from the house, and I know she can't hear me.

* * *

In a swift reversal of fortune, I end up in hospital with Emma by my side. Izzy was admitted briefly, but other than a few cuts and bruises and a hacking cough, she emerged from the ordeal unscathed. I, however, am all the worse for wear, having not only inhaled a shedload of smoke, but also having suffered some second-degree burns and a cracked rib.

Two days after the incident, the police come and interview me. I wish I could have got my stories straight with Izzy and Max first, but Emma tells me that they've come clean. I don't even pretend to comprehend all of the optical illusions they set up to haunt Rookswood – if they get through this ordeal with only a slap on the wrist, Max must have a hell of a promising career in special effects ahead of him.

Apparently, Izzy and Max were regular trespassers at Rookswood all during the time that Emma and Philip were focused, not on their children's whereabouts, but on their own problems. Izzy and Max were the ones who found the creepy old photos and portraits, along with Ada's notes, and Max decided to try his hand at 'haunting' Rookswood. He honed his skills in the chemistry lab, trying out Ada's techniques. As for the incidents at the house, Izzy confessed to the fake sleepwalking and locking me in the cellar. Max took responsibility for the phantasmagorical apparition on the stairs, and the tricks of the woman on the landing who released the debris and body parts on Charlie and me.

Charlie too was questioned under caution, but ultimately released. In his account, he 'forgot' to tell Emma about the repairs on the stairs that resulted in the loose floorboard, and 'accidently' spilled some nails and glass that I tripped on. He also brought into the house the petrol can that Max used, planning to use it to burn some debris outside. He had 'no idea' that the cupola wasn't safe before instructing demolition works to begin. Finally, he 'didn't get around' to properly securing the place, which is why Izzy and Max could get in pretty much at will. In the end, the authorities chalked him up as less of a criminal mastermind than a crap builder. I hope that's a blow to him.

Some of this I learn from Emma, some from a friendly police-woman, and some from another visitor – Matthew Whitford. He comes to visit me the afternoon of the second day. As soon as he enters the room, I grow short of breath, and not from the smoke.

'Kate!' he cries, rushing to my bedside. He leans down and

kisses me on the forehead. 'I can't believe this has happened. I was so worried. It's just awful. I wish I'd been there.'

I breathe in deeply the scent of his aftershave, coughing a little.

'I'm glad you weren't. It wasn't exactly a fun experience, ergo, I ended up here.'

He takes my hand and squeezes it gently. 'Good to see your sarcasm is still intact.'

'I guess a brush with death makes you take things less seriously.'

He laughs. 'Oh Kate, I'm so glad you're safe.'

'I've kind of lost track of time,' I say. 'Did I miss our date?'

'I'm afraid so.'

'Sorry about that.' I squeeze his hand back. Suddenly, I feel desperate for this chance. Death comes to all of us – I came close to experiencing that first hand. But right now, I want to live.

'Matthew,' I say, 'I appreciate how you've "played along" with my rantings about the ghost. I haven't told the others, but I want you to know the truth. Ada saved us. It wasn't flame retardant on an old dress. It was her.'

'I suspected as much.' He strokes the hair back from my forehead. 'I couldn't get too near the wreckage, but what I did see – well, I don't see how you could have survived.'

'So you believe me? It's important. I don't want you to think I'm a raving lunatic.'

He smiles; I melt. 'If I do, it's only in a good way. And not because of that. You went into that house to "rescue" Izzy. That might have been a little bit of lunacy. But brave too.'

'What's going to happen to Izzy and Max?' I say.

'It hasn't been decided,' Matthew says. 'And I'm going to do everything I can to advocate for them. I believe that Max didn't intend to harm anyone, not seriously, but because of his actions, harm was done. There will be consequences.'

'Yes,' I say, sighing. I pluck up the courage to ask the other question I've been dreading... 'And what about Rookswood? How bad was the fire?'

'It didn't help the old place, that's for sure.' He frowns. 'The central section was seriously damaged, especially the staircase and the first-floor gallery. But because the roof was open, it acted like a chimney and the fire didn't spread too far.'

'Is it possible to repair it?'

'Anything's possible, but it's going to take some serious cash. Emma said the house was insured, but there will need to be a full investigation before any insurer pays out, especially since Izzy and Max were involved.'

'Gosh.'

'So, the short answer is, I don't know. But that old place has been through a lot in its time and weathered some major storms. Hopefully, this is just one more memory for it to store in its walls.'

'I hope so.'

'Yes, and there's one more thing. I've got a lead on Camile.'

'Really?' I try and fail to sit up.

'Relax,' he says with a smile. 'Ada's dead. I think she can wait a little longer.'

'Maybe, but I can't. Tell me what you've found.'

'It might be nothing,' he says. 'And in any case, it was totally random. I was looking at some online photography archives, trying to find some stock photos for the school's centenary festival. I found some old daguerreotypes and gelatin silver prints that I thought might work for the publicity flyer. And then I found this.'

He withdraws his hand and takes out his phone, swiping

open a file. I stare at the photo, gazing into the eyes of the woman staring intently back.

Dark-haired, sharp-nosed, and prim in a black dress with a lace collar, I'd recognise the woman anywhere. But I haven't seen this photograph before – or, more accurately, this *half* of a photograph. Along her right side is a jagged rip, a severing down the middle like half of a broken heart.

'It's Ada,' I say. 'The other half of the torn photograph I found.'

'Yes,' Matthew says. 'I wasn't totally sure at first, but then I looked again at the photo you found on the floor in Ada's bedroom. It's definitely part of the same whole.'

'So who uploaded it? Can we track them down?'

'I'm already on it. The uploader is a regular contributor to the archive site, and I emailed her, asking about the photo. She got back to me last night; apparently she owns an antique shop near East Grinstead.'

'Where's that?'

'East Sussex. About an hour from here.'

'Can we go there?' Excited, I try to rise, but the breathing tubes, IV drip, and the sharp pain in my ribs bring me back to unpleasant reality. I breathe out a long sigh, which immediately makes me start to cough. 'Sorry,' I say.

He strokes my hand. 'Nothing to be sorry about. We'll visit the antique shop just as soon as you're able. Until then, Kate, rest up.'

Then he leans in and whispers into my ear. A slow smile creeps across my face. For what he has in mind once I'm fully recovered, I'm going to need to brush up on my Latin and be in tip-top physical shape.

XII

I saved her – saved them both. The sister who was so like me; the child who was like the daughter Camile wanted but never had. I am the dark one, the sister of shadow. But I am not evil. I never was. I did not do it out of some misplaced notion of karma or a balancing of the invisible scales. I did it purely because it was the right thing to do.

I could not save Tanya. I could not find Camile. My life was the poorer for those things.

But I could do this for Kate, and so I did.

31

Two weeks later, Matthew and I walk hand in hand down the medieval high street in East Grinstead. It's the Easter holidays, and both of us are taking some much-needed time off. Which, for me, means working harder than ever on all things Rookswood related, plus accompanying Matthew on a few outings with his son. Even the 'new me' is having to evolve quickly, but so far, so good.

We reach our destination: a twee, half-timbered shop called 'Country Treasures'. The bottle-glass bay window and hodge-podge of antiques inside is straight out of Dickens; a bell tinkles on the door as we enter.

Inside, the shop smells of old things. It's the kind of place I previously would have avoided, but Matthew is like a boy in a sweet shop. He browses eagerly the Aladdin's Cave of 'country treasures', most of which to me look like charity-shop rejects.

'Can I help you?'

From the back of the shop, half-hidden behind a bin of old maps, a woman is sitting behind a till. She looks as elderly as her wares, with wiry, grey hair pulled back into a prim bun, her face wrinkled like an old apple.

Matthew barely looks up from a display case of old camera equipment, but I'm not here to browse. I walk stiffly (my ribs still hurt) over to the woman.

'Hi,' I say. 'I think you spoke to my friend on the phone. I came here to show you this.'

I lay the torn photo of Camile onto the desk. The old woman stares at it for a long time before looking up at me, her eyes wide.

'Where did you get this?' she says.

Matthew comes and joins me, but makes no move to intervene. This is my quest, and I'm going to see it through.

'At a house called Rookswood. Near Lewes. This photo was originally of two sisters. Adaline and Camile Havelock. They lived there.'

'Ada,' the woman mutters. 'I can hardly believe it.'

She beckons me towards the back of the shop, where two wingchairs are placed in front of an ash-dusted wood burner. I sit down, grateful to be off my feet, and she takes the other chair. Matthew finds an old stool and pulls it up.

'Ada lived in the house until her death,' I say. 'But Camile was lost. What can you tell me about her?'

'She was my great-aunt by marriage,' the old woman says. 'My granddad's brother's wife. I knew her when I was a girl. She was like a woman out of a dream.'

'How so?'

'Beautiful, pale, and fragile,' she says. 'I remember she used to sing – her voice was high and clear like a bell. But the songs she sang were sad, and I recall there was always a sort of sadness about her. When my sister, Elizabeth, was born, Aunt Camile gave me a big hug, which was the only time I remember her doing that. "Your sister is precious," she said. "Never let her go."'

The old woman stares down at the photo, her eyes cloudy with memories. 'Aunt Camile got ill shortly thereafter. I'm not sure she was ever that robust. But before she died, she gave me this.'

The woman reaches under the counter and withdraws the original half of the torn photograph. Touching the old photographic paper, I feel a jolt of recognition: a vestigial response, as if a trickle of Ada's energy has been stored inside me. Matthew and the old woman watch as I lay my photo of Camile beside it, the two severed halves creating a whole. Two sisters, reunited at last.

Tears bead in my eyes. 'Camile left Rookswood and never came back,' I say. 'I don't know what happened between them, and Ada never knew Camile's fate. She waited her whole life for her sister to return. For a reunion that never happened.' The sheer tragedy overwhelms me.

Matthew leans over and puts a hand on my shoulder.

The old woman stands up stiffly. 'I think we all need a cup of tea.'

Matthew goes to help her. Left alone, I stare at the flames flickering behind the glass door of the stove, the wood consumed so quickly by the heat. In the Japanese art of kintsugi, broken porcelain is repaired using veins of gold, creating beauty and strength from destruction. Looking down at the torn photograph, I realise that life is so short, so precious. I want to learn all about Camile, but right now more than anything, I wish Emma was here.

As they make the tea, Matthew takes care of the introductions. The old woman's name is Henrietta Cottingham. She's married with two grown-up children and four grandchildren. I gather they aren't related by blood to Camile. But it's a legacy of a sort.

When we're all seated again, I let Matthew fill Henrietta in on our side of the story. It immediately becomes apparent that they share a number of interests: photography, history, old things. Because Camile died young, Henrietta has few first-hand memories of her. Still, she manages to fill quite a few gaps in my knowledge of the Weird Sisters. 'I knew she lived in an old house that she ran away from,' she tells us. 'She and her sister were photographers back before she married my great-uncle. She had a little box full of old photos, mostly of her sister. My great-uncle kept them, and when he died, they came to me. I thought they deserved to be published, so I put a few of them online. I never imagined that one day, you would come here with the other half of that photograph. Or the story.'

'I only wish we knew more,' I say. 'We know that Ada and Camile had a falling out, and that Camile left. But we don't know why.' I press the photos tightly together.

'Well,' Henrietta says, 'I've lived a fair few years and seen a fair few fallings out amongst friends and family members. Not my own,' she clarifies. 'I suppose subconsciously, I took Camile's words to heart and always tried to heal things over with my sister if there was a rift. But to me, it seems that most irreconcilable differences are caused by a broken heart.'

I nod in concurrence. Certainly, my and Emma's experience backs up that hypothesis. Nearly twice, in fact.

'So you think Ada and Camile quarrelled over a man?' Matthew asks.

'Or a woman.'

As soon as she says it, it all clicks into place.

'I've seen her,' I say. 'In the last pages of Ada's photo album. She looks formidable.'

'Her name was Countess Tatiana Bischoff,' Henrietta says. 'She was a very wealthy socialite, I understand. But Camile called her "The Woman on Fire." She recounted at least part of the story to my great-uncle, though I'm afraid that many of the details are lost to history.'

I sit forward in the chair. 'Will you tell us what you know?' I say. 'We're trying to piece together the sisters' story.'

'I can do one better than that,' she says. 'My great-uncle kept diaries, and some of them tell of his time with Camile. They met in Brighton, and for him, it was love at first sight. For her, it was slower to unfold. She was traumatised by what had happened to her. Apparently, she blamed herself for causing a fire at the house where she lived with her sister. Part of some photography illusion gone wrong. The set caught alight, and the countess, who was also Ada's lover, went up in flames – literally. Camile was scared for herself, but also for Ada. She fled from her home so that people would blame her, not her sister. As it was, the countess wasn't killed by the fire, but she did die not long thereafter. In any case, the damage was done. Camile convinced herself that Ada would never forgive her for what happened. She thought Ada would be better off just to forget about her. I believe by the end, she regretted that decision and wished to be reunited with her sister. But by then her health had begun rapidly to decline. Her lungs were never strong, perhaps from long exposure to darkroom chemicals in her girlhood. She died peacefully, though she was very young. My great-uncle always said, "She was too pure for this life."'

I brush away a tear from my cheek. It's all so tragic. Camile dying without ever healing the rift with her sister. Ada not knowing what happened and spending all those painful years waiting. All for nothing.

'It's so sad,' I say. 'Camile and Ada ripped themselves apart, just like the photo. If it was happening now, it would have been harder for Camile to disappear. But back then, I guess it was pretty easy.'

Noticing my distress, Matthew reaches out and takes my hand. Henrietta pours me another soothing cup of tea.

'If it's any comfort to you, dear,' she says, 'Camile and my great-uncle had a good life together, even though it was cut short. I think she was happy in her marriage, though they weren't blessed with children.' She sets down the teapot. 'Her one great sadness, however, was "losing" her sister. I think she wanted a reunion, but left it too late.'

'Your great-uncle sounds like a wonderful man,' I say. 'Ada will be glad to know that.'

'Ada?' Henrietta frowns. 'But surely she's...?'

'She's restless,' I say, glancing at the united halves of the photograph. 'All these years, and she still doesn't know what happened to her sister. They're both dead, obviously, but Ada can't cross over to the other side. Not without Camile.'

Henrietta takes a long sip of her tea. 'So you're saying that Ada is a ghost?'

'I know how it sounds, but yes, that's it exactly.'

Henrietta stares into the fire, the reflected flames leaping in her eyes.

'A few times, when I was young, I thought I "saw things" at my great-uncle's house. Felt them too. Camile was dead by then.'

'Sometimes houses can retain the energy signature of someone who's died,' Matthew says.

'Maybe Camile was restless too,' Henrietta says. 'Two sisters who longed to forgive each other. When all was said and done, they wanted to be together.'

She trails off, lost in her thoughts and memories.

'Can I take the photo?' I say.

She closes her hands over mine. 'Do, child, please do.' She shakes her head. 'Ada and Camile. Their reunion wasn't meant to happen in this world. See that it happens in the next.'

XIII

Her name is Kate, this woman who has closed the circle. She and the man, Matthew, enter the house in silent reverence, and their energy resonates with mine. She begins to speak to me; she holds out the thing that was lost. Half of a torn photograph. I cannot touch it, but I can see into her heart and feel what she is carrying with her. A tiny spark, curled up inside her... a story.

My story.

And as she speaks, I feel another presence here with us. A consciousness of pure light. It unfurls slowly, tentatively, but gathering strength. I cry out in silence, weep invisible tears. But they are tears of joy, for I can feel her. She is here, she is with me...

* * *

Come dearest, come to me. I can feel you here at last. That you too have been longing, waiting. I cannot take your hand; I cannot kiss your cheek. Not here, and not where we are going. But let us put our minds together now, our spirits, our energy. Do you see it there before us? A dark rectangle: the doorway to the world beyond. And through it, beyond it, shines the endless light. Let us go together, forever always. Two sisters. In light, in shadow. Two sisters. Let us go together in love...

EPILOGUE
CHRISTMAS EVE

Eight months later

It truly is a lovely Christmas. The best Christmas ever. The tree in Emma's sitting room is festooned with white lights, paper chains, and cream, purple, and pink Victorian glass baubles. The room smells of fresh pine and woodsmoke; the fire is lit and candles flicker from the mantel. Beside me on the sofa, Matthew puts his hand on my knee. Before us on the rug, his son, Daniel is playing with a bag of antique marbles, making swirls and patterns, occasionally stopping to watch the sparks fly up the chimney, occasionally smiling up at us, or even coming over for a cuddle.

And I marvel at this thing called love, and how it could have come upon me so quickly, so unknowingly. For this boy, who is different, for his father who is more of a kindred spirit to me than I ever expected to find. For all the people who have joined us here tonight.

Laughter filters in from the kitchen as Emma and Henrietta

finish cooking, and cutlery clatters in the conservatory as Max and Izzy set the table for dinner. Henrietta's husband, Frank, brings in a newly opened bottle of wine and refills our glasses.

'We should go and help,' I whisper to Matthew.

'Yes, we should.'

Instead, he kisses me, long and meaningfully...

'Get a room.' Izzy comes in with a tray of mince pies, rolling her eyes at us. Eight months on, and her ordeal is all but forgotten in the blur of teenage activities, which, thankfully, no longer include trying to fake-haunt a house. Daniel rushes over to her and she holds up a mince pie just above his head, making him jump for it. At first, Izzy tolerated Daniel as a source of babysitting money, but in only a short time, she's become almost like a big sister to him. Together, they collapse in a fit of giggles, which warms not only my heart, but the entire room.

While they're at it, Max comes into the room. 'Dinner's ready,' he says, his smile a little tentative, broadening when I smile back. Max is a good egg – I still believe that, though I no longer see him as a Christmas-card angel, or as an idealised version of his dad. Instead, I see a boy who is healing, a boy who is searching for his place in the world. A complex human being, just like the rest of us.

After the incident at Rookswood, Max narrowly escaped having to appear in juvenile court, and both he and Izzy were required to undergo extensive counselling. Max learned to process and release his pent-up emotions, and after a few tense weeks of working through his feelings about his parents splitting up, he instigated a heartfelt apology to the people he'd hurt. And while therapy is definitely helping, Dr Whitford organised something that, I believe, has proved even more formative: a community service placement at a homeless shelter in Lewes. For the last few months, Max (sometimes with Izzy) has been spending his Saturdays serving meals, doing laundry, chatting to people who have it a lot worse than he does, and taking video footage for a documentary he wants to make about the people he's met. It's definitely given him perspective – and a new direction in life.

Izzy too seems to have finally got the memo that there are people around to help her navigate her difficult teenage years, and it's been good to see her and Emma spending time together and strengthening their bond. And my bond with her is pretty strong too. At the start of the Christmas holidays, Izzy dumb-founded me by announcing that she wants to be a lawyer just like me, and work in the criminal prosecution service. While I felt obliged to point out that that's nothing like what I do, I encour-aged her definitely to go for it, and enjoyed the feeling of actually having inspired someone.

Tomorrow, Max and Izzy are flying off to Florida to see their dad, and Emma and I will spend our Christmas Day like we spend much of our spare time – working on the restoration of Rookswood House and our ambitious dream of opening a cafe, bookshop, and exhibition devoted to the Weird Sisters in the summer.

For Rookswood, it's been a long road back. The fire damaged the structure of the building, and the insurers have yet to pay out. For several months, it looked like the house might go the way of so many other historic homes lost to time, dereliction, and devel-opers like Charlie. (Following the shenanigans at Rookswood that gave him a bad reputation in the local market, Charlie upped sticks and moved his floundering property development empire to Essex.)

But following some legal magic on my part, setting up a char-itable trust to preserve the house, and Emma's tireless work to procure grant funding, we managed to cobble the funds together to start on the restoration work, which is now well under way. Thanks to the work of a skilled local craftsman, a new stained-glass cupola is being created for the house, and once the place is watertight, restoration of the staircase will begin. For now, I'm funding the day-to-day expenditures for the project, but as an early Christmas present to Emma, I started delving a little deeper into the world of family law. I took it upon myself to verify Philip's sob story that he was bankrupt, and surprise, surprise – I discovered that his Florida development was actually quids-in and that he'd been hiding the profits offshore. It may be some time before Emma sees any money, but even so, going after a deadbeat dad cum deadbeat human being has proved cathartic for both me and my sister.

'You coming, Kate?' Emma says. I realise that while I've been staring into the flames reminiscing, everyone else has moved to the table.

'Yes,' I say. 'Sorry. Just lost in thought.'

The tears take me unawares, as they do sometimes when I look at my sister and see her. For the beautiful spark of life that she is, and the true gift I've been given. A gift that I once threw away, and I will always regret those lost years. But fate has given us a second chance – for forgiveness, appreciation, and love. And for that, my gratitude is infinite.

'Oh honey,' she says. 'Are you OK?'

'Yes.' I smile. 'Absolutely. And so are they, I think.'

Standing side by side with my sister, I look at the framed photograph that has been given pride of place on the mantel. The last photo of Ada and Camile. Two sisters of light and shadow. Two sisters, torn apart, but reunited at last. I will never forget the moment it happened, the moment they passed together from this world to the next. I will never forget the lesson Ada taught me – to value those I love with everything I am, and to hold them close, but not too tightly...

'How did you do that?' Emma says, frowning at the photo.

'What?'

She points to the rip down the middle, the tear between Ada and Camile. Except, when I look closer, there is no rip. The photo is as sharp and whole as the day it was taken.

'Oh, that.' I laugh it off, trying not to look surprised. And in a way, I'm not. When I think back to everything I've experienced at Rookswood, the rational part of me knows that all of it can be explained by human acts and the laws of physics.

But I know what I know.

'I'm just working my magic,' I say.

Emma gives me a sideways smile, and I see in her the girl she once was, looking up to me, the big sister. And I feel a remarkable sense of joy just being in her presence. That's where the real magic lives.

'Good to know,' she laughs.

We stand there for a moment longer looking at the photograph. A sudden draught comes down the chimney and the flames leap skyward. For a moment, I perceive something in the room with us. Almost like an energy, almost like a consciousness. But it's no longer trapped at Rookswood. Together, Ada and Camile have become part of the great unknown. Together, Ada and Camile are at peace.

Emma takes my hand; I smile at her with all the love in the world. Hand in hand, we go to the kitchen, where our family, old and new are waiting to start the celebration.

* * *

MORE FROM LAUREN WESTWOOD

Another spellbinding historical mystery from Lauren Westwood, *The House of Second Chances*, is available to order now here:

https://mybook.to/HouseofSecondChances

A LETTER FROM LAUREN

Thank you for reading *The House of Light and Shadows*. If you enjoyed this book, please can I ask that you leave a review. It really helps other readers find my books and might help someone discover their perfect next read. If you want to keep up to date on my new releases, or are interested in becoming a beta reader for my books, please sign up at the following link. Your email address will never be shared and you can unsubscribe at any time.

https://www.laurenwestwoodwriter.com

I am privileged to live in an old house built in 1604 that has its own quirks and foibles, just like a human being. I enjoy writing books where the house is a character in its own right, whether inhabited by a real ghost or not. Both Rookswood and my human characters in *The House of Light and Shadows* are entirely fictional, but the bizarre world of Victorian photography that I've touched on in the book is based on historical fact. Looking at these photos today, the fashions and fads seem odd to us, but I'm sure our Victorian ancestors would find our modern obsession with photoshopped images and selfies equally strange. I have attempted to accurately describe the work of some of the early pioneers of photography, but in creating a work of fiction, I have inevitably taken some liberties with the timeline, technology and historical record, and any mistakes are entirely my own.

I am grateful to Francesca Best and the team at Boldwood Books for believing in me and my work, and seeing the book through to publication. I would also like to thank my agent, Kiya Evans, for her support. Other people who have helped me immensely over the last few years include Ronan Winters, Sally Orson-Jones, Jin Ong, Antonia Stefanova, Chloe Xhauflaire and Alison Smith.

Finally, I would like to thank my family for their ongoing love and support. This has been a difficult year for us, but I continue to hold the vision for a brighter future, and believe that each day we grow stronger and more resilient together.

ABOUT THE AUTHOR

Lauren Westwood writes about old houses and quirky historical mysteries. She is also an award-winning children's author (Laurel Remington), a mother of three, and works as a lawyer in renewable energy. Lauren is originally from California, and now lives in the UK, in an old house built in 1604.

Sign up to Lauren Westwood's mailing list for news, competitions and updates on future books.

Visit Lauren's website: www.laurenwestwoodwriter.com

Follow Lauren on social media here:

facebook.com/Lwestwoodbooks

instagram.com/lwestwoodwriter

goodreads.com/laurenwestwood

tiktok.com/@laremington

ALSO BY LAUREN WESTWOOD

Secrets and Love Series

The House of Second Chances

The House of Hidden Secrets

The House of Love and Dreams

Standalone Novels

The House of Light and Shadows

Letters from *the past*

Discover page-turning
historical novels from
your favourite authors
and be transported
back in time

*Join our book club
Facebook group*

https://bit.ly/SixpenceGroup

*Sign up to our
newsletter*

https://bit.ly/LettersFrom
PastNews

Boldwood

Boldwood Books is an award-winning fiction publishing company seeking out the best stories from around the world.

Find out more at www.boldwoodbooks.com

Join our reader community for brilliant books, competitions and offers!

Follow us
@BoldwoodBooks
@TheBoldBookClub

Sign up to our weekly deals newsletter

https://bit.ly/BoldwoodBNewsletter